FINAL JUSTICE

Ray Weaver

FINAL JUSTICE

The Fifth Novel in the Justice Series

Ray Weaver

Sirena Press

For information:
Murmaid Publishing
Murmaid@tampabay.rr.com

Other books by Ray Weaver:
Tightrope to Justice
Miami Justice
European Justice
Justice 4 Willis

ISBN # 978-0-9856851-5-7

Cover and Book Design
theMurmaid ™
for Sirena Press

Printed in the United States of America
First American Edition

Dedication

Final Justice, is the fifth and last book in
the Justice series.

My next novel will take a completely
different direction.

I wish to thank my wife, Ellie, for helping me
to put together these five books featuring the
Willis family.

A special thanks to all who purchased these stories
and to those who have so kindly offered positive feed-
back and constructive critiques.

And lastly, a special thanks to my editor and
publisher, Nancy Frederich, for her enhancement
of the stories and the exciting covers.

Contents

Chapter 1

"Your Honor, can you please instruct Mr. Willis to permit me to finish my question?" Ashley Willis asked the judge shaking her head in exasperation.

The judge answered dryly, "Yes, Mr. Willis. Please allow Ms. Willis the courtesy of being able to complete her question before you interrupt."

"She is leading the witness, your Honor," Phil Willis said simply, no arrogance in his voice.

The elderly, short and stout bald headed judge was meek looking in appearance, but the Honorable Harold Mercer was known for his loud masterful voice and his strict control over the demeanor in his courtroom. His motto was — "Keep the Flow Going."

Now, standing in front of him, was Ashley Willis, attorney for Sherry Wine, who was suing Diego Salasar, her live in boyfriend, for abuse. Diego's attorney was none other than Ashley Willis's father, Phil Willis.

Years of experience in the courtroom had enabled Phil to be at the top of his game and he had lost only a few cases in the past couple of decades. Now faced with an exceptionable opponent, his own daughter — Ashley, Phil was focused on proving his client innocent.

The court room, in which Ashley and her client were

pitted against her father and his client, was in the old downtown Syracuse Courthouse, which was scheduled to be demolished in a few weeks. Serving Syracuse for over fifty years, the foundation of the brick building was showing immense cracks, and the inside walls were slowly starting to exhibit signs of mildew.

A contemporary six-story courthouse, with state of the art security system, had been constructed across the street on the large lot that once contained the city's decrepit senior center.

As the trial moved along, Ashley, tall and slender with her auburn hair pinned back in a neat knot at the back of her neck, practiced all the skills she had learned in law school to win the law suit.

Diego was over six-feet tall. His forebearers must have had Mediterranean blood — his hair was almost bluish-black and his skin had a faint olive tinge. His good looks seemed to attract women without any effort on his part. He had the reputation of being an abusive womanizer and had discarded as many former lovers as he had fingers on his hands. When he was through with a woman, he just dropped her abruptly and took up with another.

Sherry Wine, a model, in her late twenties, was a tall willowy blonde with flashing blue eyes and a beautiful clear, creamy complexion. She had become famous for her figure and beauty; and was in great demand in the modeling industry, after posing for skin care commercials and Victoria's Secret magazine ads.

After her relationship with Diego fell apart, Sherry was determined not to just meekly become one of his discarded lovers. She had decided to hire Ashley Willis, an aggressive attorney, from the well known firm of Tyson and Tyson, to help her make Diego pay for the time and efforts she had spent being his lover.

Because of the impending move to the new courthouse, Judge Mercer felt pressured to move this trial along quickly. He looked at his watch and announced, "Because of the hour, we will take a lunch break. We will resume at one-thirty. Court is adjourned."

The bailiff instructed the court, "All rise." The judge stood up and strolled into his chamber.

Ashley turned to her co-counsel, Lanex, "Let's head downstairs to the cafeteria for lunch. I don't even remember if I had breakfast this morning."

Ashley would tell anyone who would listen that she had always wanted to be a lawyer and follow in her father's footsteps. She had attended Georgetown University, one of the highest rated schools in the legal profession. After graduating in the top five percent in high school, she was offered a full scholarship. The letters her father had solicited from a state senator, retired judges, and other prominent people testifying to Ashley's strong character helped to obtain the scholarship.

In spite of her closeness to her parents, Ashley was determined to take her own direction in life. She lived on campus. When she had free time she would sit in on local trials, taking notes constantly. She knew from the start, trial law was her destiny.

Phil's wife, Kelley, still worked at his side in his law practice. The two of them were now contemplating retiring to Florida. Phil had decided defending Diego Salasar, Argentina's most famous and richest soccer player, would be one of his last major cases. Defending a celebrity such as Diego would give him a large fee. Diego just wanted the case over so he could go on with his career. Since money was no object, Diego had authorized Phil to hire whoever he wished to serve as second chair.

Phil had contacted Michele Bain of the prestigious law firm of Bain and Bain to be his co-counsel. She had won a favorable verdict in a high profile case the previous year for Emil Rodman, a well known hockey player. After hitting a spectator in the stands with a hockey stick, Emil had been sued for several million. Michele had won the case when the jury decided the action was not intentional. The hockey stick had merely slipped out of Emil's hands, as he waved it in frustration over a play, as the photos obtained from a fan's camera proved.

When he agreed to take this case, Phil did not realize the opposing attorney would be none other than his daughter Ashley, of whom he was so proud.

Both Ashley and her older brother, Alan, had made their parents proud with their excellent grades, in high school and in college. When asked about his two children, Phil always said, "In this age, I'm just happy they kept their noses clean."

Alan, now turning twenty-eight, was still trying to pay off his college debts and was not dating anyone seriously. He lived in a studio apartment and drove a small Honda motorcycle. Fun and games were not on the top of his list. Like his father, he was noted for his thrift and lived on simple frozen dinners.

After college was complete, he concentrated on his police work. Alan was working in the Syracuse Police department and would soon take over as head of the SWAT Division. At six-feet-two and weighing two hundred pounds, Alan looked very fit and capable in his uniform. His blond, straight, thick hair always fell across his face until he had it cut. He said all men on his SWAT team wore their hair short with a military look.

In the couple of years he had been at the Syracuse Police Department, he had received many accommodations. He was one of the most respected officers in the department. Alan always made it a point of doing everything by the book and maintaining a very professional appearance.

Like her brother, Ashley was tall; reaching almost six foot, with legs that appeared to reach almost to her arm pits. She was well-toned, thanks to her habit of working out at the gym almost daily. She was employed at the small, but well known law firm of Tyson and Tyson, which had been delighted to snag her. Berry Tyson Sr. had heard Ashley's commencement speech at Georgetown and had decided there and then he would hire her right out of law school before any other firm could snatch her up.

In the three years she had been with the firm, Ashley had helped them earn several victories. She was elated when the partners offered her the opportunity to take on Sherry's case against Diego Salasar. It was a daring move for the firm that had a reputation of winning their client's cases. Both Berry Sr. and Berry Jr. had a full docket to cover. They decided this was the opportune time for Ashley to spread her wings. They had asked her to find her own co-counsel.

Ashley was committed to her work and lived alone in a rented condo. The only slight rift between Ashley and her parents occurred when she had started dating a married man. "Oh Mom, don't worry about me. I know what I'm doing," Ashley snapped at her mother.

With love and affection for their parents, both Alan and Ashley made it their priority to follow family tradition and have dinner with their parents once a month on Sundays.

Chapter 2

Judge Mercer was determined to keep this trial under control at all times and was prepared to do everything in his power to ensure that. The room was packed with spectators and countless people from the news media.

Both sports and entertainment magazines had sent reporters to cover the trial involving the famous soccer player, Diego. News media trucks with high antennas and countless cameramen filled the parking lot outside of the courthouse, prepared to cover every moment of the trial.

The judge pounded his gavel to commence the trial. Everyone in the room knew he was prepared at short notice to clear the courtroom if any of the Paparazzi tried to take a photo inside the room. His voice vibrated with firmness. "I wish to remind all of you you're invited guests. If any of you scream out during the proceedings, or misbehave in any way, you are out of here. Now, let's proceed."

Ashley knew she would have her hands full trying to prove Salasar abused Sherry on several occasions. But, winning this case could make Ashley and her firm highly regarded in the future. This case was being covered both nationally and internationally.

Because the alleged abuse took place in Syracuse, instead of Diego's home country, where the pair had sometimes resided, the trial was taking place in the State of New York.

Diego had hired the well seasoned and competent Phil Willis. It was only after he had accepted the case, Phil learned the opposing attorney would be none other than his daughter, Ashley. In return, when Ashley heard her father had taken the case, for the opponent, she was determined to quickly overcome her fear of facing her father in court and maintain her sense of control.

Diego entered the court room wearing white linen slacks, a blue blazer, and a white-collared open-necked sport shirt that showed off his chest filled with dark curly hair. Seeing the handsome athlete, one teenage girl cried out, "I love you, Diego." She was quickly escorted out of the room by security.

Everyone could see why most of the major magazines fought to put Diego on their cover. He was a god in his homeland, Portugal, where the media had made him a living legend. Now the prima donna of the sports world, Salasar was the highest paid soccer player in the world.

When the sports media talked about the greatest sports figures in history, Diego's name was listed next to Jordan, Ruth, Unitas and Muhammad Ali. Barbara Walters had put Diego on her top ten list of the world's most interesting people this year.

Thanks to his fame, his endorsement of a product brought him huge compensations. His business agent had made Diego even richer and more famous with all the deals he had obtained for him. At first Diego's only endorsement was Nike, but now he represented about fifteen giants of the commercial world, including Pepsi, Gillette and Nationwide Insurance Company. His agent had even obtained a book deal for Diego that was said to be worth ten million.

Consequently, it was no wonder Sherry Wine was suing him for twenty million dollars—to Salasar that was just a drop in the bucket. His homes in Portugal, London, Sicily, and an expensive apartment in New York across from Central Park, made travel all over the world easy. Wherever Diego would go, groupies would follow his every move and the tabloids hounded him in every city. Police escorts were needed to keep people at a distance.

Diego had two ex-wives he had paid off generously to leave him alone. His relationship with Sherry Wine, not her given name, but one she had taken for her career as a fashion model, had led Diego into even further legal difficulties. Sherry had met Diego at his surprise birthday bash. After the party, she spent the night with him and never left his side, accompanying him on his ten-city book tour.

As the tour progressed the two spent almost every waking hour together. Sherry soon discovered another side to the charming soccer player. He was extremely jealous when she so much as talked to another man. Before long, she developed a fear of his physical abuse. His controlling nature overcame him. Occasionally, he would lock her in the hotel room, watched by one of his many body guards, while he went out with other women.

When Sherry first confronted him about the affairs, his temper would flare. He would yell and slap her. Later, he hit her several times across the face as the violence escalated. The final straw for Sherry was when he knocked her to the ground, kicked her several times and threatened to slash her face—thus ruining her modeling career.

During this last incident, a hotel housekeeper accidentally walked into the room and had witnessed the assault.

Sherry entered the court room dressed tastefully in

a beige business suit, with a cranberry silk blouse and neutral colored stilettos. Not wanting Sherry to appear a loose woman who made a habit of co-habiting with famous sports figures, Ashley had instructed her to dress as a professional business woman so the jury might view her as such.

With the trial almost ready to take place, Ashley and Phil were getting ready to present their witnesses. Ashley had spent a considerable amount of time preparing her case against Diego. She knew he was loved by all his fans and the media couldn't get enough of him. So popular opinion would be against Sherry. Ashley also knew her evidence had to be strong in order to convince the jury of Diego's guilt in the abuse case. To help her she sought the assistance of her old mentor from law school, Lanex Fox, to be her co-counsel.

Lanex was a former judge from New York City. After the death of his wife from cancer, Judge Fox hit a downward spiral. It had been a debilitating blow to lose the love of his life. He left the bench, started drinking heavily and eventually ended up in a flop house on the lower East side. There he had tried to commit suicide with an overdose of pain medications.

When Ashley heard of the attempted suicide of her long admired mentor, she rushed to visit him in his hospital room. This once highly regarded judge was sitting in his hospital bed, just staring up at the ceiling.

"Hello, Judge Fox."

"You're wrong Ashley. It's just plain Lanex Fox now."

"You'll always be Judge Fox to me." Her chest squeezed with emotion.

For a moment, he couldn't bring himself to speak, not trusting his voice. Then he said simply, "Not much hope left for me."

Ashley tried to sound sincere and upbeat. "Well, that's

about to change my friend. I need you to help me with a case."

He shook his head slowly. "No." His voice was somber.

His answer echoed in her head. She thought long before answering, "Do you remember when I almost gave up trying to become a lawyer?"

He nodded; a hasty embarrassed nod.

She continued, "You gave me a good talking. I finally decided to continue with my studies. Boy, do I owe you."

He tried to regain some sense of control. "You don't understand Ashley. When I lost my wife, I lost my appetite for life. Now, I just want to be left alone."

Ashley reached over and took his hands in hers and took a quick breath, "You must begin again my friend." Then she added, gently, "I really need you to assist me. I'm helping a model sue her former boy friend, a rich soccer player for abusing her. It's a big trial and an enormous amount of money is involved. And you need me as much as I need you. It's time to get back on your feet and come to work with me. And I won't take no for an answer."

His expression suddenly eased. He started to rethink his situation and saw a faint light at the end of his deep tunnel of depression.

Ashley smiled broadly. "Now, let's get you out of this hospital. I've got three weeks before the trial begins and I need you to do some investigative work for it and be my second chair."

He sighed and leaned back on his pillow, his features set in a line of expectation. "You think I can really help you with the trial?"

"Hell, man, not only help. But, we're going to take this Salasar guy to the cleaners. We've going to hit him hard in his money pockets where it will hurt him and show him he's not invincible. I know you watched many high profile attorneys handle cases like this."

After a week in rehab, Lanex finally pulled out of his depression and Ashley welcomed him as second chair.

With the former judge's assistance, Ashley was prepared to pull out all stops to win her client's case and obtain a large cash settlement. Twenty million dollars was considered small payment for all the physical and mental abuse Sherry had suffered at the hands of Diego.

Lanex had brought in one of his former students, Matt Blake, who now was a top undercover investigator. No secret could remain hidden from Matt. Still attending college, this part-time investigator had proven his worth on several cases in the city. He zipped around on his motorcycle with great ease finding witnesses and clues that helped win his clients' cases.

Chapter 3

The character witnesses Ashley brought in to testify against Diego Salasar seemed very impressive to the jury. They included a top sports magazine writer, a soccer coach, and, of course, several ex-girl friends, who Diego had failed to buy off. The ex-wives, naturally, had been paid to remain silent about Diego's many vices in return for his generous alimony. Consequently, they were not permitted by their agreements to testify.

The cross examination of these witnesses by Michele Bain, Phil's co-counsel, did not seem to move the jury very much.

On the other hand, Ashley could see Sherry had not overwhelmed the jury so far. The character witnesses Phil brought in to testify about Sherry had painted her as obsessed with Diego's fame and money.

As everyone sat in the courtroom, immersed in the case, the intense looking sixty-nine-year old Lanex Fox's cell phone suddenly rang.

His voice vibrating with fury, Judge Mercer immediately reprimanded Lanex on the spot. He reminded him he had previously ordered all cell phones be shut off.

"No cell phones were to be left on Ms. Willis. Advise your counsel of this."

Her features set in lines of exasperation, Ashley turned to Lanex and whispered to him. He sprang to his feet and ran outside of the courtroom to take the call.

Within a few minutes, he re-entered and slipped into the chair beside Ashley, leaned over and whispered briefly to her.

Ashley smiled broadly, dimpling with pleasure and stood up. "May I approach the bench your honor?"

The judge frowned, then nodded his agreement. Ashley, followed by Phil approached the bench.

"My associate has just located our last witness, a housekeeper at the hotel. She saw Diego punch Ms. Wine around. She's agreed to testify. I can have her here first thing in the morning."

"Well, it is late in the day, so this is agreeable to the court. Is this okay with you, Mr. Willis?"

Phil hesitated, swallowed, and forced himself to nod. "Yes. I have no more witnesses to present your Honor, so if Ms. Willis calls this witness and I have the opportunity to cross examine her, I feel I will be ready to present my closing statement."

The judge looked at Ashley. "Are you planning to call Ms. Wine to the stand to testify, Counselor?"

"No, your Honor."

The judge sighed, and leaned back in his chair, unhappy the trial was not progressing as rapidly as he had expected. "Please return to your seats, Counselors," he ordered.

Ashley and Phil resumed their seats. The judge pounded his gavel on the bench and announced to the courtroom, "Because of the late hour, this trial will adjourn for today. We will resume at nine-thirty tomorrow morning. At which time, Ms. Willis will present her final witness. After cross examination by the opposing counsel, we will start the closing arguments." Staring at the wall clock, he slammed his gavel down once again.

"Thank you, your Honor," Ashley said. She stacked up her papers and placed them in her briefcase, then leaned toward Lanex, cupped her hand around her mouth and whispered in his ear, "Good job. They haven't seen our best yet. There's a conference room next door. Let's go over there and you can bring me up to date."

"Yes Counselor," Lanex replied, his lips curved in a pleased smile.

"Boy, have you got my juices flowing now," Ashley said grabbing her briefcase from the table and starting to head out of the courtroom with Sherry behind her.

Following, Lanex said, "After our conference, dinner is on me."

As they walked out of the courtroom, their investigator, Matt Blake, rushed out of the elevator and headed toward them. Surprised at Matt's sudden appearance, Lanex paused, "Didn't expect to see you until tomorrow, Blake."

"Just wanted to tell you I've got our star witness all lined up. She's staying at a local hotel. On our expense account of course," he drawled, leaning closer to Ashley.

"Of course." Ashley's gaze narrowed slightly, her expression revealing amusement.

"And, she's ready to testify," Matt added.

"Good. I'll plan to see her later today," Ashley replied.

They entered the conference room and sat down on the far side of the round oak table. Sherry slid into her chair and casually crossed her legs. Ashley put her briefcase down and looked at Matt Blake. "You told me our witness's name was Marie Montoss. What does she look like?"

"An Hispanic lady in her late fifties, dark-haired, little and plumb with a friendly smile. Clean and neat. Should make a good, reliable witness," Matt answered.

Ashley thought for a few moments. "Okay. Let's treat her to supper tonight and brief her."

"The chef at the restaurant on the first floor of the hotel, where I put her up, makes great Mexican cuisine. Why don't we order room service. We can go over her testimony with her at the same time," Matt suggested.

"I like that. Let's map out our strategy first and then go over it with her," Lanex added. "And by the way, Ashley did you see the look on Diego's face when his attorney told him about our final witness?"

Ashley hesitated, then smiled and chose her words carefully. "Yes. I think he never expected us to find anyone who witnessed one of his rages. But it was an excellent piece of detective work on your part, Matt."

"It wasn't too difficult," he answered with a slight grin. "Once I got Sherry to remember the date the attack happened, I just had to find out which housekeepers were working on that floor of the hotel. After a few questions and a little coaxing, I got her name and number from the head housekeeper."

A little bit bored at the conversation, Sherry sighed and looked down at one of her chipped fingernails.

They looked up when they heard a sharp knock on the conference room door. Lanex walked over and opened it. Standing in front of him, was the attorney for the opposition, Phil Willis. Behind him were his co-counsel, Michele, and the defendant, Diego Salasar.

"May we come in?" Phil asked.

Lanex blinked at him in disbelief and glanced over his shoulder at Ashley. Her mouth dropped open in surprise, she stared in amazement at her father.

"Attorneys Willis and Bain and their client wish to know if they can come in," Lanex repeated to Ashley.

"Of course." She stood up and walked toward her father. "Well, this is a surprise. What can we do for you?"

Phil walked slowly into the room, his gaze was sharp and his expression determined. "My client wishes to negotiate a deal between Ms. Wine and himself."

Sherry looked up, now very much interested in the direction the conversation had taken.

Ashley raised one eyebrow is disbelief. "He's prepared to offer a monetary settlement?"

"No." Phil spoke softly. "Something we feel will be much more satisfactory to Ms. Wine. May we sit down?"

"Certainly." Ashley sat down and waved toward the chairs on the opposite side of the table.

As Phil, Michele and Diego were about to sit down, Lanex jumped to his feet. "Please Mr. Willis we feel this is a little premature. We haven't even thought about a settlement at this point. We're prepared to let the trial continue." His expression said he wasn't fooled by the opposing attorney.

Phil's mouth twitched. He glared at Lanex. "Oh, but we aren't. We're not going to offer a sum of money, nor will Diego admit to any guilt in this manner."

Ashley leaned forward and shook her head in rueful amusement. "In that case Attorney Willis, I think this discussion is over before it even started. Maybe you better leave."

Phil waved his hand at her. His sly grin said he wasn't fooled by his daughter's response. He knew he had gotten her attention. "Please Ashley, let me finish. I'm sure Sherry will find Diego's offer acceptable."

Sherry lifted her head, bitterness tainted her features. "I thought you just said — no money."

Michele looked at Sherry and smiled calmly. "Please just hear us out. If we can come to an arrangement, we can all meet in Judge Mercer's office, tell him the details, and have the case against my client dismissed. I'm sure the judge would like to see the case come to a quick conclusion."

"Drop the case!" Sherry exclaimed, glaring at Diego.

Her eyes bulged and her complexion grew mottled with rage. "Not in this lifetime."

Diego laughed and raked his hands through his hair and grinned at Sherry. "Just hear my attorney out, sweetheart."

"Yes. Just look this deal over," Phil said. He slid a manila folder over to Ashley and one to Sherry. "This is an agreement to drop all charges against Diego. In return, he will not admit any guilt. But he will set Sherry up in Paris with her own boutique and will give her financial support for her own designer clothing line."

He looked over at Sherry, who was now calmer. She listened with interest to the direction the offer had taken.

"Something I understand you have wanted for a long time," Phil continued. "He will let you hire your own staff, pay all your costs for two years, including two fashion shows. After that time, you will be on your own, and you can then decide if you wish to continue with the endeavor."

Sherry looked at Diego with suspicion, her eyes narrowing. "There must be some catch to this."

Phil shook his head. He knew he had skillfully turned the case in his client's favor. "No catch. Mr. Salasar will not be involved in the project in any way, other than financing it."

Ashley looked through the folder and studied the papers thoroughly. "This appears to be a great offer if you are interested in accepting it, Sherry."

Now all aglow, Sherry thought for a few minutes, then jumped to her feet and nodded her head in agreement.

"There, of course," Ashley said, "will be many details to work out and contracts to sign before we can proceed further with this."

Phil stood up. His eyes became faintly hooded and a slow smile curved his mouth. "I realize that. Why don't you look everything over tonight Ashley, and discuss this with your client. We can meet tomorrow morning about eight-thirty. If everything is agreeable with you and your client, we can sign the deal and meet with the judge before nine-thirty when the trial is scheduled to resume."

Ashley looked up at her father. It was difficult to hold back a broad grin. "We just might have a deal."

Chapter 4

The next morning, Ashley was up early—anxious to meet with Lanex and Sherry. Athletic like her parents, Ashley took great stock in remaining in fine physical condition. She dressed quickly, eager to head to the bike path that ran through Syracuse for her usual 3K run.

Back home, she ate a bowl of Special K, topped with dried cranberries and walnuts, accompanied with a cup of hot tea. During her warm shower, she thought extensively about the offer her father had made the previous afternoon on behalf of Diego Salasar.

Ashley decided the offer to send Sherry to Paris to open her own boutique was an extremely generous one. Not only that, but ultimately it would probably be worth far more than any monetary compensation Sherry might have received from a jury if they decided in her favor. The deal would offer a prompt and complete resolution of Diego's situation. He could resume his normal life and retain his many endorsements while he headed back to Portugal to train for the next soccer season.

Ashley, Lanex, and Sherry entered the courthouse. They found her father, Michele and Diego, waiting just inside the doorway on the first floor. Phil escorted them to a private conference room.

After everyone was seated, Phil squared his shoulders and studied his daughter. "After we reach a final agreement, we must meet with the judge and see if he will agree to drop the charges and dismiss the case against Diego."

After discussing a few points of the agreement, and changing a few lines of the contract, the matter was soon resolved. The parties agreed to settle the case out of court. Both Sherry and Diego signed the papers after two officers of the court were called in to witness them.

They all entered the courtroom. Phil escorted Ashley to the judge's chambers for a private meeting before the court was scheduled to start. Phil's expertise around the courthouse was apparent as he led Ashley to Judge Mercer's personal chambers. After they explained the situation, and reviewed the signed papers with him, Judge Mercer agreed to dismiss the case.

The courtroom was called to order and the case was resumed. Then, Judge Mercer announced the two litigants had reached a compromise and the case was dismissed. Hitting his gavel on the bench, he announced that court was adjourned.

Ashley and Lanex gathered up their papers and left the courtroom with Sherry. Diego and his defense team quietly left the court house by a side door. Diego was whisked away in a black limousine to avoid the media and the paparazzi.

Standing outside the courtroom was Ashley's star witness, Maria Montoss with Matt Blake. Ashley approached Maria and gently placed her hand on her arm. "Thank you for agreeing to testify for Ms. Wine; however, the case has been resolved and we will no longer need you. My investigator will see that you catch a ride home. Here is a check for one thousand dollars to compensate you for your time and inconvenience."

Maria mumbled her thanks for the generous check and she and Matt turned and left the courthouse.

Sherry, standing nearby with Lanex, seemed to be beaming with joy. Her relief came out in an explosive sigh. "I'm so glad the case is finished and I didn't have to take the stand. I hope never to see or hear from Diego again. And I'm anxious to be on my way to Paris. You both did a great job and have offered me the opportunity to get my life back together again."

"We're delighted to have been able to settle the case to your advantage," Ashley answered.

"Now, what about your fee?" Sherry asked.

"Oh, that's taken care of. Diego has to pay all fees for both sides, as well as court costs, as part of the agreement. Why don't you join us for lunch and we can toast to your new adventure?"

"No thanks. I've got a lot of packing to do and phone calls to make. I'm leaving for Paris this week." She gave Ashley a big hug, shook hands with Lanex and strolled out the front door of the court house. She did not try to avoid the news media; but, instead, took the time to pose for pictures and to announce that the case had been settled. According to the terms of the agreement, she could not discuss the settlement with the public; but the broad grin on her face indicated to everyone that the situation had been resolved to her satisfaction.

After Sherry left, Lanex turned to Ashley, "Why don't we do lunch?"

"Later, I need to talk to the judge about my next adventure. I promised him I would take a pro bono case," Ashley replied.

As she gripped her briefcase, her cell phone rang and vibrated incessantly.

She answered the call. "Hi Mom. What can I do for you?"

"I would like you and your brother to both stop by the house on Sunday for dinner. I'm going to put on a big roast for your victory dinner."

"Okay Mom. What time?"

"Three is good." Ashley hung up the phone and bid Lanex good-bye.

As he started to walk away, Ashley grabbed his arm. "Say, how would you like to come to my folks for dinner on Sunday. I'd love for my mother and brother to meet you."

"I'll take a rain check on that, Partner."

"Oh, now we are partners?" Ashley regarded him steadily.

"I wouldn't have it any other way, Counselor."

Entering her apartment, Ashley saw her land phone was blinking with recorded messages. She hit the button and listened to the first message that was from the Clerk of Courts. The message indicated that she was scheduled to be in court next week for a pro bono case in which she would represent a Calvin Moss.

The second message was from her brother, Alan. "Hi Ash. Just wanted to tell you that I'll see you on Sunday at the folk's house for dinner. Also, wanted to remind you that Mom's birthday is coming up next week. I booked our parents on a five-day cruise. You can go halves with me on the trip. I got a birthday card for both of us to sign."

The third recorded message was from the Life Ways Gym, reminding her that her membership was due for renewal.

Ashley dropped down on the sofa and grabbed a pillow. "Wow! I need a nap. It's been a long week." Her head was spinning. "Gotta slow down."

Just as she started to doze off, her land phone rang again. "Yes, this is Ashley Willis. Who is this?"

"Captain Garrett Grogan of the police department. I wonder if you could stop by and see me on Monday at the main precinct? I have something important I want to go over with you."

Ashley paused for a few moments. "Sure. What time?"

"Make it around eleven."

"Will do."

After she hung up, Ashley sat there thinking about this unexpected call. "Who is this guy and why on earth did he call me? I wonder what's going on."

Chapter 5

"Good morning, Captain," the desk sergeant said to Garrett Grogan as he entered the Syracuse Police headquarters early in the morning. Smiling, she stood up and extended her hand to the newly appointed Police Captain. "I'm Marge Olsen. Welcome to your first day."

With a large torso, great brawny shoulders in a tight police jacket, and dark hair on a large head, Captain Grogan stood silently, listening to her as Marge droned on with her welcoming speech.

Then, he held up his hand signaling her to be silent. "Please, Ms. Olsen."

"Oh, you can call me Marge. Everyone does. And how would you like to be addressed, sir?"

After a moment's pause, he grinned at her. "Captain. Just, Captain."

"I have your keys," she said, and led the way down the hall to his office and entered, with him following.

"Your office key opens all these doors." She walked over to the closet and opened it. Inside, sat a huge floor safe. "The safe combination is in your top desk drawer. The former captain stored his weapons in here."

Looking inside the closet, Captain Grogan could see that on hangers were a dress uniform as well as a khaki jacket, shirt and pants.

"Five boxes from your old office in Montgomery arrived for you yesterday. I unpacked them and arranged your things. I put your Auburn University pennant up on the wall. Placed some of your photos on the back desk."

He grinned sheepishly at her. "Anything important going on today that I should know about?"

She whirled around and pointed toward his desk. "There on your desk, you'll find today's agenda. You're scheduled to meet at ten fifteen this morning with the commissioner. I'll have a city map ready for you later in the morning, with all the precincts outlined."

"Thanks. That will be very useful," Captain Grogan said as he sat down on the swivel chair behind his desk. Then, he reached his hand across the desk to shake hers. "I think we're off to a good start."

Marge just nodded her head and turned to walk toward the door. "I take an hour for lunch at noon. There's a cafeteria in the basement. A menu is in your top drawer under the phone list. The gold pass in there entitles you to two meals daily."

"Is that everything now?" He tried to suppress a smile.

"Oh, yes. Your secretary replaces me when I go to lunch." Marge had delivered her indoctrination speech to the captain and left his office.

Captain Grogan broke out in a hearty laugh after she closed the door. "Sounds to me like I don't really need a secretary. Marge should be enough."

He walked over and opened the door to his private bathroom. "Never had an office this grand before," he muttered aloud. "My own private john."

Captain Grogan exited his office and walked down the hall, looking into the various rooms. At the end of the hall, he opened a double door that led into the room where the detectives were working. Looking around, he saw that this building was top rate and had all modern equipment.

He spoke briefly to several of the men, one of them gave him a tour of the facility. Returning to his office, he turned on his computer, started to look through it, when he heard a beep on the intercom system. He recognized Marge's voice as she announced, "Commissioner Dillard Hennasey here to see you, sir."

"Well, send him right in." He got up and shook hands with the Commissioner as he entered the room. "Well, Garrett, are you getting all settled in?" "Yes sir. One of the men gave me the royal tour. Please have a seat." He directed Hennasey to a chair across from him as he took his seat behind the desk.

"Hope that was enlightening," Hennasey said. "Just wanted to inform you the city council met to hammer out the new city budget. They're asking the police department to make a few cuts."

"Different city. Same routine," Grogan said, exhaling slowly.

Hennasey slid a manila folder across the desk to the captain. "Just spend the rest of the week studying how the department works. Then, take a quick look at these figures. See if you can find anywhere we can cut down on expenses without weakening the integrity of the department. I realize these figures are new to you, but do the best you can. We'll get back together in a week and work things out."

Captain Grogan briefly looked through the papers. "Anything else?"

"Have you met with your men yet?"

"Talked briefly to a couple of them. I'm calling a meeting for all the personnel in the squad room early tomorrow morning for a briefing. So far, it looks like I inherited a good team. I plan to meet separately with the detectives in the afternoon."

"Good. Sounds like you've got your future actions somewhat formulated," the Commissioner replied. "Let's plan on getting together next week to discuss your ideas for cutting our budget. Also, I have a few suggestions for you on how we can make the City of Syracuse even safer in the future. I just hope that you brought along some good ideas from Alabama's good old Southern Justice."

"I plan to do my best."

"I'm sure you will. That's why we recruited you. By the way, have you meet Lt. Willis yet?"

Garrett shook his head. "No why?"

"He's put together one hell of a SWAT team," the Commissioner said as he stood up.

The Commissioner headed for the office door, then after a brief pause, added, "You've probably got lots to do and I'm due at a luncheon. But, I just wanted you to know that you can call me anytime—day or night. Your predecessor never liked to follow the book—if you get my drift."

"I've got it." Grogan stood up, walked over and shook the Commissioner's hand. "I look forward to working with you, sir."

"Same here."

After he left the office, Grogan sat back down and looked through the file the Commissioner had given him. Before he had a chance to get fully absorbed in the report, he heard a brief knock on his door. "Come in."

The door opened and a young woman stuck her head inside. "I'm Mary Meyers, your secretary, sir." Grogan put down the papers. "Please come in."

She entered slowly. "Sir, I was wondering if you had any typing for me? Memos to put out. Any notices?"

He looked up at her and smiled gently. "Just one right now. I want to call a meeting for tomorrow at eight in the morning for all personnel except for the detectives. And by the way, I'm expecting an attorney, Ashley Willis, about eleven this morning. Please show her right in when she arrives."

"Fine. And I'll post tomorrow's meeting notice at once. Everything that I put out, I'll see that you get a copy first."

Later that morning, Ashley entered the police station and approached the duty officer. "Hi. I'm Ashley Willis. I have an appointment with Captain Grogan."

Marge looked up. "Right. You're early. His secretary told me he was expecting you. I'll buzz him, see if he's free now."

After talking briefly on the phone, Marge led Ashley down the hall to the captain's office, knocked and ushered her inside. "Ms. Willis, here to see you, sir."

The captain stood up, walked briskly toward Ashley and reached out to shake her hand. "Willis? Willis? Say are you related to Lt. Willis, the SWAT team commander?"

"Yes, sir. He's my brother," she answered proudly.

"Didn't associate the same last names until now." He motioned for Ashley to have a seat in front of his desk, as he walked around to the back and sat down.

"One of my fishing pals," he said, "Judge Mercer told me about you. He said you are one sharp young attorney. That you had a good handle on what goes on in the city. He told me to look you up if I needed some help or advice."

Ashley nodded.

He took no time at all to come to the point. "You're probably wondering why I asked you to meet with me."

"Yes, Captain. How can I help you?"

He leaned forward in his chair and looked at her intently. He rubbed his jaw, contemplating what to say. "I heard from the grapevine you did an excellent job in court the other day and that you have a great rapport with the mayor and judges in the area. Consequently, I was hoping that you could offer some help to me in my newly acquired position."

A short silence. Then Ashley replied, "Of course. If I can."

"I would like for you to give me a run down on the mayor, the city council, and the judges in this town. I'm from Montgomery where our police force had a tough time obtaining writs and search warrants from some of the good old boys. I was hoping that you could tell me what judges here would be most receptive to working with us."

"I could discuss this with my father, who is also an attorney, and get his thoughts on it. He's been around the city a lot longer than I have."

"Sounds like a good idea to me. I'd like you to sit down with me next week, after you have time to think this over. We could discuss how our police force can work effectively with the political and judicial systems in this town."

Ashley was stunned and overwhelmed that the new police captain had sought her advice.

"By next week, I should have some information gathered for you. I'll try to fill you in on what I can learn about the past communication lines between the systems. Was there anything else?" Ashley asked.

"No. That covers it," he replied simply.

Ashley stood up, leaned across the desk, and shook his hand. "It was good to meet you, Captain. I'm certain you'll find Syracuse a good place to work."

Late that afternoon, Captain Grogan heard a knock on his door. Before he had time to say anything the door flew open. It was Marge. He instantly realized that she was both out of breath and very excited.

"Captain, sir, we have a situation."

"Yes?" He gasped and jumped to his feet.

"Townsend Middle School on the East Side has a hostage situation. I wanted to brief you on it. Thought you might want to go to the scene."

Without another word, he grabbed her by the arm. "Brief me. But make it quick! Then, I'm out of here."

Chapter 6

Marge waved her hands in the air as she shouted, "Urgent state of affairs, Captain. A hostage situation at Townsend Middle School."

Her words echoed in his head. "I heard you. How do I get there?"

She raced to the desk, pointed at the phone and took a deep breath, trying to compose herself. "If you press the second button it will hook you up to the motor pool. You have two cars at your disposal at all times. One an unmarked plain black car and a second black and white one with our police insignia on it. Your driver, most likely Jimmy, will answer."

Captain Grogan picked up the phone and hit the second button. "It's Captain Grogan. Please bring the black car around to the front of the building and meet me. I'll be right out."

The captain walked over to his closet, grabbed his police jacket and headed for the door. His brow furrowed. His jaw tensed as he ran out of the office and to the front door of the building. Parked at the curb was the black car. Its driver was standing beside the open front door.

"Jimmy," the captain said. "I need to get to Townsend Middle School and quick."

"Yes, sir. Glad to meet you Captain Grogan." His voice was cool and collected, but his stance let Grogan know that Jimmy was ready to move.

After the captain climbed in, Jimmy slammed the door shut and ran around to the driver's side. He jumped in and turned on the ignition. Looking over at the captain he spoke sternly, "Better buckle up sir. We're only twenty minutes away from the school. I'll keep the police radio on all the time. Should I use the siren?"

Grogan glanced over at him and smiled broadly as he braced his feet on the floor. "Yes. Now go."

When they arrived at the scene, they found the news media had arrived there ahead of them. Jimmy pulled the car up in front of the school and Captain Grogan jumped out. Immediately a police sergeant ran up to him, his voice welling with relief, "Glad you got here, sir. I'm Sergeant Edwards, sixth precinct. I was the first at the scene in answer to the nine-one-one call."

Captain Grogan looked around, assessing the situation outside the building. His pulse quickened with adrenaline. He saw numerous police vehicles stationed nearby, and the scene was already taped off. With an unruffled voice, he commanded, "Okay, sergeant, brief me."

"Well, Chief..." Sergeant Edwards's voice dropped as he continued.

Grogan waved his hand and interrupted. "I prefer to be called Captain."

"Yes, sir." Edwards forced himself to slow down. "Well, Captain, the lady that made the call into the emergency system is right over there, June Tagert, assistant principal of the school."

"Let's go talk to her."

They approached her. Sergeant Edwards introduced the captain.

Aware that she was on the verge of losing control of

her emotions, the captain gently asked, "Can you tell me what happened inside the school building?"

Mrs. Tagert took a deep breath and tried to organize her thoughts. "After the bell rang dismissing the students, I helped them into the buses. Then, I went inside and headed down the hall toward the principal's office. Mary August is her name. That's her office over there." She pointed to the last window in the row, left of the school door.

"Yes. Go on."

"Well, sir, when I got just outside her office, I heard loud voices. Someone seemed to be shouting angrily at her. I peeked in the door window and saw our maintenance man, Jose Gonzales, in there with her. He was holding a gun and it was pointed directly at her."

"Anyone else in the room?" Sergeant Edwards asked.

For a moment, she could only nod, almost too nervous to reply. "Yes. Our part-time physical education and health trainer, Kelley Willis."

"Now, why does her name sound familiar to me?" Grogan frowned and took a step closer to her. "Do you know of any reason why this man would be holding the two ladies hostage?"

She began to tremble. "Maybe, it's because Mary told him she was considering firing him and she was going to get in touch with the police about him. The mother of one of our female students called her and said Jose had sexually molested the girl in the gym after school yesterday. I saw Jose leave the building early this morning—he must have come back later with a weapon. However, I believe that no one except the two women and Jose are in the building now."

"Good. Anything else I should know?" Captain Grogan asked.

"Yes. For what it's worth. Mary is my sister—my twin

sister." Tears began to fill her eyes. "I just can't believe that Jose would do this—he and his wife are such nice people."

"That's rather unusual isn't it? For two sisters to be assigned to the same school?" Sergeant Edwards interrupted.

"I guess so. I was working here first. Then, the school district made Mary a principal and transferred her here. We always thought that it was fate that we both choose teaching as our profession. Then we were placed in the same school. Today fate doesn't seem to be dealing Mary a very good hand. Everyone adores Mary. She has helped make this school one of the top high schools in Syracuse."

Captain Grogan squeezed her hand, quick to reassure her. "Don't worry. We'll get your sister out okay. And that's a promise."

Turning to Sergeant Edwards, he ordered, "Sergeant, make sure no one from the media crosses into the roped off area. And find out where Mr. Gonzales lives—have his wife brought here immediately."

"On it."

By now, police cars were surrounding the entire neighborhood around the school. A large police vehicle marked, "Syracuse Police Department—SWAT team" pulled up.

Captain Grogan gave a little gasp of relief. "Who is in charge of that team, Edwards?"

"Lt. Alan Willis, sir."

"Bring him to me at once," Grogan ordered.

Edwards whirled around and headed toward the truck.

Within a few minutes, he returned with the SWAT team Officer walking behind him. The man was dressed from head to foot in SWAT team gear including metal tipped combat boots and a heavy bullet proof vest.

He walked up to Captain Grogan and stuck out his hand. "Good afternoon, Captain. I'm Lt. Alan Willis and that's my team setting up the perimeter. We await your orders."

"I thought that name, 'Willis' sounded familiar to me. The janitor, Jose Gonzales is holding the principal and a Mrs. Willis hostage inside the building, Lieutenant."

"Oh, my God. That's my mother. She teaches part-time here."

"So Willis. What's your usual procedure in a hostage situation?"

"If you will follow me into the van, I'll explain, sir. I can't believe that my mother is in there, now I have to act quickly and calmly. I just can't let anything happen to my mom."

With Grogan behind him, Alan walked quickly up to the van, threw open the double doors in the back and climbed inside.

Alan turned on a computer and pulled up a program. "Sir, here's a layout of the inside of the school. Here's the principal's office, where I've been informed that two hostages are being held."

Then looking at Alan, Grogan asked, "Did you bring a negotiator with the team?"

Alan shook his head. "He's out of town. His grandmother passed away. But, I've had training at negotiating, so I was planning on handling it. Just say the word."

"Yes. Go for it," Grogan agreed, struggling to sound optimistic. "We don't have a minute to lose."

"Great. Here's my plan. I already have all four sides of the school covered with sniper shooters in place. As we speak, my team of fifteen men is ready for action. Also, in case we need them, I've brought a chemical team along. We should be prepared for anything and everything."

"It appears that you have a solid plan, Lt. Willis. Let's do it."

"First, I need to communicate with Mr. Gonzales and

try to negotiate the situation with him peacefully. My number one job is to get the women out safely." Although his voice sounded extremely confident, Alan's heart was pounding wildly.

"Good. I've instructed Sergeant Edwards to make sure that no one is allowed to cross the yellow tape," Captain Grogan added.

"Let's get going then," Alan said, as he threw open the door to the van and climbed out. Captain Grogan followed him.

Alan looked solemnly at the captain. "Sir, we can't take the chance on spooking the hostage taker, so I must proceed cautiously."

Grogan nodded in agreement. "I understand that Gonzales is married. I instructed Sergeant Edwards to have his wife brought here in case we need her."

"Excellent. She could be a great help," Alan added.

"Well, it's your show now Lt. Willis."

Inside the principal's office, Kelley Willis was trying to reason with Jose. "So far, Jose, you haven't done anything that can't be made right. The story about you and the girl is all just hearsay. There's no proof that you have done anything wrong to her."

Mary August, nodded. "Yes. Perhaps there has just been a misunderstanding. If we talk to the young girl who's accusing you we might be able to clear this all up. And you've been a good employee for years. I'm certain I can get the school board to allow you to continue working for us once we clear this mess up."

He took a hasty step backwards and the gun shook in Jose's hand as he considered what the women had just said. "I'm so afraid. And, I don't know what to do now."

"Just give yourself up and end this right now," Mary

said as she struggled to keep her emotions under control.

Outside the school building, Lt. Willis grabbed a bullhorn. "Jose Gonzales, this is the Syracuse Police Department. Please release Mrs. Willis and Mrs. August and surrender yourself. This is no way to try to remedy your situation. And there is no way out for you. The school is surrounded by police. I have ordered everyone not to shoot. Come out with your hands up."

Alan laid down the bullhorn and waited for a response from Jose. Ashley walked up behind him. "Oh my God, Alan. I can't believe this. I heard on television about this hostage situation. They mentioned that Mom was one of the ladies being held. What are you going to do? Please—please don't let that man hurt our mom."

He smiled grimly at her. "I hope that I've got the situation under control."

She leaned toward him. "I'm confident that you do. But, I think I have an idea on how to get Mr. Gonzales to give up." She whispered in his ear for several minutes.

There was a moment of silence before Alan's eyes widened. He looked at her with interest. "You think this might work, Ash?"

Nodding, she simply said, "It's worth a try."

Alan picked up the bullhorn once again, "Jose, a local attorney is standing next to me. She said she would represent you free of charge She is certain that if you have a clean record, she can prove that you acted on the spur of the moment and help prove that you're innocent."

Ashley grabbed the bullhorn from Alan's hands. "It's true, sir. You can trust me. Mrs. Willis is my mother and I promise I'll help you," she shouted.

The front door opened and Kelley and Mary came slowly out with their hands held high in the air.

"Don't shoot. He's letting us go free," Kelley yelled out.

"All SWAT team—hold your fire," Alan shouted out as

he rushed up to them and motioned for his men to escort them to safety behind the SWAT team truck.

Suddenly, Jose appeared in the doorway of the building. He threw his gun to the ground and raised his hands high in the air. With his weapon at a ready position in front of him, Alan approached the man.

"I wasn't going to hurt anyone," Jose said, as he dropped to his knees and started to weep. "I just got frightened and didn't know what to do. I panicked."

Jose's wife ran forward, knelt down on the ground and threw her arms around him. Jose turned to her and said in Spanish, "I swear, I'm innocent. I never touched that girl."

His wife patted him on the shoulder as she was now sobbing. He looked up at Alan and asked, "Are you going to handcuff me?"

Alan nodded his head and replied quietly, "I'm sorry, but I have to."

Followed by several of his men, the captain ran up to them. "Take Mr. Gonzales to headquarters. We'll work all of this out there."

Two of the policemen walked up, grabbed Jose gently by the arms and started to lead him toward a squad car. The others followed closely behind them.

When they got to the car, Alan motioned for Ashley to come forward. "This is my sister, Ashley, Mr. and Mrs. Gonzales. She'll go with you to the police station. I hope that she can get some of the charges against you dropped."

Jose looked at her with remorse in his eyes. "I'm innocent. I didn't do anything to the girl. And, I meant no harm to the two ladies, Miss."

Ashley smiled confidentially at him. "I believe you. I'll try to help."

After the squad car pulled away, Kelley rushed up to Alan. She gave him a hug. "Thank God, you came Alan.

Great job, Son."

The principal, Mary August, and her twin sister, June Tagert, walked up to Alan and offered their thanks to him for his efforts.

Mrs. Tagert put her hand on Alan's arm. "I want to tell you that the mother of the young girl who accused Jose of molesting her was in the crowd. She just came up to me and told me that her daughter falsely accused Jose. It seems that the other girls in her little gang dared her to make up the story and she did. It was all just a childish prank."

"Not so childish if you ask me," Ashley said sternly. "Almost ruining a man's life and reputation is not a childish prank. Plus, after taking two hostages; he is now in very serious legal trouble. We'll need a written statement from the young girl regarding her false accusation. I'll go get the girl and her mother and have them accompany me to the police station where the girl can make her statement."

Mrs. Tagert nodded. "I'm certain that the girl and her mother just want the whole mess cleared up quickly. "

Alan sighed. "I just hope that my sister can straighten things out for Jose. He seems to be the innocent party in all this."

Within the next half hour, the school lot gradually cleared out of spectators and the media.

"Good job, Lt. Willis," Captain Grogan said, patting Alan on the back. After shaking hands with all his men, he said, "Gentlemen, it's time for me to get back to the office.

Willis, I'll see you and your SWAT team at tomorrow's meeting?"

"Yes sir."

During the evening news, the media gave a glowing account of how the Syracuse Police Department and Lt.

Alan Willis and his team handled the hostage situation.
It stated that the incident was handled efficiently and no
one had suffered any physical harm. They even mentioned
that perhaps Lt. Alan Willis and his team should receive
an accommodation for their work.

But as she watched the news coverage of the event,
Ashley knew that it was going to take all of her expertise
to help Jose Gonzales.

Chapter 7

Ashley spent the next few days trying to help Jose Gonzales through his legal problems. Fortunately, the school declined to press charges as did Mary August and her mother, Kelley. After a long talk with Chief Grogan, Judge Harold Mercer decided to put Jose on probation for six months and send him to anger management classes. After his hearing with the judge, both Jose and his wife sobbed as they expressed their gratitude to Ashley for her expert assistance.

Jose was embarrassed when he first returned to the school to work, but, he discovered that both the teachers and the students received him with great warmth. He was soon back to his old job in the maintenance department, replacing light bulbs and cleaning floors.

On a Saturday morning, several months later, Ashley spent several hours doing her usual week end chores of grocery shopping and laundry. After lunch, she decided to take a three mile jog.

As she ran along the scenic Syracuse bike path, her mind

went over the two pro bono cases that she taken from Judge Mercer in return for his assistance with Jose's case. In the first one, she was to defend a homeless man who had stolen a loaf of bread from a bakery. The second one that she had agreed to take on was representing a woman who had taken a fall on the wet floor in the downtown mall and was suing for her medical bills.

After her run, Ashley decided to head over to Life Way's Gym. Bobbie Clark, her mother's old friend, was now managing the gym. She knew that Bobbie had hired two new male fitness instructors. She was anxious to see what program each of them could offer her.

Arriving at the gym, she went to the locker room and slipped off her jogging outfit. Entering the work-out area in form-fitting workout shorts and a top, she was aware of the fact that a lot of the male members of the gym were giving her the eye. Her strict diet and exercise regimen had apparently paid off.

A good-looking blond fellow jumped up from his workout machine and approached her. She decided that he could be somewhere in his late twenties. "Hi. I'm Don. Can I offer you a free workout session?" His blue eyes crinkled at the corners as he smiled. "I'll get you on a program that will keep that great body toned."

She bit her lip, felt her throat thicken. "That would be nice. I would appreciate it."

Ashley spent the next hour with Don, trying out the various machines with him and following his suggestions on how to exercise.

When she glanced down at her watch, she saw that it was almost three o'clock. She had just time enough to head home and shower and change before it was time to go to four o'clock mass.

"Catch you next week, Don," she said. The previous week had been long and difficult for her. Ashley was anxious to return home after mass, and enjoy a simple supper and a quiet TCM movie. She saw that "Double Indemnity" with Fred McMurray was scheduled for later that evening, it was one of her favorites. After that she planned to hit the sack early and sleep in until noon the next day.

Shortly before six, Ashley walked into the kitchen, opened the refrigerator and took out her supper—a big salad and vegetable lasagna. Gotta keep working on the figure—it was now the best that it had ever been.

She was disappointed when her mother had nagged her the previous Sunday about being too thin. "Are you eating three good meals a day, girl?" Kelley asked.

Ashley simply replied, "Yes, Mom."

Now, she sighed as she thought about the rest of the conversation with her mother., Kelley started questioning her daughter about her love life. "Ashley, our next door neighbor saw you having lunch and holding hands last week with someone she recognized. She said that his name is Jerry Albright and that he sells cars."

Ashley was surprised that her mother so boldly brought up the subject. "That's right, Mom. I did have lunch with a guy named Jerry. So?" Her stomach churned.

"My neighbor says that she bought a car from him, he's a fast talker and a bum, she said. And she said he's married. She asked him about the woman's picture in his office, and he said that it was his wife. I certainly hope you're not getting involved with a married man."

"Slow down, Mother. I just had lunch with him." The room had begun to spin at the sound of the anger in her mother's tone.

"Next you'll be telling me that he's getting a divorce."

Ashley half-smiled, but despite her best efforts to sound calm, her voice quavered. "As a matter of fact, he is. I met him when I went into the dealership to look at new and used Toyotas. I was considering trading in my old car."

Utilizing the right argument to a nice Catholic girl, Kelley had found the very weapon to use. She gave Ashley a fifteen minute lecture on dating a married man, and breaking up a home.

Ashley swallowed around the tremendous lump filling her throat. It felt like her mother was trapping her with words. "Mom, nothing serious is going on between us. So don't make a big deal out of it."

Kelley made a soft incoherent sound, and dropped the subject. But still, she gave Ashley a skeptical look.

Ashley, now concentrating on her nice quiet evening at home. Sitting at the kitchen table in her pajamas, robe and slippers, she ate her vegetable lasagna and sipped on an iced tea. As she ate, she reflected that sometimes her work seemed to overpower her. It certainly didn't leave her much time for dating. And so far, no prince charming was in sight.

When she finished eating, she took her dishes to the sink, rinsed, and placed them in the dishwasher.

After walking into the living room, she took a seat on the sofa and picked up the clicker for the TV. She heard the downstairs door buzzer for her apartment sounding. Not tonight, she thought. Please go away. But the buzzing continued.

She lurched to her feet and walked over to the wall speaker. "Who's there?"

"It's me, Jerry Albright."

She blinked in surprise, her eyes narrowed as she said into the speaker, "I wasn't expecting you Jerry. I told you that all our future contact should be business related. Call me at the office."

"Hey. It's starting to rain out here, babe. Let me in," he pleaded." I really need to talk to you now."

Ashley sighed and reluctantly hit the buzzer. "Come on up."

Ashley had met Jerry Albright when she entered the Toyota dealership and quickly discovered that he had a way of getting close to people. "People. I love people," he told her. Apparently, his manner endeared him to most of his clients, for he was a very successful car salesman. He acted like he was a ladies' man and was a very smooth talker. Sometimes Ashley thought that he came on a bit too strong.

She was walking around the dealership looking at all the cars when he approached her. After talking with her and showing her several cars, he invited her to join him for lunch at the small neighborhood restaurant next door. He told her they had a six-ninety-nine luncheon special with all- you-can-eat soup and salad. When they entered the restaurant, it was packed.

Jerry spotted an empty table, rushed over and grabbed it without allowing the nearby busboy a chance to clear it. After the table was cleaned, the waitress walked over and took their orders.

Eating lunch, Jerry did most of the talking. Ashley glanced at her watch and gave him a bland smile. "I've got to go. Thanks for inviting me for lunch."

As she started to leave, Jerry fell into step beside her and grabbed her by the arm. "You're a lawyer. Right?"

"Yes. Why?"

He paused and she saw indecision in his eyes. "You got a card? I think I might need your legal services." He took her silence for the agreement that it was. She reached into her purse and gave him a card.

Three days later, Jerry called her and asked her out to lunch again. His charm slowly won Ashley over and she continued to meet him. Finally, Ashley bought a used car from him that had low mileage and was still in warranty.

"You'll look terrific behind the wheel of that blue Corolla," Jerry said.

After learning Jerry was married, she decided not to continue their relationship. When she finally questioned his marital status, he admitted that he was married, but tried to explain. "The reason I mentioned that I might need your services, is because I'm in the process of getting divorced. I'm not happy with the lawyer that's working for me. In fact, I'm planning to dismiss him and hire you."

Ashley look startled. "Jerry, right now my plate is full. I have lots of new clients. I can, however, give you the names of some fine divorce lawyers. But thanks for helping me get the car. It's running good."

She was disgusted Jerry had the nerve to show up on her doorstep, late at night. She decided it might be better to let him in, rather than have him wake up all the neighbors with his insistent ringing of the downstairs buzzer.

Realizing she had on only a nightgown, robe and slippers, Ashley dashed into the bedroom and quickly changed into a warm-up suit.

Returning to the living room, she heard loud knocking on the door. "Hold on. I'll be there in a minute."

She went to the door and looked through the peep hole to be sure that it was Jerry. She unlocked the chain and opened the door and faced him boldly. "What do you want, Jerry? It's late."

He walked in and gave her a quick kiss on the cheek. "Thank God you were home, babe."

She glared at him and anger clouded her thoughts. "I

told you before, I'm not your babe."

"Ya. Sure." He stood inside the entrance way as the rain dripped from his coat.

Something was wrong. She could feel it in her chest and the skin at the nape of her neck. "Take off your raincoat and shoes. I'll put your coat in the bath tub to drip. Leave the shoes in the hall. Don't need you tracking up my clean carpet."

He slipped off his raincoat, handed it to her and reached down to take off his shoes. Ashley headed to the bathroom with the raincoat in hand. He yelled out to her, "I need a drink, honey. Where do you keep the booze?"

Without answering him, she threw the raincoat over the shower head and left it to drip in the tub and returned to the living room. When she arrived there, she saw that Jerry had already slouched down deeply into one of the chairs.

Held by a thin thread, her anger snapped. "Jerry, don't get comfortable. Tonight's not a good night to visit."

He leaned back in the chair and his mouth curved in a half smile. "I've got news my sweet. But first, I need a drink."

Ashley looked at him with apprehension. "It better be good this late at night."

"My wife tossed me out. So here I am. Brought my suitcase. Hope you don't mind, honey. It's outside in the hall."

Ashley's temper exploded. She stood in front of him and put her hands on her hips, as she glared down at him. "First of all, I told you not to call me honey or sweetie—ever. Second of all, you're not staying here to night."

He looked positively insulted. "But I need you, Ashley. I don't have any other place to go. My wife, or I should say, my soon to be ex-wife, will take me for all I've got. You've got to represent me in the divorce case. I'm counting on you to be my savior."

Ashley threw her hands in the air in disgust. "I repeat—you are not staying here tonight or any other night. And secondly, I am not getting involved with your divorce case."

His upper lip curled. His expression hardened, turned mocking. "But you nailed that case months ago with the soccer player didn't you?"

"That wasn't a divorce case. Those two weren't ever married."

"But you could make an exception for me if you wanted to. Couldn't you?" His features hardened. "I told you I really need your help."

Ashley remained determined not to get personally involved with Jerry Albright. Her voice dropped. Became ice cold. "I'm sorry. I can't help you. I won't help you. Now I'm asking you to leave."

Ashley stomped out of the living room, went into the bathroom and grabbed Jerry's still dripping raincoat off the shower head.

She returned to the living room and threw it in Jerry's lap.

He looked up at her. He laughed, and it was a brutal sound. "You can't throw me out. Where will I go?"

She shot him a long disapproving glance and snapped, "There's a hotel in the next block. Try there."

He stood up slowly, raincoat in hand. "But, what about a drink first?"

Ashley remained firm in her determination. "No drink, Jerry. Time to go."

He hung his head. "Please?"

"No. No drink. No stay. Just leave," she ordered.

He walked slowly to the hall, bent down and put his wet shoes back on. After slipping into his raincoat, he turned and asked, "When will I see you again?"

Ashley knew there was no sense in giving Jerry any hope for a future with her. "Probably never."

"I helped you buy a car remember."

"And I paid for it. Right?"

Looking humble, he asked, "Can I say or do anything to change your mind, Ashley?"

She shook her head. "Please Jerry. Just go." She walked to the door and opened it for him. Jerry slowly left the apartment.

After closing the door behind him, Ashley slumped down on the couch. "Now, I need a drink," she muttered. "I'm definitely going to put my love life on hold. I'll call Mom tomorrow and tell her that."

Reflecting on her recent experience, she sighed. "Why can't I find a good guy like Dad?"

Chapter 8

The next morning, Ashley heard a loud knocking on the door of her apartment. She forced herself to open her eyes and looked at the clock on the bedside stand. Once her eyesight came into focus, she saw that it was after eleven. It had taken her until after two to get to sleep as her mind kept reviewing her encounter with Jerry the night before. She definitely knew that her future did not include Mr. Albright. She hoped that the person knocking was not him again.

The knocking on the door continued insistently for several minutes. Ashley grabbed her robe, threw it on and dashed into the living room. "Who's there?"

Looking through the peep hole, she saw her brother, Alan.

She opened the door, and was amazed to discover that her parents were standing beside him.

She wondered why they had showed up, unexpectedly, at her front door, on Sunday.

"Hi guys. Sorry, it took me so long to answer the door. I just woke up. What brings you here?"

Her mother smiled sweetly at her as she entered the room. "We're here to take you to brunch. Alan's treat."

"I didn't hear the downstairs buzzer. Did someone let

you into the building?" Ashley asked, feeling completely at a loss.

Alan looked at her and his lips curved. "No silly. Mom still carries that master key that she got when she worked undercover years ago. That damn thing can open any door."

Ashley motioned for her father and brother to come in. "I'll put on some coffee. Mom, you said that Alan is going to take us to brunch? He must have something special to tell us."

Kelley nodded and shot a long approving glance at Alan.

Ashley stared at him as a sly smile came across his face. Then Ashley noticed that standing in the doorway was Alan's girlfriend, Laura Reid.

Ashley rushed over to her. "Goodness. Please forgive me. I'm half awake. I didn't even notice you standing there ."

The two women hugged briefly, as Ashley drew Laura into the room. "You look radiant. My brother must be treating you well."

She broke into a big smile. "Yes. You could say that."

Phil stepped forward. "Boy, does Alan have some news for you, honey. Your Mom and I will put on the coffee. You get dressed. Then, we'll all sit down and talk."

"Well, okay," Ashley said, her eyes shining with anticipation. "Brunch, you said. I'll go clean up and get dressed. I can't wait to hear the news."

A short time later, Ashley walked into the living room, dressed in dark blue slacks and a beige turtle neck sweater. She found Alan and Laura snuggled close together on the sofa. Phil and Kelley were seated comfortably in nearby chairs.

"Ready for that coffee now, Ashley?" Kelley asked. Then added in a deceptively quiet tone, "No wonder you're so thin, I couldn't find any sweets in the kitchen to go with our coffee."

Kelley handed her a cup of coffee. Ashley ignored her mother's comment and squeezed onto the sofa beside her brother and his girlfriend.

"Now, Alan, you can tell your sister the big news," Kelley ordered.

"No Mom. I'll let Laura tell it."

Laura's face broke out in a big smile, and held her left hand out to Ashley. "Last night, Alan and I got engaged."

Ashley's brows shot up in amazement as she took hold of Laura's hand and looked carefully at the ring. "Wow! Quite a rock. I need more details." She gave both Laura and Alan a hug.

"And I would like you to be my Maid of Honor," Laura said to Ashley. "I feel like you're the sister I never had."

"I would be honored." Ashley was stunned and overwhelmed with emotion. The request was so touching that she couldn't hold the tears back.

"Now for the rest of our news," Alan said. "Laura just got off the phone before we came over here. She confirmed the church and in a month, we're going to be married at St. Cecelia's."

"A month? Can you get everything arranged that fast?" Ashley eyed Laura with concern.

"Why the rush?" Phil asked.

"Why not Dad?" Alan replied, without losing a beat. "Mass at eleven in the morning, followed by a reception in the community hall."

"Then, we're off for a four-day honeymoon cruise," Laura added.

"So, still—why the big rush?" Ashley asked.

Alan ran his hand through his hair and a smile grew in his eyes. "That's the other big news. After the honeymoon, the new Mr. and Mrs. Alan Willis are moving to Tampa, Florida."

"Whoa! You're moving to Tampa? Just like that?"

Ashley asked, somewhat bewildered. "Isn't that kind of a hasty decision?"

Alan leaned forward, his face flushed with excitement. "No. I was offered a new job that I just couldn't turn down. The governor of Florida is starting a new training program throughout the state, called, 'Florida SWAT teams in Action'."

"And what will you be doing?" Ashley asked.

"My job is to get all the major cities in the state up and running with a top SWAT team. I get to carry over all the time that I've put in on the police force here toward my future retirement. And not only do they pay the cost of my moving, but I'll have great benefits and a terrific salary."

"But the part that I like best is getting Alan off the streets," Laura chimed in.

Alan smiled at his folks, the hundred and fifty-watt version. "We've got lots of calls to make to set up the wedding. But, I'm sure that we can pull it all off. Now, Dad, it's your turn. Tell Ashley your news."

Ashley sat upright in her chair, as she tried to absorb what had just been said. "Wow, Dad—there's even more?"

Phil raised his head and looked at his daughter. "We got a buyer for the house. We decided to purchase the condo we looked at the last time we were in Bradenton, Florida."

"Oh, my gosh. Everyone's moving away from me," Ashley gasped as her lips parted in surprise.

"That's just part of our news," Kelley added. "Your dad got a job teaching a couple of law courses at the nearby community college and I lined up a part-time job at the local hospital in their physical therapy department."

Ashley drew a long shaky breath. "You four seem to be on a fast moving treadmill."

Phil stared at her solemnly. "It may seem fast, but we feel that it's the right time and the right move. But, not too much downsizing for us. We want a nice size place where we can have our growing family visit us."

For a few moments the room got quiet. Ashley stared at the group wide-eyed and tried to collect her thoughts.

Alan decided to soldier on and reached for the coffee pot on the table. "Anyone for more coffee?" Everyone shook their heads. "No."

Phil turned toward his wife. "Time to ask Ashley the question, dear?"

"Best that you ask her," Kelley said . "She'll understand better where we're coming from."

Ashley looked at both of them with a puzzled question on her face. "Ask me what?"

Taking a deep breath, Phil put his cup down, grinned wickedly, then sobered and said, "Okay. Here goes. We want you to follow us down to Florida eventually. Once the four of us are settled in, we'd like you to join us."

Silence filled the room as Ashley tried to contemplate what her father had just said. Finally, she asked, "And what would I do in Florida?" She jumped up and started to pace the room.

"You tell her Kelley," Phil said as he moved to the edge of his seat.

"Your father would like you to take the bar exam in Florida. He can help you study for the test. He renewed his license there and he's certain it wouldn't take you very long to pass the Florida Bar."

"You could clerk at a law firm there while studying for the exam. It might be a slight reduction in your income for a little while, but I'm confident that you wouldn't have any trouble passing the bar there," Phil added.

They could hear the reservation in her voice as Ashley responded. "Well, I would love to live close to all of you. And a change of pace might be good for me. I just have to think over the situation and weigh all my options."

Kelley leaned forward and asked hesitantly, "By the

way, Ashley, you're not still seeing that married man are you?"

"No." Ashley shook her head and shot her mother a long, disapproving glance. "But, let's slow down a bit."

Phil glared at Kelley. "Now dear, Ashley is a grown woman, it is her career and her life. But, she's right about one thing. Let's slow down a little."

Ashley gave her dad a look of gratitude. "I love you guys, but I need time to think. No quick decisions for me. Maybe by the time you land and get all set up in Florida, I'll know what my next move is."

Alan stood up and chuckled. "Good idea, Ash. I have one last announcement. I won a drawing at work. First prize was two hundred fifty dollars to be spent at the classy Harrison Hotel. I'm told that they have a great brunch from eleven until three today. So, my treat. I'm sure that everyone has a healthy appetite now."

As they started to leave the apartment, Kelley took Ashley gently by the arm. "Don't worry, dear. Everything will work out for you. Sorry I pressed you on your personal life."

"That's okay," Ashley answered in a soft voice. "Right now, that's the least of my problems."

A half smile curved her mouth as she turned to Alan. "Say big brother, does that buffet have the all-you-can-eat crab legs?"

"I called them to ask that. And the answer is yes. Okay group, let's take my van."

Chapter 9

After six months, all of the Willis family's plans had been fulfilled. Laura and Alan had gotten married in a quiet ceremony and had moved to Tampa, where Alan started his new job .

They settled into a two-bedroom apartment in South Tampa. The headquarters for his newly formed division would be housed in a nearby police substation. He was delighted to learn he had been assigned both a secretary and an assistant to help set up his SWAT team program.

Kelley and Phil sold their home in Syracuse and moved into a two-bedroom, two-bath condominium in a gated community in Bradenton, near Tampa. The condo was perfect for them with a modern kitchen with granite counter tops and stainless steel appliances. The community pool and nearby golf course had also been a deciding factor in their selection. And the activities offered many entertaining programs, including week end cook-outs.

They sold most of the furniture from the house in Syracuse. After the move, they spent a lot of time purchasing new and modern furniture for their new home.

Even leaving the two-car garage behind had not been a setback since they had sold the oldest car of their two automobiles. Kelley planned to walk or ride her bike to the nearby hospital for her part-time job.

Kelley and Phil, and Laura and Alan, were busy getting settled into their new lives. Ashley's life seemed to be on hold. After its many delays proved a real challenge, she finished up the pro bono case that she had taken for the woman who fell in the mall. In the meantime, finding new clients for the firm had proved a real problem in spite of the numerous ads that the company had placed.

Today, with a light rain falling outside, Ashley immersed herself in a new John Grisham novel. As she was reading, she heard her land phone ringing from somewhere. She heaved a sigh. "Where are you little buddy?" she muttered out loud as she looked around the living room. Suddenly, she remembered that she had left it in the bathroom earlier. She ran in there and picked it up.

"Ashley Willis here."

The voice on the other end responded, "Good day, Ms. Willis. This is Gina Bella. You don't know me, but I know your folks. I'm staying at a hotel not too far from your residence. I live in Dolphin Springs, Florida, where your parents used to live and still visit occasionally. In fact, they suggested that I give you a call when I arrived in Syracuse."

"Oh, why is that?" Ashley asked politely.

"I have something personal that I wish to discuss with you. Any chance that we could dine together tonight? We can talk then. There's a Tai restaurant downstairs in the hotel where I'm staying. Maybe we could meet there. That's if you like Tai food?"

Ashley thought it over for a few seconds. "Sure. Why not? What's the name and address of the hotel and restaurant, Ms. Bella?"

"Call me Gina," she replied. "It's Thai Town, off the main lobby of the Dexter Hotel. Does six work for you, Ms. Willis?"

"The name is Ashley. Six is great. And I know the restaurant well. I've been there before. I'll make the reservation for us and will meet you there, Gina."

Ashley did not know it, but Gina was smiling as she continued, "I have a lot of things that I would like to talk over with you. And, I'm really interested in getting to know you."

Ashley hung up the phone, and mulled over what Gina had just said. "Who is this woman; how does she know my parents?"

Ashley drove to the hotel, parked in its underground garage and made her way upstairs to the restaurant. She arrived promptly at six and asked the hostess if a Gina Bella had arrived yet.

"Yes. She just got here. I'll take you to her table." She motioned toward a tall and slender young woman who appeared to be in her mid-thirties, sitting at a table against the nearby wall. With her long black hair, dark eyes, and olive complexion, Ashley decided the striking woman definitely looked as if she was Greek.

Ashley approached her. Gina stood up and extended her hand. "Ashley Willis. I would have known you anywhere. You look so much like your mother. Please have a seat."

Sitting at a nearby table were two young men who Ashley recognized as attorneys that she often encountered at the courthouse.

Both of the men waved at Ashley and she waved back. Then, they stood up and walked over to the ladies. "Hi there Ash. How about you and your friend joining us for dinner?" one of the men asked.

Ashley swallowed uncomfortably and grinned. "Maybe another time."

Ashley could tell the local attorneys wanted to meet this beautiful six foot beauty. She smiled sweetly and introduced Gina to them. She added in what she hoped was a very courteous tone, "Gina and I have some private business that we have to discuss."

The men returned to their table. Gina raised a cool eyebrow and whispered, "Maybe, I should consider moving here. I'm surrounded by senior citizens and trailer parks where I live. And you seem to have some attractive looking guys here."

Ashley replied with a faintly ironic little smile, "Attractive, yes. And young and struggling. I hope they didn't annoy you."

"As a matter of fact, I'm rather flattered. I live in Dolphin Springs, where most of the elderly men are not looking for a wife, but rather a nursemaid or housekeeper."

Ashley raised her head and looked into Gina's eyes. "Oh, I've heard my mother talk often about Dolphin Springs. She and my father used to live near there years ago. She just loves returning to that area. She always talks about the Epiphany Festival."

"Yes. That's in January. When the archbishop throws the cross into the bayou and the young boys dive for it. Retrieving the cross is supposed to give them a year's good luck." Gina picked up the menu. "Now, let's eat. I'm famished. You said that you were familiar with this restaurant. Can you recommend something?"

Ashley pushed back her hair and pointed to an item on the menu. "I usually get the crab Rangoon for an appetizer, then follow it up with Phah Thai... a noodle dish with chicken."

Gina studied the menu, and then placed it down on the table. "What you recommended sounds good. Make it two."

The waitress, dressed in a Thai sarong, approached them and took their order. She returned in a short time with the appetizers and two hot teas. They both quickly consumed the appetizers and went on to eat the entrees with relish.

Finally, Gina wiped her mouth on her napkin and glanced at the empty plates. "Looks like neither of us need a takeout box."

"I love this kind of food," Ashley said with a heartfelt sigh. "And it's both filling and easy on the figure. Working out daily and eating sensibly is my continuous objective."

The waitress removed their empty dishes. "Do you wish some dessert," she asked. "Maybe some coconut custard or Thai ice cream?"

"Both are delicious, I highly recommend either of them," Ashley said to Gina.

"I think I'll pass," Gina answered.

"Me too," Ashley chimed in. "But I will have a Thai coffee. How about you, Gina?"

Gina nodded. "Sure. And it will give us a chance to talk about why I called you."

The two women sipped their coffees and leaned back in their chairs.

Finally, Gina said in a low voice, "As I mentioned earlier, I know your parents. My grandparents are Mr. and Mrs. Gus Katalolis. Your parents knew them when they worked as private investigators years ago in Dolphin Springs. My brother, Dino, and I own a small law firm in Dolphin Springs—'Bella and Bella.' And I'm here in Syracuse doing some investigative work on a case that he's handling."

Their waitress stopped by the table with the coffee pot in hand. "You like more coffee?"

"No thank you," Ashley replied. "But I do love your attire."

After the waitress walked away, Ashley exhaled slowly. "You know it's getting kind of noisy in here, Gina. I don't live too far from here. Why don't we go to my place where we can talk quietly? I'll drive you back to the hotel when we're finished."

"That sounds good. I do have a lot to discuss with you. But better yet, why don't we go up to my hotel room and chat there."

Ashley stood up. "That's even better."

Gina grabbed the check on the way out. "My treat. I'll write it off as a business expense."

Once they were comfortably settled on the sofa in the hotel room, Gina wasted no time before she told Ashley why she had wanted to meet with her.

"I understand that you know a Jerry Albright," she said.

Ashley felt the color drain from her face. She couldn't hide the discomfort that the words had inflicted. "Yes. As a matter of fact, he was trying to get me to handle his side of his divorce. How do you know him?"

Gina smiled without humor. "His wife was originally from Dolphin Springs and moved back there recently. She has asked my brother to represent her in the divorce case since he is licensed to practice both in Florida and New York. He went to law school up here and worked in New York City before he moved back to Dolphin Springs where we set up a joint practice."

"So. Why are you asking me about Jerry?" Ashley nibbled on her lip nervously.

"I'm here to investigate him. My grandmother told your mother that Dino, my brother, was going to represent a Mrs. Jerry Albright in her Syracuse divorce case. Your mother said that name was familiar to her. In fact, she said you had been going out with some married guy named Jerry Albright. She told grandma how she wasn't too happy about that."

Ashley frowned and she contemplated that statement. "Yes. Mother made no bones about how she felt about him."

"Anyway. We soon figured out it *is* the Jerry Albright you know. He was indicted several years ago for picking up a prostitute and raping her. He eventually paid her off, and she refused to testify against him."

"Wow! I didn't realize that he had a past like that," Ashley exclaimed with a look of disbelief. "He helped me to get a good deal on a car. I only went out with him about three times before I discovered that he was married."

"I guess you were lucky that you didn't get seriously involved with him," Gina said, leaning forward.

"I suppose you're right. About six months ago, he came to my apartment and wanted to stay the night. He said his wife threw him out. I sent him off to a hotel and said goodbye to him. That's the last that I saw of him. Wish I could give you more information ."

"Well, he and his wife will soon be in court. And Dino is busy digging up all the dirt that he can on Albright to help the wife's case. Actually, my brother would like them to settle out of court, if possible," Gina replied earnestly. "No messy hearing; just split the assets fifty-fifty."

Ashley inclined her head. "I still have his business card, Gina." She reached into her purse. " Here's where he works."

"Thanks. I'll try to find out what he's up to." Gina looked briefly at the card.

"Now, I have something that I would like to confer with you about. You probably know my parents and my brother and his wife now live in Florida. I was thinking of moving there myself and I wonder if you know of any law firms near you that are looking for some assistance. I would have to study for the Florida bar before I could practice law there, but in the meantime, I could work as a law clerk."

Gina thought for a few moments before answering.

"Gal, you must be a mind reader. That's one of the things that I wanted to talk to you about. As, I told you, my brother and I have our own office in Dolphin Springs and our practice is definitely growing. We could use a sharp gal like you on our team. Maybe you could work for us, while you study for the Florida exam."

"That sounds like a great idea," Ashley said.

"I'm certain that we could work out a satisfactory arrangement for you. Just think about it."

A smile broke across Ashley's face as she stood up. "I would love to live near my family and avoid the cold winters in Syracuse. And other than my job, there's not too much holding me here. The lease on my apartment is month to month."

Gina looked directly into Ashley's eyes. "I hope you'll think seriously about it. I'm certain that you would fit into the Dolphin Springs community easily." She reached into her pocket. "Here's my card with my number on it. Keep in touch."

Ashley took the card. Her eyes narrowed and she hesitated briefly. "Well, I better be going. I've got a big day tomorrow. Thank you for the kind offer. I'll think about it seriously and get in touch with you soon about my decision."

Gina followed her. "And if you decide not to make the move, I hope that you'll at least visit me soon. And bring your bathing suit. You know those white sandy beaches are waiting for you."

"Thanks. I'll call you soon with my decision."

On the drive back to her apartment, Ashley contemplated Gina's offer. She knew moving to Florida would mean a big change for her. Maybe this was the right time to do it. She was single and nothing was really holding her in Syracuse. By moving, she would be near her family and getting her Florida law license should be a snap with dad's help. Yes, she would just up and do it.

Chapter 10

After her discussion with Gina Bella, Ashley thought constantly about the offer and what she planned to do with her future. The rest of her family was now permanently settled in Florida.

Her father, Phil, was teaching three days a week at the local campus of USF. Her mother, Kelley, was working part-time at the Bradenton Hospital doing physical therapy. They both planned to work a few more years until their Social Security benefits kicked in. And for the present, they needed to keep working for the health care benefits. Besides, they said, living in a gated community made them feel like they were already retired.

Alan and Laura had settled into a two-bedroom apartment, but were now looking for a home to purchase. To hear Kelley talk, all the dreams of the four Willis's were right on track.

With winter rapidly approaching, Ashley could easily remember the record breaking snow storms of the previous year in Syracuse. The more she thought about moving to Florida, the more she was inclined to believe it would be a wise decision.

After carefully thinking the situation over for a couple

of weeks, Ashley picked up the phone and called Gina in Dolphin Springs.

When she told her that she was ready to make the move, Gina replied, "Come on down, gal. We need you."

That statement was all that Ashley needed. She dialed her folks and told them of her decision.

"Just bring your clothes and computer and fly down. The fresh start will do you good, honey," Kelley said with joy.

Hanging up the phone, Ashley knew that she had made the correct decision. Somehow living in Syracuse had run its course. She was now in her late twenties. It was time for her life to take a new direction.

There was no turning back as her ticket from the Syracuse airport to Tampa International was one way. She had closed up her apartment, sold most of her furniture and her car. Boarding the early morning flight, she exclaimed, "Lookout sunny beaches—here I come!"

After arriving about noon, Ashley picked up her luggage and placed it on a cart. When she walked outside the baggage area she discovered a short heavy-set man waving a sign with her name on it. She rushed over to him. "You must be Wayne. I'm Ashley Willis. Gina said she'd send you to pick me up."

"Yes. The name's Wayne Recker. You're in my hands now," he smiled and grabbed Ashley's bags off the cart. "My carriage is at your disposal."

Amusement flickered in Ashley's eyes. "Carriage. I'm not Cinderella."

"I know," he croaked. "I'm just trying to be real friendly. Ms. Gina told me to give you the royal treatment."

He led Ashley outside the terminal to the curb where a blue van was waiting. The sign on the side of the van read, "Blue Streak Vans. Let us drive you—it's faster and safer."

Wayne opened the back door of the van and threw Ashley's luggage inside. Then came around to the passenger door and opened it for her. When he spoke his voice was filled with enthusiasm, "Hop in. I have a surprise for you."

Ashley stepped on the running board and climbed inside. Wayne went around to the driver's side, jumped in, shut the door and turned on the ignition. "Buckle up, lady."

Ashley snapped her seat belt on. "Do you know where to take me?"

"I do. Indeed, I do. In fact, I have a little treat for you. Now just sit back. You're in for a mini tour of the area. Have you ever been here?"

Smiling at the recollections that came to her, she answered, "When I was little, my folks brought my brother and me here for vacation. I especially remember the fantastic beach. I loved the birds, the white sand and playing in the surf. Anxious to see the beach again."

Wayne tilted his head to the side and chuckled. "You're lucky. You came at a great time of the year. We have extraordinary weather here now. Not too hot and humid. But before I take you to the place that Gina rented for you, I'm going to give you a quick tour of Tampa. Nice city. Known for its Gasparilla pirate parade in January and its busy Ybor City. Then, we'll head over to Clearwater Beach. That's where I live."

"And what about the so-called surprise? Why all the mystery?"

"You'll see," he answered with a big grin on his face.

After a short tour of the city, Wayne started across one of the three bridges leading from Tampa, west to the Gulf Coast. Ashley noticed that the sign on the Courtney Campbell Causeway read "To Clearwater Beach."

"You said that you lived on Clearwater Beach," Ashley asked. She looked excitedly at the beautiful blue waters on both sides of the Causeway.

Wayne nodded. "Yup. Love it there. I came down from New Jersey about ten years ago. Bought a small cottage about a block off the water. My brother and his family will be moving here soon. I gotta find him a job and a place to live. But for you, that's all taken care of."

Ashley sighed. "I'm glad to have a job lined up. Don't know yet where I'm supposed to stay. But Gina said that she took care of that for me."

Wayne smiled. "You did bring some suntan lotion, didn't you? And your swim suit?"

"Yes," Ashley answered. The traffic started to get more congested as the van approached the beach area.

"It's really busy here this time of the year," Wayne said as he maneuvered the van through the round-a-bout on Clearwater Beach. "Lots of snow birds and vacationers."

He turned down one of the side streets and pointed to the water at the end of it. "Look, there's the Gulf of Mexico. Did you ever see such white sandy beaches?"

"Yes, a long time ago. And you've convinced me. I'm staying." Ashley threw her hair back out of her eyes and laughed aloud as the van pulled into a parking spot in front of a small beach house.

"Well, here we are Miss," Wayne said as he turned off the ignition.

"Call me Ashley and I can call you—Wayne. Okay?"

"You got it." Wayne jumped out of the van, walked around to the passenger side, and opened the door for Ashley.

He retrieved her bags from the back of the van, slammed the doors shut, and pointed to a small white clapboard house across the street. "By the way. That's my house. Now follow me."

Carrying her suitcases, he led her up the sidewalk to a small yellow one-story stucco beach house. "Here you are," he said.

"Here I am. Where am I?" Ashley asked.

"It's your surprise. Your new digs. Follow me. You'll live in the small apartment at the back. It's a one bed-room and bath with a large living area adjoining a small kitchen. Your patio faces the water. This is the surprise that Gina arranged for you. Not bad, huh?"

Wayne led her down the walk on the side of the house and around to the back.

Ashley stood there with her mouth open, staring at the small addition that looked like it had been added to the bungalow in recent years. Then she swallowed and said, "I'm, going to live here? Right on the Gulf of Mexico?" She inhaled a long breath, concentrating on the warmth in the air.

"Your landlady, Nellie McClosky lives in the main part of the house. She's away for a few days. But she gave me the key. Said she would be back about four today and would come over to meet you."

He opened the apartment door with the key that Nellie had left with him. He put Ashley's bags inside. "Here's your key. I've got to get back to work now. But, I'm right across the street in case you need anything. I'll be home in a couple of hours. Here's my card with my cell phone number in case you need to reach me."

"What do I owe you for fare, Wayne?"

"First ride is free. But here's a bunch of my business cards. Tell all of your friends about my friendly service."

Ashley looked inside the open door to the apartment. "This is just charming. You were right; Gina is full of surprises."

"I'm sure there are more to come. Oh, and if you're looking for a place to have a quick sandwich there's Frenchy's Café in the next block—bright blue building with orange trim. You can't miss it. Great grouper sandwich. See ya."

After he left, Ashley muttered, "Well, I'm going to be living here. So I guess I better take a look around."

Entering the living room she noticed the blinds were down over the window. Only the light from the open door illuminated the room. She quickly stepped over to the large picture window in the living room and opened the blinds. "Got to get some light and air into this place."

She looked around and whispered out loud, "This looks like a mother-in-law addition." She chuckled and added, "Yea. That's me. Mother-in-law."

She walked slowly through the apartment. The kitchen cupboards were stocked with a complete supply of dishes, silverware, and pots and pans. This must be a furnished rental, she thought. And on the beach too. I wonder if I can afford it. New in town. Low paying job as a law clerk. Looks like Mrs. McClosky could get big bucks for this place."

She opened the refrigerator and the rest of the cupboards and saw there were no food supplies. It was now after one and Ashley's stomach was growling.

It looks like 'Frenchy's here I come,' she thought. And, I better find a grocery store around here so I can stock up on supplies.

She looked out the patio door, and noticed a couple of lounge chairs leaning against the wall. "Great. I can't wait to head to the beach. But, first, I've got to look like a Floridian. Let's see—shorts, a tank top and flip-flops. Got to blend in with the locals."

She ran to the bedroom, unpacked part of her suitcase and changed her clothes. She was ready to depart for her new adventure. She locked the door and headed up the side street to the main thoroughfare. The sun was shining as bright as a brass lamp. There was a glorious breeze that cooled the skin considering the heat. What wonderful weather she thought.

Walking around the corner, Ashley spotted the blue wooden building with orange trim around the windows and a large red awning in front with the words "Frenchy's Café" in yellow lettering.

Wayne was right—she couldn't miss it. Approaching the building, she stopped to admire the mural of a colorful bird painted on the side wall. She stared at it and decided the bird with the vibrant orange and red bill was a toucan. It seemed to fit right into the color scheme of the building. A glass pane in the large window overlooking the outside patio with tables and benches had an insert of a huge colorful fish. Ashley could not decide what kind of fish it was.

Before she opened the door to the restaurant, Ashley noticed a police car parked across the street. Maybe the cop can point me to a bank and a grocery store after I finish eating she thought.

The small café was fairly dark, even in the daylight. Its floors and walls were of highly polished cedar planks. Entering, she noticed a small curved bar with a highly polished wood lacquered top on the left side of the room. Against the wall were some counter height tables with tall stools around them. The right side of the room was filled with a number of wooden tables and chairs. Against the wall were several spacious booths with wooden benches.

"Bar or booth?" a robust middle-aged man with graying hair and a small mustache asked. He was wearing dark colored shorts and a black and white striped t-shirt. Ashley looked him over and decided that he reminded her of a debonair looking little Frenchman. Later, she learned, that was exactly what he was.

As she stared at him, she muttered to herself, "Nice tan. You can see he lives on the beach."

But aloud, she said, "Booth please."

He picked up a menu and led her to a booth. "The name is Frenchy Preston. I own the place."

He looked down at her pale looking legs. "If you're going to be here for a few days, I suggest that you invest in some good suntan lotion. It doesn't take long to get burned here."

"Thanks."

Then, he studied her face closely. "Never saw you in here before."

"Maybe it's because I've never been here before," she responded.

He whipped around. "Then we should get acquainted." But instead of shaking her extended right hand, Frenchy bent over and placed a tender kiss on it. "Glad to meet you, Mademoiselle?"

Ashley grinned. "Ashley. Ashley Willis," she said as she took a seat in the booth.

He cast a quick glance from the corner of his eyes before he asked, "Visiting our fair city? And by the way, do I detect a Jersey accent?"

"No. New York. Are you psychic?"

Frenchy placed the menu in front of her. "No. I love people. So I usually ask them a lot of questions when they come in. Tory will be with you shortly to take your order."

"Well, if the food here is as good as my friend Wayne Recker said, you'll be seeing a lot of me in the future."

"Ah, yes. Wayne. I must warn you about him. You see he likes to flirt with all the ladies."

Ashley chuckled to herself, thinking that of the two men, this little man was by far the worst flirt. "Well, thanks for the warning."

A few minutes later, the waitress, a tall, young girl with long brown hair and wearing Jean shorts and a crop top walked up to the booth.

"Hi, I'm Tory. What can I get you?"

Ashley looked briefly at the menu. "I'll have an iced tea and a regular Grouper sandwich."

"Do you want it with mayo, lettuce and tomato?"

"Give me the works."

Tory walked away.

After she left, Ashley glanced over at the very young girl who was sitting at the bar, sipping a beer. The girl appeared to be in her teens. Concerned, Ashley motioned for Frenchy to come over to her table.

"I know it's none of my business, but did you check that girl's ID? She looks a little young to me," she said hesitantly, careful with her words.

He stopped cold and expelled a disgusted breath. "Oh, shit. I'll bet that the bartender was so busy writing up the liquor order that she didn't check her ID."

"I think that you ought to know that there's a cop car right across the street. You might want to get her out of here," Ashley added .

Distinctly uneasy French asked, "You a cop or an attorney?"

"Attorney—licensed out of state now. Hope to soon be practicing law in Florida." She glanced over at the front door. "For what its worth, that cop just walked in."

Frenchy looked over at the young girl seated at the bar, with panic written over his face. "Kids can sit at the bar if they're underage in Florida, but we can't serve them."

She stood up and whispered, "You get rid of the girl, I'll distract the policeman for a few minutes."

Ashley slipped out of the booth, scooted across the room and approached the policeman. "Oh, officer." Then looking at his badge, she continued, "Sergeant Toliver. I'm new in town. Can you tell me if there is a bank close by?"

His gaze settled on her. "When you leave here, turn left and walk about a block up the street. On the right, is the Beach Bank. Grey stucco building, on the opposite side of the street from the beach."

While they talked, Frenchy quietly grabbed the young girl by the arm and pushed her out of the back door of the building.

"Thank you, officer." Ashley strode across the room to her seat, as the policeman walked up to Frenchy, who was now standing behind the bar.

"Afternoon, officer. I don't think that I know you," Frenchy said cheerfully.

"Sergeant Toliver. Filling in for Bell this week. He's on vacation. How about one of those famous Grouper Sandwiches that he raves about?" He turned back toward the door. "Make it to go. I'll be back for it in about twenty minutes."

"Sure thing," Frenchy said as he picked up a wet cloth and wiped off the bar.

After the officer left, Frenchy walked over to Ashley sitting comfortably in the booth. "Thanks for the warning. Never can be too careful in this business."

Ashley smiled as he continued, "Toliver was right. We are well known around here for our huge grouper sandwiches. It comes with cold slaw and fries"

"That's what I ordered."

Within a few minutes, Tory arrived with an enormous grouper sandwich on a soft French bun with tomato, lettuce and mayonnaise.

Ashley took one look at the big sandwich and decided to cut it in half. However, it was so large that she still had trouble wrapping her mouth around it.

After enjoying the large dish of cold slaw and the big helping of French fries, she decided that the grouper sandwich was too huge for her to finish, so she decided to take the remaining portion with her. She waved Frenchy to come over to the table.

"All set Miss?"

"Yes. I'll take the check now please. And a doggie bag for the rest of my sandwich. You're right. It was gigantic. And delicious too."

"Glad to hear that. But, no check. And, thanks for the tip about the cop. One favor deserves another. And maybe I'll see you again soon."

"Plan on it. I'm going to be living around the corner. At a place on the beach."

"Say, I could use another waitress part-time, if you're looking for a job. This joint is the original Frenchy's, but I own a couple of more restaurants on the beach."

"Thank you, but I've already got a job. Right now, I'm heading to the bank. Then off for a little shopping. I noticed a nice little shop on the way here. It had a great looking bathing suit in the window and I could use another one."

"Tell them that you're a friend of Frenchy—they'll give you thirty percent off the ticket price. And, don't be a stranger."

"Don't worry, I'll be back. You said thirty percent?"

He nodded as Ashley picked up the remainder of her sandwich, and headed outside into the Florida sunshine.

"Boy, this really beats the cold weather up in Syracuse," Ashley muttered to herself. "I think that I'll watch the sun go down over the Gulf tonight. But first, I'll call the folks and give them my new address. Mom was right—they sure are friendly down here."

Chapter 11

After visiting the bank, where she withdrew a couple hundred dollars from the ATM, Ashley stopped at the nearby In and Out Store and picked up a six-pack of Diet Pepsi, low fat yogurt, milk, a couple bags of salad, and numerous staples. Returning to the apartment, she placed some of the groceries and the remainder of grouper sandwich in the refrigerator. She put the rest of the groceries away and took a second look through the furnished one bedroom beach efficiency.

The bed was freshly made up with clean sheets and blankets. The beach apartment that faced the street, with its back patio looking out over the Gulf of Mexico, seemed ideal for the present time. Not only was it fully furnished, but it was also neat and clean. I should call Gina and thank her for locating it for me, she thought. Right now, I need to take a short nap.

A short nap. But where? Opening the patio door, she discovered a large beach umbrella leaning against the wall and next to it a folding lounge chair. "Ashley Willis—you have arrived in Paradise," she muttered to herself. Having not slept much on the plane, the white sands of Clearwater Beach called to her. She could use some R and R.

She went to the front hall closet and pulled out the beach bag she had noticed there earlier. Inside were two beach towels, a half empty bottle of suntan lotion and a beat up Danielle Steele paperback.

How nice of the prior tenant to have left this for me, she thought. She raced into the bedroom and to her suitcases on the bed.

She removed a bikini that she brought with her and put it on. She went to the kitchen, opened the refrigerator door, pulled out a can of soda, and put it into the beach bag together with her jogging shoes and towel . She headed down to the beach carrying the beach chair and umbrella under one arm and the beach bag over the other shoulder. She set up the lounge chair and umbrella several feet back from the water and placed a towel over the lounge.

Sitting back, she looked around—it was a bright sunny day with just a trace of a breeze and few clouds. This is heaven, she thought. I hope that Mrs. McClosky lets me stay here forever. She pulled out the suntan lotion and lathered it on—remembering Frenchy's warning about the sun. She knew that it would be best to tan gradually.

After reading for a while, she turned the umbrella around to block the sun, settled back on the chaise lounge and drifted off to sleep.

Later she awoke, took her jogging shoes out of the beach bag and slipped them on. A short run on the beach would be good exercise. This place is definitely not New York. Starting today Ashley Ann Willis, one of your top priorities is to look great—especially in a bikini.

Following the run, she gathered up her gear and headed back to the cottage. The white sugary sand seemed to cling to her body making her feel like a sugar cookie and she decided that a nice hot shower would feel good.

As Ashley reached to open the sliding glass door, she found a note taped to it. "Ms. Willis, Anxious to meet you.

Come to the main house for supper at five. Meat loaf." It was signed Nellie McClosky.

"Now, that's southern hospitality at its finest," Ashley muttered to herself as she slipped inside the house. "I'll save the rest of my sandwich for lunch tomorrow. But, I'm going to make sure that I only take a small portion of meat loaf. I don't want my jogging to have been in vain."

Before showering, Ashley placed her underwear and small items in the dresser drawers and hung the balance of her clothes in the closet. Because she had brought down only a few summer clothes, she would have to hit the mall later in the week to spruce up her attire. In fact, a whole new professional wardrobe would probably be in her near future.

Exactly at five o'clock, Ashley knocked on Nellie McClosky's front door. A short, rotund, gray-haired woman, who appeared to be in her early sixties, opened the inside door and smiled sweetly, "Oh, you must be Ashley. Come in."

Ashley pulled on the screen door. It wouldn't open. "I think that you still have the screen latched."

Nellie laughed. "Oh, so I do." She unlatched the door and opened it. As Ashley stepped inside, Nellie exclaimed, "My God, girl. You're even prettier than Gina said you were."

She threw her arms around Ashley and gave her a hug. "I'm so glad to have you here."

Ashley immediately took a liking to this warm and friendly lady. "No. I'm the one who should be thanking you. It was so nice of you to allow me to stay in your little cottage until I can find something more permanent."

Nellie smiled. "Stay as long as you like. My daughter used to live here but she moved. I miss her very much. But, I do expect her to come by tonight for short visit."

"I'm so sorry that I didn't bring you a bottle of wine for

inviting me to supper," Ashley replied.

"Not necessary. After all, you just got here and haven't had time to settle in yet. Please follow me into the kitchen."

In the kitchen, Nellie proceeded to bark out orders to Ashley like a drill sergeant. "Go to the china cabinet in the dining room and get the dishes. Set the table for five. Gina and Dino Bella and my daughter will be joining us. Then grab the good silverware out of the top drawer and use that. Hope they get here soon, supper is almost ready."

They heard a soft knock on the door. "I'll bet that's them. Let me introduce you."

Ashley followed Nellie back into the living room. Nellie threw the door open and a tall thin girl in her twenties with long, blond hair sprang inside. After a brief hug and kiss, mother and daughter just stared at each other. " I sure missed you," they both said at the same time.

Nellie turned around and signaled Ashley to step forward. "Megan, I want you to meet my new tenant, Ashley Willis."

"Ashley, this is my daughter, Megan Foster."

Behind Megan stood Gina and a tall young man with raven black hair framing a face that was both perfect and coolly sensational. His eyes were gray and watchful and he reminded Ashley of an ancient Greek God.

Ashley rushed to Gina and hugged her warmly. Gina withdrew from the embrace and nodded toward her brother. "Ashley, this is my brother and law partner, Dino."

"Glad to meet you," Ashley stammered, as she stepped forward and shook his hand. "I'm looking forward to working with you and your sister."

His eyes brightened as he said, "Same here." Then he turned to Nellie."I took the liberty of bringing a bottle of my favorite wine. It's chilled too."

"That was very thoughtful of you. But, enough chit chat. The food will be getting cold." She put her arm around her daughter's waist and led her into the dining room. The others followed.

"Everyone please sit down." Nellie ordered, "Megan, get some wine glasses out of the china cabinet."

"Oh, Momma before we eat there's something important that I must tell you."

"A little later, dear. A little later."

"I hope everyone likes the vino. It's red," Dino said, as he pulled out chairs for Ashley and his sister.

"So is my meatloaf," Nellie said, smiling wistfully. "In fact, it has a little kick with both green and red peppers in it."

For the next hour, they made small talk as they enjoyed their meal. Ashley ate a large helping of salad, but, as she had promised herself, she ate only small portions of the meat loaf, scalloped potatoes, peas, and corn bread.

Noticing that she had eaten little, Dino said, "You must eat more, Ashley. We Greek men don't appreciate skinny women." He started to put an extra slice of meat loaf on her plate.

She put her hand in the air to ward him off. "I'm far from skinny and I've had plenty to eat. Thank you."

In an effort to detract from Ashley's discomfort, Nellie exclaimed, "Oh, my goodness. We forgot to say grace before we started."

Dino smiled graciously and put the slice of meat loaf back on the serving platter. He wiped his hands on his napkin. "It's never too late. Let's join hands and offer a brief prayer now."

The others put down their utensils and linked hands.

"I'm so grateful that my Megan is home," Nellie said after the brief prayer. Then looking at her daughter, she added, "I missed you, honey."

Megan sighed and looked at her mother. "You know Mom, I wish I could stay longer."

"Yes. Yes." Nellie looked around the table and asked, "Seconds for anyone?"

All of her guests shook their heads, declining her offer.

"It looks like the leftovers will be tomorrow's sandwiches," Nellie said.... pushing her chair back and looking at Gina and Dino. "You two head for the living room and get comfortable. Megan and Ashley can help me clean up here."

It didn't take long for the three ladies to clear the dining room table, rinse the dishes and put them in the dishwasher. When they were finished, Nellie said, "Ashley, I'm going to give you some leftovers to take back to your place. But right now, let's go into the living room and talk with Gina and Dino. I'll fix some coffee and dessert later."

After they were settled comfortably in the living room, Nellie dominated the conversation as she proceeded to tell Ashley her whole life story.

"My first husband was a staff sergeant at Fort Sill, Oklahoma, when I met him. After twenty years of moving around the states, he was transferred to MacDill Air Force Base in Tampa. Two years later, he was sent overseas, where he was killed by a land mine. After his death, I found this small beach front property and purchased it with the proceeds of his life insurance."

Gina and Dino sat by quietly listening as Nellie continued telling her story to Ashley.

"A couple of years later, I met Tom Foster, a traveling salesman, who had a twelve year old daughter, Megan. Soon, Tom and I became involved and Tom, together with Megan, moved into my house.

Tom was on the road for business all the time. Megan stayed with me and went to school here. Tom was involved in a hit and run accident while he was drinking. He was sentenced to fifteen years in prison."

Megan sat silently with tears in her eyes as Nellie continued. "After a couple of years in prison, Tom got into an argument with another inmate and was murdered. So, I adopted Megan and raised her. Tom and I never married. Megan decided to keep the last name of 'Foster'."

"But all that is water under the bridge. And I have been very grateful to have this wonderful girl in my life. She's been the perfect daughter." She turned toward Megan. "Now, tell me, what you just couldn't wait to tell me before."

Megan looked at the two lawyers and took a deep breath. "Well, here goes."

Nellie saw Dino and Gina look at each other and flinch.

"This looks serious," Nellie said with a worried look.

"I'm not sure where to began," Megan replied softly.

"At the beginning, dear," her mother answered. "Remember you're among family and friends."

Chapter 12

Nellie scooted over on the sofa and sat closer to Megan. "Now, you and I have got some catching up to do. You know that I'm here for you."

"It's a long story. And kind of stupid on my part." Megan cringed and bit her lip.

Her mother paled and sat upright with concern. "Now, Megan, tell me what's going on. And I don't care how long the story is."

Megan struggled, trying to find the right words. "Well, Mom, about nine o'clock Thursday night, two guys, one who lives in my apartment complex, met up with me when I was doing my laundry. They wanted to know if I would like to go with them to a party at one of the local clubs in Ybor City. It sounded like more fun than just doing laundry and the night was young, so I agreed to go."

"Go on," Nellie said curtly.

"The guys needed a ride. So, like a fool, I volunteer to drive my car and the three of us headed over to a club called 'The Aces' about ten thirty. The guys were buying 'shooters' and beer and I had a few. Needless to say, they soon took their toll on me. I got pretty drunk."

"You should know better than to go alone with two

guys and drink too much." Nellie shook her head to clear it, troubled by the direction of her thoughts. "I'm afraid to hear what happened next. Do these guys have names?"

"Please Mom, just let me tell the story. The one that lives in my apartment complex is named Rick. The other one was his cousin. I don't remember his name."

Megan looked over at Gina and Dino, who already knew the story, and were listening intently.

She let out a short breath and her eyes narrowed, "I guess that it was around midnight, when Rick suggested that we leave the club and head to a private party on Clearwater Beach. They took me by the arms and helped me to my car."

Nellie's face bleached of color as she stared at her daughter, "My God, what got into you girl?"

Megan hung her head in shame. "I realize now how foolish I was. And the next thing I knew Rick was driving my car toward Clearwater. After we drove over the bridge to the beach, they said that they were going to stop at a convenience store for some beer. I guess I was passed out in the back seat when they went in and purchased the beer.

"I woke up as they drove up to the party at the motel. After a couple of drinks, my head was really spinning. I thought I was going to be sick, so I decided to leave. I staggered out of there, and somehow I got back to your house. I don't remember if I walked or if the guys brought me here. I guess that I used my key to get in. The next thing I remember was waking up in your bed in the morning."

Nellie raked her hand through her hair with a gesture of savage disbelief. The others sat nearby listening to Megan's story in silence.

Megan squared her shoulders. "Wait, you haven't heard the worst yet. The next morning, my roommate called me on my cell about seven. She was screaming her head off at me. She wanted to know if I was hurt and where I was. After I told her that I was safe and at your place, she calmed down at bit. Then she said that the cops had found my car abandoned."

"Oh, my God, Megan. Was it in an accident or something?" Nellie asked, looking completely distraught.

Megan paused for a second, stood up and started to pace around the room. "Please, Mom. Here's the rest of the story. The cops checked out the license plate and found out the car belonged to me. In fact, they were at the apartment looking for me. They said that my car was seen the night before leaving a convenience store that was robbed.'"

That statement brought Nellie up short. She shot up straight in her seat, her voice shaking with alarm. "Oh, my God, Megan, I can't believe that you're involved in something like this."

Megan looked away abruptly. "First of all, I'm innocent of any crime. I learned that the two guys didn't just go into the store and buy some beer. They robbed it and knocked the clerk unconscious."

Nellie sat forward in her chair and stared at her daughter. "Is there more?" Her eyes turned dark and moody.

"Yea, my roommate raced over to your house, picked me up and we went to the police station down on the beach." Megan paused for a moment. "And boy, did they try to drill me with questions."

Nellie felt as if a cold hard weight had settled in the pit of her stomach. "You know, I thought that someone might have been here the other morning because my bed was messed up. Then, I decided maybe I just forgot to make it before I left." Her expression softened a fraction. "What happened next?"

"I told the police that the car was mine and that I was driving it earlier in the evening. I remembered that Rick drove it to the convenience store, but I didn't remember the guys going in or out of the store, since I was pretty well looped. And, I had no idea they had robbed the store. But, I don't think the police believed my story because they were talking about arresting me."

At his point, Nellie's shock turned to anger. "Why are you just telling me this now, Megan? Why didn't you call me and tell when this happened?"

"I tried calling you, but you didn't answer your phone."

"Oh, I was out of town. I went to Ft. Myers for a couple of days. I had a call from a real estate lady about selling the condo your dad owned down there. I forgot to take my cell phone with me," Nellie replied, her voice softening. "But, what did you do Megan? Did you get arrested?"

Megan leaned back, almost exhausted and shook her head. "I called your friend, Wayne. Remember, you gave me his number because he keeps an eye on you and the house. He said you left a couple of days before."

"Did he come to the jail and help you?" Nellie rubbed her forehead wearily.

"No. He said he couldn't come because he had some people in his van and was on his way to the airport. But he did have Dino and Gina's number, and he gave that to me. So I called them."

Nellie looked over at the two attorneys with apparent relief. "Thank God."

At this point, Gina smiled and interrupted the conversation, "Of course, as soon as we heard about Megan's situation, we rushed right down to the police station. When the detectives on the case heard that Megan had called an attorney, they waited until we got there to interview her any further."

Megan looked pale and nervous as she continued the story. "I tried to explain to the detectives that I was just friends with Rick and his cousin. And that I wasn't even conscious when they robbed the store."

Nellie sighed in disgust. "My God, Megan, I thought you had more sense."

Megan looked over at the two attorneys, and then hung her head, looking very contrite. "I agree. It was very stupid. But I knew Rick for some time and trusted him."

"What happened after you gave the police your statement?" Ashley asked, keeping her voice very neutral.

Dino leaned forward, his enthusiasm taking over, "While Megan was being interviewed by the detectives, the police chief came into the room and said the same two guys had attempted to rob a second store that morning and were apprehended. They had just confessed to both robberies and confirmed Megan had been passed out in the back of the car during the first one and was not aware of what transpired."

Megan was now sobbing softly. "Believe me, Mom, I would never have gone with Rick and his cousin if I had thought they were capable of doing something like that."

Gina took Megan's hand in hers. "Megan realizes now that she was very foolish. Lucky for her, the two young men told the police she wasn't involved in any way."

"The detective did have Megan sign a statement and agree to testify at the trials," Dino added. "All told, she's a very lucky young lady. And very smart to turn herself in."

Megan looked directly into her mother's eyes. "I promise that I'll be more careful about who I run around with in the future. I've learned my lesson. I won't be so foolish from now on."

"And where is your car now?" Nellie asked sternly.

"The police are keeping it for the time being. Since it was part of the robbery, they're going over it for fingerprints. I can pick it up in a couple of days, I guess."

"Well, how are you getting around? Do you need my wheels?" Nellie asked.

"No. I'm using my roommate's car. She took a Greyhound bus to Atlanta to visit her sick grandmother."

"Well, I certainly hope you learned a lesson from all this." Nellie said, now relieved beyond measure.

"Yes. I'm never going to drink too much again. And I'm going to be careful of who I hang out with." Megan's face sobered.

"Good," Nellie replied. She looked directly at Gina and Dino. "And what do I owe you for helping my Megan?"

Gina responded in a mild tone of voice. "No bill, Nellie. You're a good friend, and you're providing a temporary home for Ashley. We were very happy to assist Megan. She identified the two robbers. Cameras inside the convenience store showed just them entering. So, thankfully the police are satisfied that Megan wasn't involved. All she has to do now is show up to be a witness in the case."

"Well, I'm so thankful to you two," Nellie said. She looked toward Ashley. "As for you Ms. Willis, I hope that you'll find your little apartment satisfactory."

Ashley broke into a big grin. "Are you kidding? With a patio facing the Gulf of Mexico, it can't get any better."

Gina added casually, "With Megan living off campus, near the college, I was very glad that your little apartment was available."

"Well, since you and your brother have been so kind to Megan and me, I've decided that Ashley's first month's rent will be free," Nellie replied as her face broke into a soft smile.

Gina turned to Ashley. "By next month, you should be able to afford the rent. We expect you to start working for us on Monday."

"I can't wait," Ashley replied with a big grin.

"That settles it then," Nellie added. "The first month's rent is free, after that, five hundred a month including utilities."

"And believe me, for an apartment on the beach, that's

very generous," Dino chimed in.

"And there's an old car in the garage Ashley, that you are welcome to use," Nellie said. "Might need a new battery. In fact, I'll get my friend, Wayne, to take a look at it. You've met him, Ashley. Remember, he's the limo driver."

"Yes. He was very helpful picking me up from the airport."

Nellie stood up and started toward the kitchen. "Now, enough of this. Time for some coffee and apple pie." She whirled around and clasped her arms around her daughter and gave her a hug. "Sorry, I was so harsh on you, dear. But, I just love you so much."

"I know Mom. Let me give you a hand in the kitchen," Megan answered, with tears in her eyes.

After they had their dessert, Megan said, choosing her words with care, "If you don't mind, Mom, I think that I should head back to school."

"If you must, dear. You must." Nellie replied with a dismissive shrug. "Call me when you get there. I worry about you."

Megan's brow furrowed and she put her arm around her mother. "I'm fine and soon it will be spring break." Her voice was now steady, sure and sincere. "I have a job lined up as a server at a nice restaurant."

Dino and Gina stood up and started for the door. "We should be heading back to Dolphin Springs now, Nellie. And thanks for your hospitality and taking care of Ashley for us," Dino said.

Gina reached into her purse, pulled out a piece of paper and handed it to Ashley. "Here's a map on how to get to our office. We'll expect you bright and early on Monday. Say about eight thirty?"

Ashley took the paper and looked it over briefly. "Looks like I shouldn't have any trouble finding my way. I'll be there with bells on."

"That's great," Gina added with a smile. When the others left her house, Nellie put her arm over Ashley's shoulder. "Well, it looks like it's just the two of us for now. I hope your little apartment seems adequate for you."

"Yes. I think I'll be very comfortable there," Ashley answered as the door bell rang.

Nellie went to the door, opened it. Wayne Recker was standing there.

"Hi Wayne. Come on in. I've got some apple pie and hot coffee left in the kitchen if you would care for some."

"Lead me to it."

She nodded her head toward Ashley. "You remember Ms. Willis, don't you?"

"Yes. Florida's newest resident."

Nellie led them both into the kitchen. After they were seated at the table, she put a slice of apple pie and a cup of hot coffee in front of Wayne. "Ashley needs some wheels to get around. I was hoping you could take a look at that old car in my garage. I told her that she could use it, but I believe it could use a new battery."

"Nellie, I'm surprised at you. You know that I'm psychic. I put a new battery in it yesterday and took it for a test run. It's good for another ten thousand miles, sweetheart."

Nellie looked at Ashley, a broad smile crossing her face. "You can see why I love this neighborhood and especially this guy."

"By the way, Nellie, the key to your car is on the front seat," Wayne said looking lovingly at her.

Realizing they appeared to have more than a casual relationship, Ashley decided to leave and give them some privacy. "I think I'll leave you two alone and head for my new digs. It seems like it's been a long day for me."

She stood up. "Wow! What an exciting and wonderful first day in Florida this has been! But, what will the coming days be like?"

Chapter 13

The following days and months passed quickly for Ashley as she worked as a law clerk for Bella and Bella and studied to take the Florida Bar. She had lived for the past several months in Mrs. McClosky's mother-in-law apartment.

Working in the Bella's law office, Ashley had met an older gentleman, Walter Huxley, who was about to enter a retirement home in Tampa. When she discovered he was going to sell his three-year old car, with low mileage, she decided to purchase it from him.

After looking at his small house in Crystal Beach, not too far from Dolphin Springs, she made an offer on it. With its open family room, two bedrooms and bath all on one floor, it was the perfect size for her. And, it was close to a beach which she loved. The small, but newly remodeled kitchen was adequate for Ashley who ate mostly salads, fresh fruits and vegetables, chicken and fish.

Completely settled into her new home, Ashley learned that Nellie had received an offer to sell her home on Clearwater Beach to a large hotel chain. So it was agreed, when the sale was complete in the late summer, Megan would return to college. She would stay on campus, and

Nellie would move in with her friend, Wayne Recker.

Walter Huxley was finally settled into a retirement home that permitted him to bring his dog, Buddy, along. Walter had to agree that whenever he and Buddy left their room, Buddy was to be on a leash.

Walter was also elated that the retirement home had a back yard for Buddy to run. He made it a point to introduce his special friend to all the residents and visitors. With a big smile on his face, he would tell everyone, "Love my dog".

Ashley found that between working for Bella and Bella from nine to five, five days a week, and studying for the bar exam in her spare time, she had little left over for a social life. Now it was time for her to take the Florida Bar. With the help of Daddy Dearest and her two bosses, Gina and Dino, Ashley had spent the last few weeks cramming for the test.

She had signed up to take her exam at the Tampa Convention Center. The test, which took place over two days, was only offered every six months, so she was determined to pass it on the first try.

Three hours of exams were scheduled for the mornings and three hours in the afternoon. The multiple choice part of the exam had over two hundred questions and was accompanied by an essay problem.

The first day of the exam was pertinent to the law in all the states. The second day covered the laws in Florida. After having passed the New York State Bar, Ashley was confident that she would have no trouble with her Florida test.

On Tuesday, she arrived at the Convention Center, walked in and found it full of eager and nervous applicants. Seated three at each table, the applicants were placed in alphabetical order from the front to the back of the room.

As she pulled out a chair at her assigned spot, a young man seated next to her looked up. "Hi, I'm John Walters, you must be Ashley Willis."

She nodded. "Looks like the W's are in the back of the room."

Making a light-hearted attempt to relieve his nervousness, John said, "Just like in Sister Janet's room in grade school." Looking around he added, "Big crowd. My first try. And yours?"

"My first in Florida." Ashley placed her purse on the floor beside her chair.

"You been living here long?" John asked, trying to make light conversation.

"A few months. Came down at the urging of my parents. And you?"

"My mom and stepfather live in New Jersey. In fact, he adopted me. I took his last name—Walters, because I love him so much. I came to Florida when I got a job offer from a friend of my folks."

"Well, good luck on the exam," Ashley said. She looked up as a tall, slender middle-aged woman sat down on the other side of John. "Good morning, I'm Juanita Valdez," she said in a voice that was a bit unsteady.

"It looks like we have our third party now," John whispered, after he introduced himself and Ashley to her.

Juanita forced her lips into the semblance of a smile. "This is my second try. So I hope I make it this time. Otherwise, I'll be a legal assistant for the rest of my life."

"I've got to pass this time," John said, his stomach fluttering with tension.

Juanita chose her words with care as she nodded. "I'm running out of time and money."

As the attorney in charge of the exam started to pass out the test papers, Ashley leaned over and whispered to John, "I have a tip for you. Don't waste a lot of time on a question if you get stuck on it. Just mark the ones you have trouble with and come back to them later. If there's a page of fifteen or more questions, hop on it."

"Thanks." John looked at Ashley and winked.

Ashley finished the morning test in less than two and a half hours and spent only about that much time on the afternoon one. The test seemed to have gone well for her as she felt adequately prepared. The intense studying had paid off.

After the second exam, Ashley headed toward home, stopping only at a Chinese takeout near her house, to pick up an order of Almond Chicken. After she finished her supper, she took the time to call her father, Gina and Dino. To all three, she simply said, "Looking good."

She went to bed early, but tossed and turned as she kept telling herself that she needed a good night's sleep so she would be well rested for the tests the next day.

After the long restless night, Ashley felt ill when she awoke. She was nauseous and had a stomach ache, fever and chills, and felt very weak in the knees.

Trying to calm her stomach down, she made herself a cup of tea and a piece of dry toast and sat down in front of the television to eat. Suddenly, what the television news reporter was saying registered with her. She sat upright in shock. There was an outbreak of salmonella poisoning connected with a local Chinese restaurant and the health department was shutting it down. A wave of nausea that brought her to her feet swept over her—it was the very restaurant that she had bought her Almond Chicken from.

Even though she had to stop to make two trips to the bathroom while getting dressed, she was determined to head to Tampa and finish the bar exam. She didn't want to wait six months to take it again. She took a couple of the anti-nausea pills she had in the medicine cabinet and headed out the door, with a determined look upon her face.

"Please Lord. Give me the strength to make it through the day," she prayed on her trip over the bridge to Tampa.

Somehow, she managed to drive to the Convention Center. She parked and walked into the room where the test was to take place. A young law clerk noticed how pale and drawn Ashley looked as she sat down. His eyes grew distressed as he approached her and asked in concern, "Are you okay, Ms. Willis?"

She slowly shook her head. She couldn't stop the tremor that rippled through her voice. "Don't feel so good. I think I have salmonella poisoning."

"Maybe you should go to the hospital." His frown deepened.

"No. I can make it. Honest."

"Ms. Willis, why don't you take a seat closer to the door in case you need the ladies room. If you do leave, my assistant, Mrs. Zook, must accompany you to the restroom."

Ashley shook her head, and drew a steadying breath.

John Walters entered the room and walked over to Ashley. As he noticed her pale and drawn face, his smile faded and his eyes look alarmed. "You okay?"

Ashley rested her head in her hands and murmured, "No. Not doing too hot. But, I think I can finish the exam today. I just have to."

With her head feeling woozy, it took Ashley the full three hours to finish the morning exam. At lunch time, she exited the building and found a bench to rest on. She knew she would never be able to hold down any food, but the pills that she had taken before she left the house were easing the cramps and nausea.

The afternoon test seemed to take forever and she took the fully allotted time to complete it. After finishing, Ashley walked slowly from the room. In the hall, she promptly slumped to the floor in a dead faint.

When Ashley came to, she was in a hospital room and John was sitting next to her bedside.

"Welcome back to the real world, Ashley. You fainted when you came out of the exam room. The paramedics brought you to Tampa General."

"Oh, my gosh. I have never blacked out in my whole life. Will I live?"

John looked genuinely worried. "Yes. They gave you antibiotics through that IV tube. You gave us quite a scare, but you're going to be okay."

Ashley tried to ease herself into a sitting position. "Thank you for rescuing me."

"Actually, I followed the ambulance here in my car," John said, reaching out to help her sit up. "In emergency, the nurse looked through your billfold and found the name and phone number of your parents. She called them and they're on their way here."

"Oh, no," she screeched in alarm.

"Any parent would want to know when their daughter is in the hospital," he answered as a nurse entered the room.

"Sir, you'll have to wait outside for a few moments, while I assist my patient," she ordered.

John stood up and left the room. As he shifted from one foot to the other, outside the door, waiting to be re-admitted, a middle-aged couple walked up to the room.

"Excuse me folks, the nurse is checking Ms. Willis over, so you can't go in."

"We're her parents, Phil and Kelley Willis," the man replied.

John reached out his hand. "I'm John Walters. I took the bar exam with Ashley and called 911 when she was ill."

"You're who?" Kelley excitedly asked.

"John Walters."

She turned to her husband. "My God, Phil, do you know who this is?"

He looked puzzled for a few moments, and then hesitantly said, "I think so. I believe this is the young fellow my Uncle Jack adopted."

When the nurse came out of Ashley's room, they entered and Phil and Kelley explained to Ashley that this John Walters was a relative of Phil's. After his Uncle Jack Walters was released from prison, he turned his life around. In his early sixties, he got married and adopted his wife's son, John, who took the last name of Walters.

After they reminisced, Kelley and Phil invited John to visit them in the near future in their home. John assured them that not only would he visit, he would bring his parents.

Within a couple of weeks, Ashley had fully recovered from her illness and was back to her regular routine of healthy eating and jogging. After she learned she had passed the Florida Bar exam, she had a small dinner celebration with family.

"My bosses, Gina and Dino, just bought the building next door to our old office. I'm going to have my own office and a large conference room to visit with clients," she told her parents.

"They hired a new clerk, Elaine Evers, to supplement the staff. She's a single mom with a ten-year-old child. She'll work as the receptionist and answer the phones. She's going to do all the duties that I did before. She should be pretty good since she worked at a Tampa law firm for eight years."

"And what are you going to do now that you passed the exam?" Kelley asked.

"Oh, I plan to dive into my role as a fully fledged attorney with the firm. I've been assigned to a hit and run case already. I don't expect to have much time for play in the near future."

Kelley looked at Ashley with a determined look. She

hoped that statement wouldn't prove to be true. She wanted Ashley to find some romance in the future.

Ashley sighed. "We have John Walters to thank for saving me. He called the paramedics the minute I passed out. They got me to the hospital quickly. And I saw in the paper where the restaurant I got my Chinese food from burned down accidentally, or so they say."

After the bar exam and her illness, Ashley had one date with John Walters. Later, he moved to Orlando to be closer to his family. He said that his step-father was now busy working with the Orlando police department, helping to solve cold cases.

John had also told Ashley that Juanita Valdez had finally passed the bar exam and was now working for a law firm in Miami.

On Sunday night, Ashley's brother, Alan, called, "Hey Ash, tomorrow is a holiday and there's a big blood drive on in the morning at the court house. The police department, fire fighters, and the city council are sponsoring it. We need all the donors that we can get. Do you think that you can drive over and help out by donating a pint? You'll get a ticket to the movie theatre and a gift certificate to a local restaurant."

Ashley did not hesitate before answering. "Sure. Be glad to. And I can always use that free stuff. Count me in."

"Be there about eight, if you can. We expect a big turn-out," Alan replied.

When Ashley arrived at the Tampa courthouse, she saw that Alan was correct. The parking lot was filled with three bloodmobile trucks, a large white tent, and numerous people and cars. The local media had shown up to film the event. The Tampa Mayor gave a short speech in front of the large crowd shortly after eight. Then the blood mobile trucks opened for business.

Ashley was second in line at one of the trucks, with Alan standing right in back of her. A long line of police officers were behind him. At the other trucks, long lines of firefighters, judges, and city politicians and even the mayor were gathered. Because of the extensive lines forming at the three trucks, a fourth blood mobile truck was called in to accommodate the immense crowd.

Alan tapped Ashley on the shoulder. When she turned around, he put his arm around the shoulder of the police officer that was standing behind him. "Ash, this is Detective Steve Clarke, we work together in the same office. Steve this is Ashley."

Steve stepped forward and shook Ashley's hand. "Morning Ms. Willis. Glad to finally meet you. Your brother speaks well of you."

Ashley smiled at the tall, sandy-haired young man, who appeared to be in his late twenties. His physique was superb, wide-shouldered and sleek hipped beneath his jeans; a white shirt was topped with a black leather jacket that shouted good taste and quality workmanship.

"Call me Ashley, please," she responded.

"Well, then, I'm just plain Steve."

Ashley decided there and then, that this handsome young detective was anything but plain.

The men followed her into the bloodmobile, where all three of them took seats on the leather lounges that lined the wall. After donating their blood, and a short rest, they proceeded outside and walked to the huge white tent.

A long buffet table had been set up with scrambled eggs, bacon, sausages, toast and juice for the blood donors. Two local restaurants had donated all the food in return for the free advertising and pictures in the local newspapers.

Ashley and the two men helped themselves to the

buffet and sat down together at one of the tables .

When they finished, Steve leaned over to Ashley and placed his arm on hers. "Maybe, you would like to take in a hockey game with me Wednesday night?"

Ashley replied coyly, "I'm busy. Got other plans."

"I've got two good seats. My treat too," Steve replied, almost pleading.

Her brother looked at her with disgust on his face. "Oh, what the hell, Ash. Give my good buddy a break. You should go."

Ashley smiled faintly and nodded her consent. "Okay Steve, I'll meet you here at the courthouse on Wednesday night after I finish work."

"Make it six. The game starts at seven." Steve had a very pleased grin on his face. "And Ashley, wear slacks and bring a jacket. Remember, it's a hockey game. You know—ice."

Ashley just looked at him and said nothing. She could see that he was a guy who liked to be in charge."

Chapter 14

"Look Mom, a few of the leaves have changed colors, even though it's Florida," Ashley said, glancing up at the trees in the park. She patted her father's arm affectionately and added, "Great idea, Dad, a picnic."

"It was your Mom's idea. Just a sneaky way to meet your detective friend." With an innocent smile, he asked, "Am I mistaken, or is there a future with this guy?"

Not answering his question in words, Ashley merely shrugged her shoulders. Then sat quietly at the picnic bench, closed her eyes and reflected on the past few months.

It was now six months since she passed the Florida Bar. She was proud to have a certificate attesting to this hanging on the wall of her office at Bella and Bella. The newly acquired building provided ample room for Ashley Willis P.A., Gina Bella P.A. and Dino Bella, P.A., to each have a private office.

The front part of the building was comprised of a reception area and a desk for Elaine, the receptionist. Down the hall were the three private offices. Beyond them were a large conference room, a kitchen area and rest rooms.

All this seemed fitting as the firm had rapidly become one of the top law offices in the region. Its reputation in Pinellas County was soaring, partly due to the numerous cases the team had been winning.

Ashley's thoughts were interrupted by her father. "It's hard to believe that it's still in the nineties in September, isn't it? I was so accustomed to the cooler fall weather in New York."

She looked up and nodded.

Phil smiled and asked, "Now, when is that young man of yours going to arrive?"

"He should be here soon." Turning to her mother, she tried to keep her voice calm and pleasant, with just a hint of authority in it. "And please, when Steve arrives, no twenty questions. Let's just enjoy each other's company and the cookout. But, to ease your minds, I want you to know that we're just dating, nothing serious."

"You said that he's a detective on the Tampa Police force," Phil said. "Does he know Alan?

"Yes. In fact, Alan introduced me to him. You'll find that Steve is one terrific guy. And one last thing, he's single. No ex-wife. No kids. But please don't cross examine him like an attorney, Dad."

Kelley grinned, her gaze never leaving Phil. "Now that we've got our orders, dear, why don't you start the grill."

Within the next half hour, Steve Clarke arrived as did Alan and Laura. After quick introductions, everyone turned their attention to the food.

Potato salad, chips, and fresh rolls were accompanied by grilled chicken. When everyone finished eating and the table was cleared, Ashley and Steve slipped away for a private walk around the lake.

"Remind me to bring you back here soon," Ashley said.

"What a great way to clear your head."

Steve smiled, took her by the arm, and guided her down the path "By the way, your parents are extremely nice. And Alan's wife, Laura, is just as terrific as he described her. They all make me feel very welcome."

His remark clearly thrilled Ashley. "Good. I'm so glad that you like them."

"And Alan is one lucky guy. He not only has a terrific job and a wonderful wife, but he's soon to be a father. Did I hear Laura say that it was going to be a boy?"

Ashley smiled, "Yes. And did you notice the gleam in Alan's eyes when she announced that?"

Ashley was happier now than she had been in the last few years. At last, her world seemed to be turned right side up.

Steve guided her to a small bench beside the lake and they sat down. Across the lake, in the distance, they could see a small water fall, cascading leisurely into the lake.

"It's so peaceful here. I just love it," Ashley said. She gazed thoughtfully at Steve. "You know you never did tell me much about your family."

"Not much to tell. I'm an only child." His face wore a mixture of emotions. "My mother passed away about five years ago and my father lives in an assisted living facility in Punta Gorda. He's doing okay."

"Do you see him often?"

"Only a few times a year. My job keeps me pretty busy and sometimes the hours are a little irregular. But, I'd like for you to meet him. We could drive down together and visit him sometime, if you like."

"I'd like that," Ashley replied. She and Steve both had busy schedules and seeing each other regularly was not always easy. It slowed the development of their relationship somewhat.

Steve looked up to the sky. "I think I just felt a drop of rain. Maybe we better get back to the others."

He jumped to his feet, extended his hand to Ashley, and pulled her up from the bench.

"Right. I think this party is almost over." Her heart lurched as she looked into his eyes.

"Not quite," Steve said, pulling her slowly into his arms and kissing her thoroughly. "I hope that we'll see each other more often in the future, Ms. Willis." His voice was filled with emotion. "I've grown very fond of you."

Ashley's heart was beating trip-hammer fast. She pulled back and said in a whisper, "You can plan on it."

The following week, Ashley was back to work, busy completing her paperwork on a couple of pro bono cases. She had taken her dad's advice and asked the court if she could handle several free cases. Judge Amos Folger readily assigned them to her saying, "You're really helping the county out, Ms. Willis, taking these cases."

One case involved a hit and run and the other was about a homeless man who had been accosted by two youths. Judge Folger was very grateful that Ashley had taken the homeless man in hand before his court appearance.

Ashley sobered him up, took him to a barbershop for a shave and haircut, then found him a place in a shelter before the scheduled trial. She even took him to a thrift store and helped him select some clothes. Finally, she helped him find a job as an assistant janitor.

When the cases were over, the judge called Ashley to congratulate her on the way that she handled them.

By Friday afternoon, the office was very quiet. Gina and Dino had left to start a long weekend. Ashley and the receptionist were alone.

"Would you mind terribly if I left early, Ashley?" Elaine

asked. "My mother hasn't been feeling too well this week. I'd like to run up to Cedar Key and visit her."

"Not a problem," Ashley responded as she relaxed and leaned back in her chair. "You go on, I'll lock up. Besides this will give me a chance to go over a couple of briefs."

However, Ashley soon discovered she could not get her mind to focus on the briefs. Rather, she found herself thinking about Steve. Her feelings for him were growing stronger by the moment.

Chapter 15

After Elaine left, Ashley slid back into her chair with little enthusiasm and thought about her personal life. Just when she thought that it was progressing nicely with Detective Steve Clarke, her love life had taken a turn for the worse.

Steve and she had agreed to meet for dinner the previous evening at a local restaurant. After waiting forty-five minutes for Steve to appear, she tried several times to reach him on his cell phone. No answer. Bitterness welled through her as she decided that she had been stood up. Without eating, she left the restaurant, climbed into her car and headed home.

About three blocks later she saw Steve walking into a bar with his arm around a tall, slender blonde woman. Slowing down, she saw him stop, pull the female to him and kiss her.

Ashley, suddenly found herself completely furious. "Nobody stands me up for another woman and makes a fool out of me," she sputtered aloud. She saw a parking spot, parked the car, jumped out, locked it and headed down the street to the bar. Inside she spotted Steve sitting in a booth next to the blonde. The two were kissing and appeared to be involved in a very intimate conversation.

With muttered oath, she strolled over to the booth and standing in front of the two, she put her hands on her hips. Her voice filled with fury, she snapped at Steve, "So, this is why you stood me up, you creep."

Steve never looked up, his face devoid of emotion. He leaned over and continued to kiss the blonde female on the neck.

"Well, what have you got to say for yourself?" Ashley was determined to get an answer.

Finally, Steve looked up and shrugged. He added a bored wave of his hand for good measure. "Go away. Can't you see I'm busy?"

Ashley swallowed and took a step back. "Yes. I can see you're busy. Oh, I'll go away alright." She felt like finding a quiet hole, crawling into it and pulling the lid on top of her. Her voice was now filled with sadness as she forced herself to speak, "Believe me, I'll go so far away that you'll never see me again."

"Well, that's good news," Steve muttered as he lifted his chin and glared at her. He appeared to have no regrets about the situation.

The woman sitting beside him asked, "Who's the bimbo, honey?"

He answered softly, "Nobody, doll. Nobody."

Ashley turned quickly on her heels and headed out of the bar. Her heart was beating rapidly and tears filled her eyes. She ran down the street, jumped in her car and turned on the ignition. A sharp flash of bitterness surged through her and a chill raced down her spine. So, this was what it was like to be jilted by someone you cared for. She sat silently staring out of the window and tried to comprehend what had just occurred. Then uttered a few swear words out loud.

After a short but thorough cry, she decided that perhaps

it was better that she had found out what an asshole Detective Clarke really was before she had gotten even more involved with him.

Yes, Mr. Detective, that's the last that you'll see of me, she promised herself.

Now the quiet of the office, and her work, were the best ways to heal a broken heart, she decided. "Damn," she whispered beneath her breath. "I'm never going to see Mr. Clarke again. Nor will I take any phone calls from that two-timing rat. I can't believe that I was so gullible."

She felt a tear slip from her eyes. Then another. She didn't try to stop them. That would be futile. She sighed, wiped her eyes, and got out her billing records. The pro bono hit and run accident she'd taken on had involved a young girl in Clearwater, who had left the scene of the accident. The case had proved to be a slam dunk for the prosecutor. The girl had no license and was driving drunk. Since she had no other violations, Ashley did get the judge to give her the smallest sentence allowed under the law.

Again, she struggled as her thoughts returned to her personal life. She felt even more devastated. Somehow, she couldn't get Steve out of her mind. "Why did you betray me?"

She sat scrunched down low in her chair, wallowing in her sorrows, when the front door to the office opened and a voice called out, "Ms. Willis, are you here?"

Ashley paled and jerked around. Who could be coming into the office looking for her so late on a Friday afternoon? She stood up and walked out to the reception area, where she saw her acquaintance, Walter Huxley, standing inside the doorway. He was quite red in the face and seemed to be beside himself with anxiety.

"My goodness, it's my dear friend, Walter. What brings you here? You look like you're upset over something."

She walked over to him and put her hand on his arm. "Why don't you come in the back room and have a cup of coffee and we'll talk this over." His step faltered as she led him to the kitchenette and guided him into a chair next to the small table. She poured a cup of coffee for him and handed him two donuts from the box on the counter.

After pouring herself a cup, Ashley sat down beside him. Looking very concerned, she asked, "What's wrong Walter?"

Moisture glinted in his eyes and he sighed. He seemed fatigued to the pit of his soul. "Ms. Willis, I need your help. I've got a big problem."

He whimpered, he couldn't keep the hurt in. "It's my dog. Buddy. Buddy's missing. Someone took my dog." His voice trailed off. "You gotta help me. Please."

Feeling completely at a loss, Ashley put her arm around his shoulders. "Walter, please calm down. I'm here for you. You know that."

A smile flickered in his eyes, he made an effort to calm himself. "You'll help me then?"

"Of course," she stated firmly.

He looked up and saw her eyes were red and her face was a little pale. "Are you alright Ms. Willis? Your eyes. They look like you've been..."

She interrupted him. "I'm okay, Walter. Let's concentrate on your problems. Now start from the beginning and tell me what happened."

Walter relaxed a bit and took a bite out of his donut. "First of all, Ms. Willis, The Oaks Retirement Home that I'm living at has new owners and they're mean. The home has gone to hell. They fired the cook, the head nurse, and the maintenance man. They put new rules into effect and the place is run like a jail."

"How do you mean, Walter?"

The look in his eyes was brooding and somber. "They took all the phones out of the rooms, we have to go to the front reception desk to make a call. And they listen in to everything you say. So, I couldn't even call you to tell you what's going on."

"What about Buddy? Ashley asked. "You said that he's missing?"

Walter took an uneven breath and leaned forward. "Yes. I went to breakfast in the dining room a couple of days ago, and when I got back to my room, Buddy was gone."

She showed a moment of hesitation, then put her hand over his. "I assume that you looked around the facility and outside. Could he have gotten out and just wandered away?"

"No. I looked all over for him. Walked around the neighborhood and asked everyone I saw. Buddy never leaves my room unless I take him out. I think one of the new owners went into my room and took him," he declared bitterly. "And two other ladies that live in there have had their cats missing for the last couple of weeks."

"It sounds like you really don't care for the new owners."

Walter bellowed, almost beside himself. "I tell you that they're mean and cruel. The food is bad now. I even saw a rat running around in the dining room."

"Is there anyone on the staff that you could question about Buddy?"

His eyes narrowed and he shook his head sadly. "No. The new maintenance man looks and acts like a prison guard. Can you do something to help me, Ms. Willis?"

Concerned about the conditions Walter described, Ashley tried to think straight. She decided to take action. Something glittered deep in her eyes. "I think you've given me enough information to get a search warrant issued for the retirement home. Now, finish your coffee and donut. You need to keep up your strength."

"Please Ms. Willis, the place has new owners, and a new name, too. I snatched a business card from the front desk. It's now called 'The Teller's Retirement Home.' Maybe, you can check them out and find out more about these people. But, like I said—they're mean—so watch out for them," he added with deep foreboding.

"Walter, you would make a good detective."

" You'll help me then?" Walter asked, his voice quivering. "You'll get Buddy back for me?"

"Yes. I'm on the case," she said firmly, taking him by the arm and helping him to his feet. "Now, how did you get here, Walter?"

"Took the bus."

"Well let's get you back on the bus. I would drive you back, but I don't want anyone there to see me or to have any idea that I'm investigating them. And whatever you do, don't tell anyone that you came to me with this."

He smiled, but not with his eyes. "I can't thank you enough for helping me, Ms. Willis. I just didn't know who else to turn to."

"Don't you worry, Walter, I'll find your dog." She managed to look completely confident. "These people can't be allowed to get away with abusing elderly people. And if they had anything to do with the disappearance of your dog, we'll find that out, too."

Walter grabbed Ashley's hands in his, leaned down and kissed them. "Thank you. Thank you. You are an angel."

Ashley smiled reassuringly. "Now, calm down and take this last donut with you to eat on the bus." She put the donut in a napkin and slipped it into his pocket. "And remember; don't say anything about this to anyone."

"I promise. How soon can you come?" His gaze rested on her, knowing the situation had taken a turn for the better.

"Tomorrow morning. I need to get a search warrant. And remember, mum's the word."

She escorted Walter to the bus stop and waited with him until it arrived.

After the bus pulled away from the curb, Ashley turned away. Her eyes narrowed, as she murmured, "Now, it's time to head home and plan my strategy. Mr. and Mrs. Teller—watch out.

You're about to see Ashley Willis in action."

Chapter 16

The next morning, Ashley picked up the phone and called Tampa police headquarters.

The voice on the other end of the phone was crisp and professional. "Good morning. Detective Ricky Johnson here."

"Good morning. This is Attorney Ashley Willis calling."

"Yes. I recognize the name. You're Steve Clarke's girl," he drawled in a deep Southern voice.

Ashley's voice rose with indignation. "Excuse me. I'm nobody's girl."

"Sorry. But how can I help you?" Detective Johnson's tone was now very cautious, as if no one usually spoke to him in such a manner.

Realizing that she had been too quick to take offense to the detective's comment, Ashley responded in a quiet and practiced manner. "I need to find a judge and get a search warrant issued for Hillsborough County."

"How far are you from headquarters?"

"About a half hour."

"Come on in. We have a couple of judges here now. Maybe one of them can issue one for you."

"Good. I'm on my way. And please don't tell Detective Clarke that I called or I'm coming in," she said, restraining herself to keep her professional tone of voice.

"Your wish is my command, Ms. Willis. Just talk to the sergeant at the desk and she'll direct you to me. Our internal phone system is out of order this morning."

Detective Johnson hung up the phone and leaned back in his chair, wondering why Ashley seemed to be so angry with his friend, Steve. He decided that he definitely did not want to get in the middle of this couple's quarrel.

Ashley grabbed her briefcase and cell phone, rushed out of the door, and drove to Tampa police headquarters. Inside, she approached the sergeant seated in the front office.

"Hi. I'm Attorney Willis. I'm here to see Detective Johnson."

The sergeant looked up and eyed Ashley briefly. "Yes. I was told to expect you. Our intercom and phones are on the blink. I'll take you to him."

Ashley followed her down the hall to the detectives' room at the end. She was amazed at how crowded and noisy it was, filled with about ten desks that were littered with papers and empty foam coffee cups. The detectives seated at the desks were either conversing noisily with each other or were on their phones.

"That's Johnson, in the corner." The Sergeant pointed to a man who was standing and facing his desk as he talking on his cell phone.

Ashley approached him and saw his teeth clench. A look of supreme irritation chased though his eyes. As the conversation continued, the man nodded several times. When he could finally get a word in, he said pleadingly, "But, honey, you're the only one."

Somewhat amused, Ashley coughed briefly. "Excuse me, Detective Johnson?"

He whirled around and plastered an awkward smile on his face. "Attorney Willis? Right?"

He whispered into his phone, "I'm busy now, sweetie. Talk to you later."

Smiling uncomfortably, he switched the phone off and pointed toward a chair in front of his desk. "Please sit. You need a search warrant?"

Ashley drew a deep breath. "Yes, and right away."

"Tell me your story and I'll see if I can get one of the judges to issue it." He took a seat behind the desk.

"Hey Johnson," one of the men yelled from the front of the room. "The computers are backed up."

"Good. Now just fix the damn intercom and phones," Johnson snarled back. Then he looked directly at Ashley and saw the lines of strain on her face. "Go on counselor," he said gently.

Ashley quickly told him the story about Walter, his dog Buddy, and the retirement home. Before Johnson could reply, a large burly man standing in the doorway, called out in a deep voice, "Hey Johnson, I need you in my office. Now!"

Johnson gasped and looked up, "That's Captain Donafrio." He replied, "Okay. Be right there."

He looked at Ashley nervously as he stood. "You'll have to excuse me for a moment. This is probably important. The captain is new and he's always changing things around."

"Sure," Ashley answered, snapping her head around to look at the captain.

"I've got Judge Folger in my office. We need you now," the captain said, masking the impatience in his eyes with difficulty.

"That's just who I need to see," Ashley exclaimed, as she jumped to her feet, grabbed her purse and briefcase, and followed Detective Johnson into the captain's office.

When he saw Ashley walking in behind Johnson, the captain said, "Sorry, miss, you'll have to wait back at the detective's desk."

"I need to see Judge Folger," she said stepping forward with determination.

The judge, who was seated at the desk, looked up. "Oh, hello there, counselor. Great to see you again. I was planning on sending you a letter commending you on how you handled those pro bono cases for me. Great job."

"Thanks." Her voice was all business. "But, now I need to ask a favor of you, in return."

The hasty smile that the judge had pinned on, faded from his lips. "Good. Why don't you let me finish my business with Captain Donafrio. I'll come outside and talk to you in a few minutes."

Frustrated at his dismissal, Ashley was about to leave the room when she heard a familiar voice. "Hi Captain, I just got back from court. Have to talk to you."

Ashley whirled around and saw Detective Steve Clarke walk into the office. He looked surprised when he spied Ashley, but he quickly regained his composure and said in a friendly voice, "Hi Ashley. I didn't expect to see you here this morning."

Her eyes narrowed. "Apparently not. And I was hoping not to see you," she replied, coldly. She fought to get herself under control. She took a slow deep breath.

"Well, I can't talk to everyone at once. And since you seem to know this young lady, Clarke, please take her out to your desk," the captain ordered. "The judge can talk to her there in a few minutes."

Steve took Ashley gently by the arm and led her out of the office and back into the detectives' room. He guided her toward a desk at the front of the room and motioned for her to have a seat.

Ashley dropped into the chair, glad to get off her quivering legs, but she was in no mood to talk to this two-timing skunk. A chill circled her heart like cold fingers.

Steve sat down in a chair beside her and asked quietly, "What brings you here, Ashley?"

Her eyes narrowed and she took a long time to answer. "Well, I certainly didn't come to see you. I needed to get a Hillsborough County search warrant."

"Tell me about it. Maybe, I can help you." Steve pulled a paper from the drawer of his desk and picked up a pen.

Ashley closed her eyes, and swallowed, the emotions threatening to choke her. Forcing herself to calm down, she took a few long breaths and told him the story about the conditions at Walter Huxley's retirement home and the fact that his dog was missing.

"This sounds like a very serious situation. And one that your friend wouldn't just fabricate," Steve said as he made notes. "What's the name of the people who run this retirement home now?"

Ashley reached into her briefcase and pulled out the business card Walter had given her. She bit her lip and tried to soldier on. "Here's their business card."

"I'll make a copy of it for the warrant," Steve said as he stood up and headed for the copy machine.

Concerned over Walter's problem, both Ashley and Steve seemed to have put aside momentarily the incident of the other night.

When he returned, Steve handed the card back to her and smiled. "You know, I'm about to become popular with you this morning. I have a dear friend at the health department and she owes me a big favor. I'll give her a call. If she's not busy, we'll take her out to the home. If that place is in as bad a shape as your friend described, with rats running around, maybe she can do something about it. Maybe, even close it down."

"I would really appreciate that," Ashley replied with a look of gratitude in her eyes.

"As soon as the judge is finished with the captain,

I'll get him to issue a search warrant. In the meantime, Ashley, why don't you head out to the sergeant at the front desk and get her to do a complete background check on the new owners of the retirement home."

Ashley lifted her head and felt her heart melt a little as she looked directly into Steve's eyes. "Thank you so much for helping me."

He nodded and smiled at her. "Later, we've got to talk about the other night. I want to explain to you what that was all about. But right now, let's take care of this problem. Get a move on."

"Sure, boss." Her face was now brittle with a false smile, she thought it would crack under the pressure. She picked up her briefcase and headed to the front desk.

Thirty minutes later, Ashley returned to Steve's desk with several sheets of paper in her hand. "Can't wait to tell you what we found on this couple."

He looked up and gave her a slight grin. "Good girl. I showed Judge Folger the facts of the case and got the warrant. And I called my friend, Tina Wilcox, at the health department. She's waiting for us to pick her up. Let's get going."

He stood up and they headed for the door, passing Detective Johnson and Captain Donafrio on their way out.

Stopping them, Detective Johnson asked, "Did you get your problem solved Attorney Willis?"

"Yes. Thanks for all your help."

Johnson smiled, now somewhat relieved at Ashley's friendlier tone. He looked at Steve and said, "And by the way Detective, we did find Judge Folger's granddaughter. Turns out she was staying with a friend overnight and just came home this morning."

Captain Donafrio walked down the hall, looked over his shoulder and ordered, "Anderson, go get me some coffee. My nerves are shattered. What a morning."

"It's Johnson, sir," the detective said. Then he whispered to Ashley, "It's his first week here. He's still got a hard time remembering all our names."

Captain Donafrio, put his arm around Steve's shoulders. "Hey Clarke care to join us for a coffee? And by the way that was good undercover work you did on that drug deal with that woman. I want to talk to you more about it."

Suddenly it dawned on Ashley what the captain had just said. Drug deal? Her head jerked up in surprise and she stared at Steve in total shock.

Steve quietly nodded his head. "Thank you, sir. Right now, I've got Attorney Willis to take care of."

"Say, Steve, do you need me to help?" Detective Johnson asked.

"Thanks. But no thanks. Got it under control. And I'll have that talk with you later, Captain, if that's okay with you," Steve replied.

"Sure, go ahead." The captain turned to the other detective, "Johnson, why are you just standing there? Black coffee."

"Yes, sir."

Chapter 17

Ashley and Detective Clarke, accompanied by, Tina, from the health department, drove to The Teller's Retirement Home. Behind them, driving in a second squad car, were two police officers who were going to carry out the search warrant.

They arrived at the home, went to the office, and presented the Tellers with the search warrant. While Steve and Ashley questioned the Tellers, the police officers and Tina scoured the facility.

One of the police officers burst into the office and interrupted the conversation in an intensely loud voice. "Flies and maggots led us to two dead cats behind a shed. We could tell from the fur, that one was a calico cat."

Ashley raged a silent battle for a few minutes, then looking grim said, "That's how Walter's friend described one of the ladies' missing cat—a calico."

Walking behind the police officer was Tina. She was carrying a dog in her arms and slowly following her was Walter Huxley. Walter was crying profusely and moaning, "Buddy, my Buddy. Look what they did to my poor dog."

The dog appeared to be near death. It was covered in fleas and feces. A wide rubber band bound his jaw shut and his mouth oozed with blood and pus.

An emotional reaction had set in with Tina, shattering her control. Tears trickled down her cheers as she said sadly, "They had this poor dog locked in the shed. It looks like someone was trying to starve him to death."

The Tellers looked up in alarm. Mr. Teller's eyes became faintly hooded. "You have no proof that we were part of this horror."

The police officer speared him with a faintly mocking gaze. "The door to the shed was padlocked so it had to be either you or one of your staff. Mr. Huxley said that his dog has been missing for several days."

"I've called someone from my department to pick up the dog and take him to a vet." Tina's eyes narrowed furiously. "But, bad news for you, Mr. and Mrs. Teller. Based on my assessment of your facility, I'm going to get a court order to shut this place down."

The anger in Tina's expression gave both of the Tellers pause. As she continued her voice remained soft and menacing. "You can look over the list of code violations I've just written down."

She handed them a paper with a long list of notations. "I've already contacted my superiors at the health department. They plan to be here tomorrow. With the aid of the Red Cross they will start moving your residents out and to new facilities."

"You don't understand. It was the last owners who left the place in a mess," Mrs. Teller said tartly, then looked even more uncomfortable.

"Well, since you took over the facility, you have had ample time to clear up the problems," Tina responded.

Detective Clarke looked at the Tellers for a moment, his mouth hardened. He shrugged and said, "Right now, I'm arresting you for animal abuse. And when the judge reads all the violations regarding this facility, he'll probably add mistreatment of the elderly to the charges. These two officers will take you in now."

Mrs. Teller's head drooped, and then she squared her shoulders, and tilted her chin as she said defiantly, "We want to call our lawyers."

"You can do that from the station," Steve replied with a half smile.

"And while you're talking to your attorneys, tell them that the health department plans to post a condemned sign on the front door tomorrow morning," Tina added.

"Damn you people," Mr. Teller muttered, with a look of outrage, as the officer pulled his hands behind his back and handcuffed him. Reaching over, they did the same to Mrs. Teller and led the two out of the building and into a squad car.

"We also caught the maintenance guy trying to leave, and we're taking him to jail, too," an officer said.

Looking into the squad car, Tina said with disgust to the Tellers, "Your son can run the place until tomorrow morning. Then, we'll have someone from the state take over."

On Monday morning, Ashley and Steve sat outside of Judge Amos Folger's courtroom, waiting for the hearing for Mr. and Mrs. Teller to commence.

Steve turned to Ashley and took her hand gently in his. "I want to explain to you about the other night when you found me in the bar with that woman. I was working undercover to purchase some drugs. That woman and her brother were both involved in drug trafficking. After you left, we arrested both of them outside of the bar for possession and selling. I couldn't let my relationship with you interfere with my job, so I had to act coldly toward you. I'm so sorry for the hurt that I caused you."

Surprised by the sudden welling of emotion his expla-
nation caused in her, Ashley bit her lip. "I kind of guessed
that's what was going on when the captain congratulated
you about the drug deal earlier."

"Thank you." Steve's eyes reflected his gratitude at her
understanding, as he continued, "Once in jail, both the
woman and her brother began to sing. Told us, where and
from whom, they got the drugs. So, we got a lead to the
entire drug operation."

Ashley put her finger on his lips. "Enough said."

A short while later, Mr. and Mrs. Teller were standing
in front of Judge Folger, with their lawyer next to them.

The judge's face deepened into a big frown as he read
the list of charges that the police and health departments
had brought against them .

Anger crept into his voice as he said irritably, "Hillsborough County has charged you both with animal cruelty
and abuse of the elderly. How do you plead?"

Mrs. Teller spoke up with defiance, "Not guilty, your
Honor." Mr. Teller stood meekly beside her and echoed,
"Not guilty."

Their attorney stepped closer to the bench. "Your Honor,
my clients have no criminal record and are not a flight
risk. I ask that you release them on bail."

The judge looked down and announced with enormous
contempt, "Bail is set at fifty thousand each. The trial will
commence four weeks from today. And, don't even think
of leaving town." He pounded his gavel. "Next case."

Ashley, Tina, and the two officers, were well prepared as
they entered the courtroom the following month as Hillsborough County prosecuted Mr. and Mrs. Teller.

The first part of the case to be heard was the animal
cruelty charge. The two veterinarians who had treated

Buddy estimated the tight rubber band had been around the dog's mouth for several days, cutting through muscles. The vet, who had removed the deeply embedded elastic, said that the odor of decaying flesh was overpowering. And it had taken over a week on IV's to bring the dog to where he could finally stand on his feet. The last vet to testify stated, "If the dog had gone another day or two without food and water, he would have probably died."

The attorney for the Tellers jumped to his feet. "That's speculation, your Honor," he shrieked.

"No. That's a medical opinion," the judge responded firmly. "Objection overruled."

After Ashley testified and showed the judge several pictures of Buddy, Judge Folger pounded his gavel. "I've heard enough about the animal cruelty charge. Now, I'm ready to hear the testimony about the exploitation of the elderly."

Tina took the stand next and testified about the conditions that the health department had found at the home in regards to the treatment of their residents. Next, Walter and two of the female residents stated under oath about how they had been treated by the Tellers. Cross examination of these witnesses by the Teller's attorney did little to rebuke their testimony.

Judge Folger brought himself up short and struck his gavel. "Enough. I've heard enough. I'm ready to rule on this matter. Mr. and Mrs. Teller, please stand up."

The couple got slowly to their feet. Mrs. Teller wrung her hands together nervously. Mr. Teller muttered a quiet curse under his breath.

Judge Folger stared down at them, unable to say a word. Then, shook his head sadly. "Never, in all my years on the bench, have I heard of anyone being so cruel to both animals and humans. I find you both guilty of animal cruelty, a first degree misdemeanor. And I sentence you to ninety days in jail, three thousand dollars for court costs and vet bills. I also order you to pay Walter Huxley, two thousand dollars for his pain and suffering and two thousand each to the owners of the cats."

The Teller's attorney groaned. "Your Honor, the Tellers are not pet owners, they run a retirement home."

The judge nodded. "I realize that. As for the exploitation of the elderly, they will forfeit their state license, and never again be allowed to care for the aged in this state. In addition to that, I sentence each of them to another one hundred and eighty days in jail."

He pounded his gavel loudly. "This court is adjourned."

Ashley, Tina, Steve, and Walter were all smiles as they left the courtroom.

"What a nice ending to an unhappy phase of your life, Walter," Ashley said cheerfully. "You have Buddy back and now you are living in a lovely retirement home in Brandon, where they can take good care of you and your dog."

After they accompanied Walter outside the courthouse, he said, "Ms. Willis, I want you to come and see me some Sunday and plan on having dinner with me. The cook at the new place makes a terrific Southern Fried Chicken. And bring Steve with you. You two make a nice couple."

Ashley smiled quietly and Steve broke out in a broad grin. Both nodded and said in unison, "We'll be there."

"You did say Southern Fried Chicken, didn't you?" Steve asked.

"Yes, sir."

After they drove Walter back to his new home, Steve said, "I've got to stop at the precinct for a minute. Gotta check in. But hang tight. After that, I have the afternoon off. And I have so much to tell you."

In the next few weeks, Ashley and Steve became close. He accompanied her on Sundays to dinner at her parent's house where Alan and Laura were also present.

"How are you feeling these days?" her mother-in-law asked Laura, who was soon to give birth, as they sat at the dining room table prior to starting their meal.

"Oh, I'm tired a lot, but, with only a month to go, I think that's normal. My mother is going to stay with me for about a week after the baby's born."

"Well, you know you can count on us to help you in any way," Kelley replied sweetly.

"We appreciate that. The baby's room is ready—walls painted and the baby furniture all set up," Alan said, unable to conceal his excitement at the anticipation at the upcoming birth.

Looking at her with concern, he added, "The doctor said that Laura needs to get a lot of rest now. With me assigned to work in Tallahassee, she could use a lot of support. Of course, I'll be home on weekends even though it's about a three and a half hour drive each way. Then, I'll be home permanently in time for the delivery, which is most important."

"What a great family I have acquired," Laura added, as her eyes misted over.

Kelley had been watching Ashley closely as the others talked. Now she glanced over at her. "You look like you have something important to tell us, dear."

Ashley looked around the room, then dropped her voice and leaned in closer to Steve. He took her hand in his as she said, "Yes. Well here goes. Steve has asked me..." Ashley paused momentarily.

"Well, hurry up and spill it," Phil yelled. "Come on. Tell us."

Ashley stuck her left hand out and flashed the large emerald cut diamond ring on her finger. "I'm engaged.

Or rather, we're engaged."

Kelley jumped to her feet in excitement. "Tell us all the details." She ran over to her daughter, hugged her and twisted her hand so that she could get a good look at the diamond. "It's gorgeous," she exclaimed.

"Now, time for a celebration!" Phil stood up, opened a bottle of wine, and filled everyone's glass except Laura's, who was drinking iced tea. He raised his glass, "Let's toast the newly engaged couple."

"Yes. Three cheers for Ashley and Steve," Alan said as he leaned across the table to get a good look at the ring. "How did he ask you, Ash?"

"During a date last week, Steve leaned over and gave me a gold cross on a chain. After he put it around my neck, he said, 'And here is something else I want you to have, if you're sure you really want it.' He opened a little blue box with the ring in it and whispered, 'Will you marry me?'"

"And you said?" Kelley prompted.

"Of course, I said yes," Ashley answered with a broad smile lighting her face.

"Hey Ash. Did you set a date yet?" Alan asked, taking a sip of his wine and leaning back in his chair.

"Maybe in the fall. We have so much to work out. But, one thing I can promise, you'll all be there," Ashley said looking proudly at her family.

Kelley looked directly at Steve. "And when can we expect to meet your family, Steve?"

He sat upright and sighed. "My mother passed away a few years ago and my father lives in a retirement home. I plan to call him tonight with the good news."

"I'm sure he'll be very pleased," Kelley added.

"Now, it's my turn for an announcement," Phil said. "I'm hungry. Let's eat."

Ashley laughed. "That's what I love about you, Dad. No matter what's happening, you never forget your stomach."

Steve looked over at her and grinned. "Like father, like daughter." Glancing at Phil, he added, "I'm with you, Mr. Willis."

Kelley stood up to go into the kitchen, and whirled around, "Oh Ashley, I meant to ask you before. What happened with your old friend from the retirement home? You know the old man whose dog was missing for a few days."

"After the owners of the home went to jail, the building was torn down. Walter and his dog are at a new retirement home now and he just loves it. And I heard that the Tellers are still trying to appeal their sentence. They plan to go back to New Jersey if and when they get out of jail."

Phil stood up and put his arm around Kelley. "Now, let's eat. I'll help you bring the dishes from the kitchen."

Leaving the room, he leaned over and whispered in her ear. "Just think, not only are you going to be the 'Mother of the Bride,' but you are also going to be 'Grandma'."

Chapter 18

Everyone in the Willis clan was all abuzz with the news about Alan, whose name was on the front page of the Tampa Tribune. The headline read "Local SWAT team Leader to meet with Governor."

Accolades were plentiful on how successful Lt. Willis and his team were on making both Tampa and the State of Florida a safer place to live. The newspaper did not indicate why the governor had asked to meet with Lt. Willis, but announced he would call a press conference shortly after the meeting to reveal what the two discussed.

On Monday morning, Alan said good-bye to his wife at five-thirty in the morning and started off on his journey to Tallahassee. He was scheduled to meet with the newly elected governor at eleven.

After the meeting in which the two talked privately for almost an hour, the governor called a press conference. He announced he had appointed Lt. Willis to be the new crime watch dog for the state. Lt. Willis would oversee crime prevention in all the major cities. Joining the crime prevention units in the cities into one central unit would save the state an immense amount of money and make crime prevention more effective.

The good news for Alan was that he would be based at a precinct in Tampa and go to Tallahassee once a month to present his reports to the governor. After their meeting, the governor and Alan were scheduled to have lunch with several of the precinct captains to get their input on the new plan. The rest of the week, Alan would spend time training the various SWAT teams at their precincts.

Alan was staying at a bed and breakfast near the police headquarters in Tallahassee. He told the Governor's staff that all he needed for lodging was decent food and a comfortable bed. He planned to spend his evenings reading a good book or working on a new manual.

Each morning, about seven, he made a point of calling Laura. "Good morning, honey," he said to her over the phone on Friday morning.

"Boy, this really seemed like a long week with you gone," she said miserably. Alan could hear the loneliness in her voice.

He sighed. "Me, too." He closed his eyes trying to picture his wife sitting by the phone in her pajamas and robe. "How did you sleep last night?"

"Tossed and turned a little. The baby kept kicking. Thank goodness it's Friday at last." Her voice seemed to be more upbeat now.

"I should be heading home early this afternoon. Why don't you stay in bed most of the day and rest," he suggested. "I should be home by five. Miss you."

"Same here. It's not much fun alone."

"I know, I feel the same. If you need company, call my mother. She can't wait for her new grandson to be born."

"Good idea, dear. Oh, Alan, before you hang up, I hope you don't mind, but I think that I've finally decided on a name for our son, Michael James."

"That's a beautiful name, honey. I just love it. Michael James Willis has a nice ring to it. But say, I have to go now. I have a group meeting with the precinct captains. I should be done by noon, then I'll head for home."

"Sounds good."

"If my mother and father are coming over today, ask Mom if she'll fix spaghetti for the four of us."

"Just like your father, always thinking of food," she rolled her eyes and chuckled.

"Love her cooking."

After he concluded his conversation, Alan took a quick shower, put on his fatigues, and headed downstairs for his breakfast. He was grateful that the woman, who owned the bed and breakfast where he was staying, provided a three course breakfast. This morning it was complete with eggs, bacon and French toast. After breakfast, he stopped at the front desk to check out and made it a point to tell the receptionist to convey to the owner how delicious the breakfast was. "'Next time I'm in Tallahassee, you can count on me staying here."

About a block before headquarters, Alan spotted a small church on the corner.

The sign in front read 'St. Michaels.' How appropriate he thought, that's the name Laura picked out for our son. He parked his car in the adjacent lot and walked through the front door into the empty church. Inside, he spotted a beautiful statute to the left of the altar. It was of St. Michael, the Archangel. Kneeling in front of the statue, he lit a large candle and prayed for the safe delivery of his son. In a box nearby, he spotted small St. Michael medals with a sign reading 'One Dollar Donation.' He took five medals. He reached into his pocket, drew out a ten dollar bill and put it in the offertory box.

He exited the church, jumped into his car, and headed to headquarters for the ten o'clock team meeting. Entering the office of Captain Jay Cunningham, he said pleasantly, "Morning, sir."

Seated at his desk, the captain looked up. "Well, your last day here has finally arrived. The SWAT teams are in the conference room waiting for their citations and your farewell address, Lt. Willis."

"Thank you."

The captain cleared his throat. "And how did they do, Willis?"

"You should be very proud of the teams, sir." Alan's voice was steady, sure and sincere. "I would rate them as some of the best that I've ever worked with."

Captain Cunningham stood up and as he and Alan started to leave office, a police sergeant rushed into the room. "Sir, we have a crisis."

"Sergeant Lopez, don't you know how to knock?" The captain glared at him.

"Sorry, sir. But, there's a Ferris wheel stuck in mid-air at a neighborhood carnival. Some kids are stranded high above the ground."

"Slow down man!" The Sergeant's voice was now frantic.

"But Captain, they need help!"

The captain paused for a few minutes, and then turned to Alan. "Don't look now, Willis, but it looks as if you're about to put that SWAT team into action."

Chapter 19

"Willis, get your men out to that carnival, at once," the captain ordered.

"Yes, sir. "Alan ran into the conference room and shouted, "Lt. Steffins, have your men gather up their gear and get to the rescue vehicle. We're needed at a carnival immediately. Ferris wheel stuck in the air and people are trapped."

Within seconds, the highly trained team was dressed in full gear. They jumped into the van and were on their way to the scene. Painted on the outside of the van were the words, "Tallahassee SWAT team."

"Take the short cuts," Steffins yelled to the driver, who had input the address into his GPS. "Just get us there fast, every second counts."

"I know just where the place is Lieutenant," the driver replied confidently.

As they drove toward the carnival, the sky turned black and green. Alan could see that a dreadful storm was rapidly approaching. Within a few minutes, Steffins and his men were at the site of the carnival. The driver brought the van to an abrupt halt at the entrance way.

The entrance sign to the church's grounds had a piece of cardboard stapled over the carnival sign, announcing that it was closing.

Alan yelled for the driver to ignore the sign and drive right onto the grounds. The van pulled up in front of the Ferris wheel. As Alan jumped out of the front seat, two men came running toward him waving their hands frantically. The remainder of the SWAT team poured out of the van and stood patiently awaiting instructions on how to proceed.

"Thank God you guys are here. I'm Spike Woods, the owner of the carnival. And this is our maintenance supervisor, Julius Statin." The pulse in Woods' neck bulged with anxiety.

"I'm Lt. Willis from the State SWAT team." He nodded toward Steffins. "This is Lt. Steffins from the Tallahassee Team. What's the situation?"

"A nearby electric transformer blew and the power went out in the whole area." Woods spoke through clenched teeth. "Before the storm approached, the operator had just started up the Ferris wheel ride and he was giving an exclusive ride to a kid celebrating his birthday. He and his sisters were the only ones on the wheel. We're waiting for the electric company to come and fix the transformer."

"Do you have a backup generator for the wheel?" Alan asked Julius.

Julius was sweating profusely. "No. We have a couple of small ones that we used to turn on a couple of flood lights, but nothing big enough to power the Ferris wheel. And there are three kids trapped inside the bucket at the top." He pointed upward. "Look! One cable has already snapped."

"Will the bucket tip when you start the wheel?" Alan's eyes narrowed, his body tensed.

"No, this is an old fashioned Ferris wheel. The weight of the kids in the bucket holds it upright. As far as I know, this is the first time it's ever stopped with anyone in it.

Gotta get those kids out and fast. They're screaming their heads off." Julius's hands were trembling.

A young woman with flowing blonde hair rushed up to Alan. "Thank God, you're here. I'm Mrs. Macy. My son and his little sisters, Lucy and Judy, are stuck up there. You've got to get them down." Her voice was filled with panic, and she swayed like a young tree in a gale. "Please, I beg of you."

Alan stepped toward her and put his hand on her arm. "We'll take care of it. Just try to remain calm." He motioned for one of his men to take her over to the side of the field.

Alan stood a step back and looked up at the wheel, as an electric company truck with a cherry picker attachment rolled into the parking lot and pulled up beside the SWAT team truck. A utility worker jumped out of the truck and walked up to Alan.

"I'm Manny Edwards. Tallahassee Electric. I brought 'Tillie', our bucket truck. Looks like you guys could use some help."

"You've got that right." Alan reached out and shook Manny's hand. "Lt. Willis, Florida State SWAT team. I understand that a transformer blew. How long before you can get it fixed?"

Manny shrugged his shoulders and shifted from one foot to the other. "No telling. Could be minutes. If we have to replace it, it could be hours." He stared up at the kids in the bucket, who were now leaning over the edge, looking down and whimpering.

"How high does your bucket reach?" Alan asked Manny, trying to concentrate on a solution to the problem.

"About one hundred thirty feet."

Alan sighed and looked over at Julius. "How high up is that top bucket seat on the wheel?"

That question stopped Julius for a moment. After

thinking carefully, he replied, "About a hundred and thirty six feet."

Alan could feel his toes curl in his shoes with tension. He stared up at the Ferris wheel that looked like two giant bicycle wheels.

The wheels were connected to the main frame by metal bars, which were positioned so that the buckets could swing freely in the air. Gravity kept the seats from swinging upside down. The wheel was run by a series of gears, belts, and pulleys all connected to each other and run by an electric motor. Only now—there was no electricity to the motor.

Alan had to think of another way to get the children down and he had to do it quickly. The children appeared to be too frantic to wait for an hour or more for the transformer to be replaced.

Alan turned toward Julius. "You're sure that no one else is on that wheel except the three kids?"

Julius's eyes widened, and he thought about the question a little more, just to be sure. "Yes. The boy's mother gave me twenty bucks to give the kid and his sisters a special birthday ride all by themselves."

A middle aged man dressed in a maintenance uniform approached. "Mr. Woods, we got everyone off the other rides okay, but we can't find a little girl that was on the tea cup ride. We've looked all over for her."

Alan screwed his face into a grimace and turned toward his team. "Steffins, take a couple of the men with flash lights. See if you can find the little girl. The rest of you get the crowd back away from the Ferris wheel."

Woods looked up into the sky, which was dark and threatening. "Looks like the storm is getting closer. Better try to get the rest of the crowd to leave the premises."

"We're on it. The rest of you men take care of it while we concentrate on the three kids." Alan sounded more confident than he felt.

"Say Willis, I've got an idea on how to get those kids down. I'll pull my utility truck as close as I can to the Ferris wheel," Manny said. "You get in the bucket and I'll hoist you up. Once you're up there, you can see if you can make your way up and over to the bucket."

Alan looked upwards and breathed deeply. He forced himself not to give in to the panic that was rising inside of him. "We've got to try something. Do you have a body harness that I can put on so that I can secure the kids to me when I reach them?"

"Got that," Manny replied

After he pulled the truck into position beside the wheel, Manny got out of the cab. He walked over to the bucket, pulled out a body harness and helped Alan put it on. The chest harness had straps that fit over the shoulder and between the legs with a waist belt.

"I think I have a plan," Alan said. "Do you have a long sturdy rope that I can fasten to myself and the harness? If I can lasso the arm of the seat, maybe I can pull myself up to the kids, grab them one by one and drop them down into the bucket. "

"Here," Manny said after he reached inside the truck and pulled out a long rope with a buckle attached to one end. He helped Alan clip it to the harness. "There are three kids up there. Do you think you have the strength to do that three times?" Manny asked.

"I've got to try. All my physical training for the SWAT team should help, but, that doesn't mean that it'll be a piece of cake." Alan paused and made a futile little gesture. "And by the way Manny, I thought you would come here with a partner."

"Oh, he broke his wrist getting a cat out a the tree a couple of hours ago. So, it's just you and me, pal." He stood back and looked at Alan nervously.

"Okay. Let's do it," Alan replied, with a determined look on his face.

Manny shrugged, stepped forward and helped Alan into the bucket. "What's your plan, Willis?"

"I'm going to lift each of the kids out of the Ferris wheel, one by one, and lower them into the utility bucket. Then you can bring us all down at once."

Manny looked up at the sky which was getting darker by the moment. "We better hurry. We need to get this over before the storm hits. It won't be too safe up there if there's lightning."

Julius had been standing nearby listening to the conversation between Alan and Manny. He stepped forward and put his hand on Alan's arm. "Try not to get inside the bucket on the Ferris wheel with the kids. Your weight may tip it." He avoided Alan's gaze. "And, I forgot to tell you that the operator said that the birthday boy's name is 'Tubby'."

Alan stared at him in shock. "Tubby? The kid's name is Tubby? You gotta be kidding."

"Well, that's what the kid's mom called him."

Chapter 20

Captain Cunningham stood nearby, trying to hold a television reporter and her camera man back from the scene. When the reporter saw the children's mother standing at the edge of the field sobbing softly, she instructed her camera man to take video of the desperate mother. At the same time, she described the scene for the audio portion of the video.

"Are you going to be okay?" Manny asked Alan, who was now standing quietly inside the utility bucket.

Alan looked upward at the Ferris wheel. "Yup. Somehow, I've got to get the three kids into your bucket." He swallowed, hoping his anxiety did not show in his face. "But, I don't like the sound of the name 'Tubby.' Sounds like a kid who eats well."

Manny shot him a quick glance. "Well. Good luck."

"Thanks. I'll need it."

Manny climbed inside the truck and turned on the ignition.

The television reporter snapped at her camera man. "Be sure you get all of the action. It'll be a good lead-in for the evening news." She flung the words at him, daring him not to miss any of the conflict.

Manny directed the bucket of the truck skyward and

toward the Ferris wheel. To Alan, it seemed somewhat like riding in an elevator outside of a building. All of a sudden, the bucket stopped with a jerk. Manny had raised it as far as it would go.

Alan looked over at the swaying car seat on the Ferris wheel. Just as he had anticipated, he was about five or six feet short of reaching it.

He looked down and made sure the rope was firmly attached to the chest harness with a clamp. He knew that throwing the rope over the Ferris wheel arm would be tricky.

He made a loop in the loose end of the rope and swung it like a lasso toward the arm of the seat. The children were peeking out of the seat at him and they let out a scream as the rope missed the arm.

"Quiet. Be quiet and don't move," Alan yelled up at them.

Their eyes widened and they stared at him in silence as he made a couple of more attempts to lasso the arm of the seat. This was a new experience for the SWAT team leader.

"Shit. I would have trained at a rodeo if I knew I was going to have to do this," Alan muttered to himself.

Finally, on the next try, the rope caught onto the arm. He gave a final pull on the rope, making sure it was firmly attached to the harness and then hand over hand worked himself up on the rope to the wheel.

After slowly pulling himself up, he was now even with the passenger seat and could peer in at the children.

One of the little girls looked up at him and whimpered, "Are we gonna die?" Her face had little color.

"No, little one," Alan answered in a low reassuring voice. "What's your name?"

"I'm Lucy. I'm five." She gulped for air.

"Five years old. That makes you a big girl. Now, Lucy, I want you to raise your arms in the air and face me."

He looked over at the other two children. "Please stay quiet and remain very still. I'm going to lift Lucy out first."

The short stocky lad's eyes filled with tears and he whimpered, "What about me?'

"You must be Tubby," Alan grinned. "Well kid, ladies first, that's the rule you know. Guys are always last."

Tubby lifted his chin. He took the back of his hand and wiped the tears from his eyes. Then, bravely nodded his head, as Alan reached down and lifted Lucy up slightly. "Put your arms around my neck and put your feet inside the harness." She slid her body into the harness. "Now hold on tight."

"I'm scared," she whispered.

"Just do it, sweetheart," he instructed gently.

With her arms around Alan's neck, she clung to him for dear life. Within a few minutes, Alan was lowering her and himself into the utility bucket.

"Good girl," he said. "Now, I'm going to lift you out of the harness. I want you to stand up against the wall of the bucket. I've got to go backup and get your sister."

She sniffled and replied in a rather squeaky voice, "Hurry, mister. I'm still scared."

A loud clap of thunder could be heard and the sky got even darker. Two drops of rain hit Alan's face as he smiled at her reassuringly. He tried to say something, but couldn't, he seemed to have run out of words.

He stepped up on the edge of the bucket and then slowly climbed hand over hand up on the rope once again. He picked up the second little girl, who said her name was Judy. She closed her eyes and shuddered as she wrapped her arms around his neck.

He lowered her into the utility bucket beside her sister. Suddenly, Alan heard a creaking sound above him. He looked up and saw that one of the cables holding the Ferris wheel seat had snapped. "Oh shit!" he exclaimed.

"Two down and one to go," Alan sighed and muttered to himself, his arms starting to feel a bit tired. He cleared his suddenly dry throat. "And now it's on to the big kid."

The Ferris wheel gave a big lurch. Alan could see Tubby peering over the side.

"Just stand still. I'm coming kid. Don't move," he yelled out. "Shifting your weight makes the seat move."

Tubby looked down at him. Alan could see sheer terror in the child's eyes.

Again, after climbing the rope, Alan found himself even with the Ferris wheel seat. He cursed under his breath as he looked over at Tubby. He knew that it would be difficult trying to get this boy down, because he appeared to weigh about a hundred and thirty pounds. No way was the kid going to fit as easily inside the body harness as the thin little girls had.

With a slow and deliberate movement, Alan gripped the side of the seat with one hand and extended the other hand toward Tubby. "I'm going to pull you up even with my chest. And when I do, I want you to put your arms around my neck and I'll lift you. Then, we'll slip your feet inside the harness."

Tubby's eyes widened even more in fear and he started to whimper.

"Listen kid. That's an order," Alan said sharply. Then in a calmer tone of voice, he added, "I know you can do it. Just take it slow."

"I'll try," Tubby stuttered.

"Okay, son. Now, I'm going to pull you up." Alan lifted Tubby a little, and helped him shove his fat legs into the harness as far as they would go. With a strong pull from Alan, Tubby thrust himself upwards and locked his arms securely around Alan's neck.

"Hang on. Down we go." Alan's arms were now throbbing. Suddenly he could feel his feet touch the rim of the utility truck bucket. He released a breath of relief, slid into the bucket and helped the boy step out of the harness.

"Stand still, beside your sisters," Alan instructed Tubby. Lucy and Judy reached over and hugged their brother.

Alan could hear the cheers from the people below as they saw that the third child was now safety inside the bucket. He leaned over the side of the bucket and waved his arm at Manny who was sitting inside the truck looking upward. When he saw that all four were safely inside the bucket, Manny mumbled, "Thank you Lord" and slowly lowered it to the ground.

As the bucket touched the ground, the children's mother came running toward it with tears of joy streaming down her face and her arms out stretched.

Lt. Steffins and the SWAT team members, who had been anxiously looking on, rushed forward and helped the children out of the bucket.

After hugging and kissing her children, a sobbing Mrs. Macy approached Alan and gave him a big squeeze. "You saved my babies. Thank you."

"You're welcome. Glad I could be of help," Alan replied as a big bolt of lightning flashed across the sky." He turned toward his men as the rain started to fall gently.

"I'm glad to report that we found the missing little girl," Lt. Steffins said. "Everyone is accounted for."

"Good," Alan replied, "Now, let's get the men back in the truck. This mission is over."

Spike Woods and Julius Statin shook hands with Alan, Lt. Steffins and thanked them for their help.

Manny walked over to Woods and said, "As soon as the storm is over, we should be able to repair that transformer. I'm waiting for a backup crew to come and help. We should have power restored to the park shortly. "

"Excellent. This was the last day anyway, we'll give this storm a chance to pass over and wait until morning to pack up the equipment."

Holding an umbrella above her head, the television reporter and her camera man walked up to Alan. She thrust the microphone into his face. "Lt. Willis, I understand that you are in charge of the SWAT team. Can you give me an interview now?"

Distinctly uneasy, Alan pointed to Captain Cunningham. "He'll fill you in Miss. But you might want to head inside that tent and get out of the bad weather first."

Alan jumped into the SWAT team's van beside Lt. Steffins, who was in the driver's seat. "Okay, Steffins, back to headquarters. You and your men will probably receive a citation for your work here today. And I'm anxious to get home. Gonna be a father soon," he said proudly.

Chapter 21

The team drove back to the precinct as the rain and thunder intensified. Alan was thankful he and the children had gotten out of the utility bucket before lighting had struck them. All the men's uniforms were soaking wet from the rain.

"Go in through the back door," Lt. Steffins barked out to his men. They dashed into the building as Sergeant Ed Lopez held the door open for them. He directed them to the lockers and shower room.

"Looks like you got pretty wet," Lopez said to Alan, glancing down at his dripping clothes. "Please follow me, sir. After you take a hot shower, I've got clean fatigues, a dry T-shirt and socks you can wear."

"Never mind. I've got dry clothes in the trunk of my car. I'll go get my suit case and I'll be all set. Thanks any way," Alan said cheerfully. "By the way, have you ever thought of joining the SWAT team?"

Lopez shook his head in bemusement. "Nope. I like working in the office. How about giving me the keys to your car? I'll bring it up to the front for you ."

"Thanks. I'm going to head back right after the awards ceremony. I'm anxious to get home to my special lady."

After changing his clothes, Alan met the rest of the team in the conference room, where he passed out the certificates to the graduates. A quick summation by Lt. Steffins on how the incident at the Ferris wheel had gone down made every member of the team proud of how they had assisted in the crisis.

Now, it was Captain Cunningham's turn to speak to the men.

He folded his arms across his chest and waited for the men to quiet down. "My speech will be short. Congratulations to all of you for completing your training with Lt. Willis. A special thanks to him and to Lt. Steffins for a job well done today. Now, please remain seated. Since you all missed lunch, I've ordered an early supper brought in for us."

He turned toward Alan. "I know you're in a hurry to get home. I hope you'll stay a little and enjoy my southern favorites—chicken fried steak with mashed potatoes, white gravy, and corn on the cob. I call it 'comfort food.' And oh yea, strawberry short cake with whipped cream for dessert. So, everyone, enjoy."

Alan's mouth started to water as he looked over at the buffet table the caterers had laid out for the men. He nodded his agreement to the invitation.

Houdini could not have made the food disappear faster than the hungry men did.

As the caterer served the dessert, Sergeant Lopez walked up to Alan and said, "Have a safe trip back."

Alan shook his hand.

Lopez took a step forward. "By the way, the rain has stopped. I think the storm is headed to Georgia."

"Glad to hear that." Alan walked around the table and shook hands with all the men. "You're a fine officer and a credit to the uniform," he added, when he approached Lt. Steffins.

"Captain Cunningham," Alan said, "The rain has stopped and I've got to be on my way. As you know, I've got an expectant wife waiting for me. I'll send my final report to the governor and a copy to you."

Cunningham shook his hand, "Thank you. And keep up the good work, Willis. The Governor thinks highly of your program. And remember to keep a look out for the State Police on your way home. I heard they're pulling people over left and right for speeding."

"Don't worry. I'll set my cruise control so I'm under the limit." Within minutes, he was on his way home to his wife.

It was about seven-thirty as Alan pulled into his driveway. He hit the garage door opener, pulled into the garage, turned off the ignition and exited the car. He grabbed his duffle bag and the gifts he had bought for Laura and ran into the house.

"Laura, I'm home," he shouted. "And I need a hug from my little mother."

Dressed in her robe and slippers, Laura appeared in the kitchen doorway. "Not your little mother yet. Your son hasn't made his appearance."

He threw his duffle bag on the floor and placed the gifts on the table as Laura rushed over to him. She threw her arms around him and gave him a long passionate kiss.

"Oh, you taste good. And I'm so glad I made it home before the baby decided to arrive." Alan took a step back and looked with joy at his very pregnant wife.

"And now, Lt. Willis, I'm in charge once again," Laura announced. "Throw your dirty clothes in the laundry room. Then, march yourself up stairs and slip into something comfy. Meet me in the family room. I've got a fire going in the fireplace and I'm going to fix you a nice gin and tonic."

Alan smiled and hurried out of the kitchen. Fifteen minutes later, with arms around each other they cuddled on the leather sectional.

"God, it's so good to be home." He gave his wife a big squeeze. "I had quite an adventure up there."

"Yes. I saw you on television. I almost chewed off my nails watching you rescue those kids."

Alan put his two fingers on Laura's lips. "I'm fine and safe. Let's talk about you. How are you doing?"

"I'm well," Laura replied softly. "And you look great."

"Did just fine up in Tallahassee. You told me on the phone you ordered a rocking chair for our son's room so you can sit in it to feed and rock him. So, I bought a CD with lullabies as a gift for you. Also, got a St. Michael's medal for you from the church I visited." He handed her the items in a small bag.

Laura took them out and looked them over. "Thank you, that was so thoughtful. The week seemed long, but thanks to your folks and my mom, the days went by fairly quickly." Her eyes narrowed. "However, the nights were long and lonely. And I mean lonely."

"Well, I'm here now. We'll just get ready for the big event."

"If I stay on schedule, the doctor said I could deliver next week. I have her phone number handy and my bag is packed." Her voice sounded very anxious.

Alan looked a little concerned. "Okay. But, I've got to go in on Monday to fill out my report about the Tallahassee SWAT team. By noon, I should be done. After that, I'll be all yours. I'm taking the rest of the week off. I can even take more time if needed."

Early on the following Wednesday morning, Laura leaned over in the bed and woke Alan. "I think it's time, Daddy."

His eyes widened as he jumped out of bed, took a deep breath. He tried to remain calm as he scrambled to gather up his clothes. Both of them dressed quickly, and Alan grabbed her bag and dashed out to the garage.

He tossed the bag onto the back seat and swiftly backed the car out of the garage. Laura called her doctor and told her she was on her way to the hospital.

Alan ran back into the house and assisted Laura out through the front door and into the car. He drove quickly through the quiet morning traffic, and headed for the emergency entrance to the hospital. He stopped the car, jumped out, threw the car keys at the valet, and raced around to the passenger side. He gently helped Laura from the car, placed her in a wheelchair, grabbed her suitcase, and rushed her through the emergency entrance.

When he told the admitting nurse their names, she said Laura's doctor was waiting for them on the fourth floor delivery area. "Okay, follow me," she instructed Alan as she pushed Laura through the double doors and down the hall to the elevator.

When they arrived upstairs, a delivery room nurse took over. She instructed Alan to wait in the hall as she led Laura into a birthing room. She helped Laura out of her street clothes and into a hospital gown. "Your first one?" she asked.

"Yes," Laura answered between the pains, which were now coming quite rapidly.

The nurse helped her into a bed, then opened the door and motioned for Alan to enter.

"I'm ready," Laura called out as he walked toward her. "Boy am I ready!" She let out a big breath.

He took her hand in his. "I'm here, dear. Just hold my hands and squeeze when the pains come."

He looked inside his jacket pocket. "Oh, my gosh. I forgot my camera. Oh well, I have my phone. I can take a couple of pictures with that after the baby is born."

"Anything you like," Laura muttered as she gasped between the pains.

"By the way, I called my folks and your mom while I was waiting in the hall. My folks are picking up your mom and bringing her to the hospital. I called Ashley too and let her know we're here. Got her voice mail. I'm sure she'll call back soon."

A couple of hours later, Michael James Willis was born. Alan gave a huge sigh of relief, thankful the labor time had been so short.

Chapter 22

"Mr. Willis, please meet your healthy baby boy—all six pounds, ten ounces of him," the nurse said as she handed him the baby, wrapped in a blue receiving blanket. Laura's eyes were beaming as she watched her husband affectionately kiss the baby on the forehead. "Bring our son to me," she instructed.

Alan laid the baby on Laura's chest. Dr. Theresa Heatley, who had delivered the baby, smiled proudly at them, "You look like you will be very caring parents. But now, I want the nurse to take the baby away. We need to clean up our little fellow."

Alan handed his phone to the nurse as he knelt down beside Laura and the baby. "Can you take a picture of the three of us, please?"

The nurse did not even have to order them to say "cheese." It looked as though even little Michael was smiling for the picture.

The nurse snapped a couple of pictures. The door to the birthing room opened and Alan's parents entered, together with Laura's mother, Catherine.

Alan looked up and beamed, "Hey, you're just in time for a couple of pictures. They're going to take little Michael away and clean him up." He looked at the nurse. "A few more pictures with the grandparents? Please?"

She smiled and nodded. Grandpa Phil removed his camera which was slung over his shoulder and handed it to the nurse. "This means so much to us," he said as his eyes started to mist. "It's our first grandchild."

Alan stepped to Laura's side. The others knelt near her and the baby for pictures.

"Michael is so beautiful. I just wish your dad was here to see him, Laura." Catherine had tears in her eyes as she thought of her late husband.

The doctor stepped forward, took the baby from Laura's arms and handed him to the nurse.

Looking at Alan, she tilted her head back. "I'm going to keep your wife and baby for an extra day. The delivery was harder on Laura than we anticipated. She needs to regain her strength before heading home. I suggest you and your family leave for now, allow Laura to get some rest. She and the baby are in good hands."

"Thank you doc," Alan said. Her words soothed him. Then he knelt down next to Laura and gently kissed her. "I'll be back later in the day, my little mother."

"Why don't you go get yourself some breakfast," Laura suggested.

Alan looked up at his parents and his mother-in-law. "You see everyone, she's still the boss. My treat for breakfast."

After an extensive maternity leave, Laura placed baby Michael in a day care facility and returned to full-time work.

Alan was working out of the Tampa's SWAT team division on a special assignment for the governor. Since he had worked around the state at many of the various city precincts, the governor wanted a report on the state-wide budget and staff morale. He was especially interested in hearing Alan's suggestions on how to make the whole operation more efficient and safe. Crime in the state was now down and the approval rating for the Governor was up. Alan's primary suggestion was better communication between the various captains and their men.

Their work schedule was perfect for them. They were delighted Alan's parents and Laura's mother were available for baby-sitting for the occasional evening out. This was the opportune time for the couple to try to build their son's nest egg. Plus Alan's parents had already purchased a prepaid college plan for Michael.

Ashley and Steve now took center stage. A group of family and friends attended the quiet church wedding of Ashley Ann Willis to Steven John Clarke in Tampa's old cathedral.

As Grandma Kelley tried to keep Michael from fussing out loud, she watched Ashley walk down the aisle on the arm of her father.

Ashley was wearing a simple cream-colored silk wedding dress. It was little more than a slip with delicate spaghetti straps and a softly shirred bodice. A small shrug worn over her bare shoulders made it appear modest for the ceremony. The color complimented her tanned complexion. The short hem, hitting several inches above her knees, highlighted her slender legs. A simple crown of baby's breath attached to a chapel length veil complimented Ashley's face and her long, flowing hair.

Two cameras were set up in the church—one in the back and one in the front near the altar to capture every minute. The ceremony was attended by about seventy-five family members and close friends.

Steve's old partner was his best man. Both stood at

the altar, dressed in black tuxedos, waiting for the bride and her father to walk up the aisle. Behind them stood the only usher, the bride's brother, Alan.

As the matron of honor, Laura was dressed in an aqua-colored cocktail dress. The maid of honor, a friend of Ashley's, was dressed in the same cocktail dress but in a shade darker. Both ladies had shoes of exactly the same color as their dresses.

The altar was decorated with aqua and white flower arrangements. After the ceremony, a sit-down dinner was held at the local country club for the guests. Aqua and white chiffon panels hanging from the ceiling and white lights wrapped around trees made the dining room a romantic fantasy. Aqua candles and white orchids glowed in the table center pieces.

Following the dinner, the newly married couple cut the four-tiered wedding cake before the dancing started. The white chocolate cake was filled with chocolate mousse. It was covered in white chocolate frosting, hand-crafted gum paste aqua-colored seashells, and cream roses.

After a three-day honeymoon to Key West, Ashley and Steve planned to live in Ashley's small home in Crystal Beach. The location made Ashley's drive to Dolphin Springs easy. Steve had only a short commute to his job in Tampa, where he was now one of Tampa's top police detectives. Their busy schedules would leave the newlyweds little time to decorate their home and to have fun together.

The following Christmas, the whole family gathered in Kelley and Phil's home for a special celebration. Phil stood up and announced, "As our Christmas gift to everyone, I would like to treat Ashley and Steve, Laura and Alan, and mother and myself to a seven-day cruise to the Caribbean. Laura's mother has already agreed to take care of baby Michael."

"Oh my goodness," Alan swallowed. "Laura doesn't like

to go on cruises. She gets seasick."

Laura took Alan's hand in hers and tried to reassure him. "That's okay, honey. I'll get a patch for seasickness. Don't worry, I'll be fine."

Kelley's relief at Laura's statement was evident as she said, "Now, let's have a show of hands. Who is ready to go on a Willis Family Cruise?"

Everyone raised their hands.

"Now, here's a list of the dates available." Phil's voice was a trifle loud with enthusiasm. "Let's see if we can find a time when we can all go at once."

Laura screamed out. "Did everyone see what I just saw? Little Michael just took his first step."

They all stood up and rushed over to the baby and took turns having him stand.

"Let's not rush the kid," Alan said, delighted with his son's progress.

After they cooed over Michael for some time, Phil said, "Now, let's head in for dinner ."

As the others left the room, Kelley lingered behind in the family room.

Phil put his arm around her. "Are you okay, Kell? Why are you crying?"

She wiped the tears from her eyes. "I'm just so happy."

"Well, you have a new job now, Kelley." He took hold of her hand, threaded his fingers through her own, and began stroking her wrist. "You are hereby assigned to be the tour director on our future cruise."

"Aye, aye, sir," she exclaimed. "You know, this is the best Christmas I ever had."

"I'll second that," Phil chimed in.

Chapter 23

Phil and Kelley were extremely pleased that Alan, Ashley and their spouses agreed to join them for the cruise, hoping this would give the family the opportunity to bond even closer.

Ashley and Steve were particularly excited about the prospect of swimming with the dolphins. Laura and Alan were looking forward to the scuba diving. Kelley and Phil wanted to just eat, sleep, read by the pool, and maybe take in a couple of excursions.

A week before the departure they all met for a Sunday dinner at Alan and Laura's home. Laura made crab linguini accompanied with thin slices of veal, coated in flour, dipped in beaten egg, then rolled in bread crumbs and quickly fried. Watching cooking shows on television had given her inspiration, and with the help of a good cook book, she felt confident enough to show off a little.

She also served an assortment of steamed vegetables and hot garlic bread. Phil brought a bottle of his treasured wine from the Rossi Vineyard in Sicily. There had been a note attached to this bottle from Senior Rossi that this would be the last of the wines from his vineyard. Now, in his late eighties, he had decided to sell the vineyard and retire to his villa to spend more time with his grandchildren. He said it was a sad day for him when he had to sell his beloved winery.

"It's so nice of your mother to watch little Michael while we're gone on the cruise," Kelley said, smiling serenely at Laura.

"Yes. It should be easy now that he's eighteen months old. Mom's girl friend, a retired nurse, is keeping her company and will help her care for him. So between the two of them, I'm confident they can take good care of him for a week. Besides, my mother finds traveling a little difficult these days and has to use a walker for long distances."

Phil and Kelley planned to drive from home the day before the cruise and stay with Ashley and Steve overnight. Phil had arranged for a shuttle van to pick the four of them up in Clearwater then drive on to Tampa to pick up Alan and Laura.

Both Ashley and Laura were taking two large suitcases—one filled with an assortment of cruise apparel and the other one half-empty to allow space for souvenirs.

Kelley and the three men each took only one large suitcase. But everyone had a carry-on bag or a laptop. The back of the van was piled high with luggage. The driver made his way east across the state to Port Cape Canaveral... the starting point of the cruise.

They prepared to board and stopped briefly for the photographer to take pictures in front of the white life preserver with the ship's insignia on it. Each couple had their individual pictures taken and then several group photos.

Kelley noticed one of the passengers in front of them had shoved the others aside as he scurried to get past the photographer. With a few curse words, he let the photographer know, in no uncertain terms, he didn't want his picture taken.

The photographer handed Ashley a sheet of paper. "Here's a brochure with the prices of the photos and the times and location where you can purchase them."

Ashley took the brochure studied it. "When we were approaching the gangplank it looked like one of the passengers just brushed past you."

The photographer didn't bother to mask the indifference in his voice. "Yeah. Some people just don't want their pictures taken. Others are in a big hurry to get to the buffet. We're instructed not to force any of the passengers nor to high pressure people to purchase them. The photos usually just sell themselves."

Boarding the ship, a young man, dressed in a white uniform, walked up to them. "Let me assist you in finding your cabins. Your luggage should be there shortly."

"Thanks," Phil replied with a quick grin. "And by the way, who do I see about having dinner with the captain?"

"I'm First Mate, Terrance Alger. I can arrange that for you, sir."

"Here's my card. We have a party of six," Phil said.

Alger directed the group toward the elevator and to their suites which were located on the Promenade Deck. "After you get settled, there's a bar and a luncheon buffet on the Lido Deck."

For the first few days of the cruise, the waters of the Atlantic were very calm. All three couples did activities on their own during the day, but agreed to meet for the early seating for dinner. Three days before the cruise was to end, Kelley and Phil were formally dressed for dinner at the captain's table. She had brought along a long formal gown, he had brought his white dinner jacket. This dinner was to be one of the highlights of the cruise.

They entered the dining room and First Mate Alger introduced them to the captain, Franz Lodger. Nodding to the captain, Phil said, "On behalf of my family, I want to thank you for making this cruise so enjoyable. We found everything first class."

"May I get that in writing, Mr. Willis? I usually hear only the negative. But, we have experienced a few challenges on this sailing. That's to be expected with this many people on board."

Waiters walked around the table and filled the wine glasses as the hors d'oeuvres of caviar and sour cream on toast were served, followed by a choice of wild rice and chicken or French onion soup. Then mixed greens with lobster and grilled artichoke were served. The main course was mignon of beef tenderloin with garlic roasted eggplant, tomato basil brochette, and roasted lamb shanks.

The Romanian violin players circled the room entertaining the guests.

"You like?" the captain asked his guests. Everyone nodded and murmured their appreciation.

Following the medley of desserts that included lemon sorbet, a superb Tiramisu, and coffee, the Willis family was quite relaxed and content. They stood up and headed out of the dining room. It was almost nine o'clock.

"I can see you ordered a full moon just for us," Alan gestured toward the sky as the captain accompanied them outside

"But, of course," he replied. "My pleasure."

They thanked the captain for the lovely evening and decided to take a walk around the deck to settle their large meal. A short time later, Kelley paused and turned to Phil. "Dear, it's starting to get a little chilly. Do you think you could get me a sweater from the cabin? I'd like to stay outside and enjoy the full moon."

"Sure." He took the elevator to what he thought was

their deck and started down the hall. Phil wouldn't admit it to his wife, but there were so many elevators on the ship he still got confused as to where to get off the elevator and what direction to take to their suite.

He started down the dimly lighted hallway and stopped abruptly when he saw two men struggling together on the floor in front of him. Approaching them he could see the man on the bottom of the skirmish was Captain Franz Lodger.

Phil paused, a long tense moment. Then he drew a deep breath. The assailant had the captain by the neck and was choking him.

Phil blinked several times as he grappled with the situation. He ran up behind them, grabbed the strange man, pulled him off, and flung him against the wall. Within a few seconds, the man jumped to his feet and ran off down the hallway.

Phil knelt down beside the dazed captain and shook him gently as he contemplated the dilemma. "You okay?"

The captain closed his eyes briefly and fell forward into Phil's out stretched arms. Finally, he regained his composure and looked up into Phil's face. He turned away silently, waited for a few moments, and then said, "Mr. Willis, thank you for coming to my rescue. Please help me up and assist me into my cabin. This is it, next door."

He handed Phil the key card. Phil helped him to his feet. He could see the fear on his face. Staggering under the captain's weight, Phil managed to open the door, drag him inside and assist him into a large leather chair.

The captain struggled to catch his breath. His lips parted soundlessly.

Phil noticed a large pitcher of water sitting on a nearby desk. He poured a glass and handed it to the captain. "Here, sir. Drink this slowly and I'll call the ship's doctor for you."

The captain grabbed Phil by the arm. His fingers closed over Phil's wrist and he managed to croak out harshly, "No. No. No one must know about this."

Phil studied him coldly and considered for a moment. "But someone was trying to kill you. Who? And why? What's going on?"

The captain said with an effort, "Sit. Let me explain my responsibilities as captain of this vessel."

Phil gazed down at him intently. "I see you have a cut on your hand. I insist upon getting the doctor."

The captain stared at him, wide-eyed and pale. "No. That bloody ass had a knife. Grab a towel from the bathroom. That will stop the bleeding."

Phil agreed, then went into the bathroom, grabbed a towel, and handed it to the captain. "Now tell me what the hell is going on." He sat down on a nearby chair.

"First, thank you," the captain murmured as he placed the towel firmly on the wound.

Phil noticed the lines of strain upon the captain's face. "For your information, sir, my family is part of law enforcement. My son-in-law is a police detective. My son is a police officer and part of a state SWAT team. And my wife and I are former private investigators. Maybe we could assist you tracking down your assailant."

The captain decided this wasn't the time to be evasive about the situation. "We have our own security personnel on the ship. "But I don't want them involved."

Phil put out his hand to him. "Well, my family is more than happy to assist you in any way we can to help you find out who assaulted you."

The captain looked down at Phil's hand covering his and took a little breath. "It is imperative we be most secretive about this. I do not want the crew or the passengers to become alarmed tonight. We can discuss this further tomorrow."

"Why don't you meet with my family in the morning? Maybe, we can put together a plan to help you with this situation."

"I would appreciate that," the captain smiled briefly.

"Are you going to be alright during the night?" Phil asked, grimly.

The captain hesitated briefly, then said, "Thank you. I think I will be okay, once I lock my door. I doubt if that fellow will be so bold as to return tonight."

"Lock your door and don't open it for anyone other than me."

"Yes, I understand." The captain swallowed. His voice was shrill and rapid as he said, "Remember, Mr. Willis, don't tell anyone other than your family about this."

Phil nodded. "Okay. I'll see you in the morning."

Chapter 24

After leaving the captain's room, Phil went to his cabin, got his wife's sweater, and rejoined his family on the Lido deck, where he had left them.

"What took you so long, dear?" Kelley asked with concern.

"We were starting to get worried about you, Dad," Steve added. "We know it's easy to get lost."

"Let's go inside to the Michelangelo Lounge and have a nightcap. I've got something important I want to tell you guys."

The others were struck by the solemn tone of his voice. They followed him into the piano bar lounge and headed toward a large booth in the back. Kelley grabbed her husband by his sleeve. "Look at the bartender, Phil. It's our old friend, Bobby Campbell."

Phil looked up and after recognizing him said to the others,"Take a seat kids. Your Mom and I will be right back."

As Kelley and Phil walked up to the bar, Bobby suddenly looked up from his work. "My God, the Willis'."

He ran around to the front of the bar and gave both of them a hug. "Sit down you two. Long time no see. We've got a lot to catch up on. Gosh, you both look great. No need to tell me what you want to drink; I remember. Two gin and tonics on the way."

He scurried to the back of the bar and in no time, Kelley and Phil each had a drink sitting in front of them.

"What are you doing working on a cruise ship, Bobby?" Kelley asked. "We're used to seeing you at Billy's Restaurant in Treasure Island."

"Yeah. You were there for a long time and we never expected you to leave," Phil added, taking a sip of his drink.

Bobby leaned his elbows on top of the bar. "The place had a fire and they closed it for several weeks for renovations. After this cruise is over, I'm headed back there. It's always been a good gig for me. I know most of the patrons and they tip me well. Now, tell me what you two have been up to lately."

Phil took a few moments to update Bobby on their lives. When he saw a waitress walking past him, he reached out and waved her over. "Miss, that's my kids in the back booth. Tell them to order whatever drinks they want. And tell them we'll join them in a few minutes."

The waitress nodded and walked away.

"So, how long have you been bartending on this ship, Bobby?" Phil asked.

"This is my third cruise with them. It's only for seven days and I make a few coins. Enough to keep me going. But, I wouldn't want to do this permanently."

"I suppose it's a little more exciting than working at Billy's," Kelley said.

"Funny, you should say that. I have to tell you what happened to me about a half an hour ago. Some guy came running into the room and slid into a seat at the end of the bar. He was shaking a lot. Then he put his hand over his face and just sat there. I walked over to him and asked, 'You okay, Mac?' He looked up, kind of stared at me and then muttered, 'A double bourbon, and make it quick'."

Phil and Kelley looked at each other intently as Bobby continued, "Sure I said. Do you want to start a tab? He shook his head, downed the drink in a big gulp, slammed the glass down on the bar and snapped, 'Give me another.' I poured him a second double bourbon and set it down in front of him."

"Then what?" Kelley asked.

"Well, a lady at the other end of the bar waved her hand at me and called out, 'Oh, Bobby, another daiquiri.' 'Coming up,' I said, and rushed down to take care of her. When I finished, I glanced up and noticed the wild guy at the other end was gone. I never got his room number, I got stiffed for the drinks. Even at Billy's that never happened to me. Something crazy must have happened to this guy because he was really upset. Shaking like a leaf the whole time and then, four shots in only a few seconds and wham. He was gone!"

Phil sat there silently, staring at his wife. Could this have been the same fellow who had just assaulted Captain Lodger, he wondered.

He mulled this thought over. "I guess lots of strange things occur on ships, Bobby. Right now, we've got to get back to our family. If you have a few minutes stop over at the table and meet the kids."

Bobby nodded. "Thanks. But as you can see, this place is really starting to get busy. I doubt if I'll be able to get away."

Kelley stood up. "Well, if we don't see you again before we get off the ship, we'll stop by Billy's."

"I'll look forward to it," Bobby said. "And by the way, the drinks are on me tonight."

Phil reached over and shook his hand. "Thanks, my friend. See you soon." Phil reached into his billfold, pulled out a twenty and dropped it into the tip jar.

They picked up their drinks, and heard Bobby's voice ring out, "Thanks guys."

They returned to the table where their children were quietly talking and sipping on beers. Kelley explained to them how they had known Bobby for years and how they had regularly visited the restaurant and bar where he worked.

Ashley noticed a smear of blood on her father's shirt sleeve. She reached over and grabbed him by the sleeve. "My God, Daddy, you've got blood on your shirt," she exclaimed in astonishment, the color draining from her face.

"Dad, what happened?" Alan sat forward in his chair.

Phil looked down at his sleeve. "I didn't realize I had gotten blood on me." He sighed. "Give me a minute to organize my thoughts, and I'll tell you what happened."

Kelley was as near to exploding as she scooted closer and grabbed his arm. "What's going on Phil? I knew right away when you came back that something had happened to you. You're driving me nuts. Now spill it."

He smiled gently at her. "Well, as usual, I got lost going back to our cabin for your sweater. The next thing I knew I came across a scuffle in one of the halls. Two men were fighting. The hall light was dim. One man was on top of the other and choking him."

Kelley's breath stopped in her chest, her eyes widened as Phil calmly continued, "The guy doing the choking had his back to me. I didn't get a close look at him. I reached down and yanked the guy off. After I threw him aside, he jumped up and ran off. Only then, did I realize the man on the floor was none other than the ship's captain."

"Oh, my gosh," Laura sputtered and put a hand to her mouth.

"Wait until you hear the rest of the story," Phil said. "Well, I picked the captain up and helped him into his cabin which was nearby. All he had to say was—'The bloody bloke tried to kill me'."

"Is the captain okay?" Ashley interjected, looking shocked. "Is that his blood on your shirt?"

Phil sat back in his seat and nodded. "Captain Lodger got a cut on his hand. Just a flesh wound. The bleeding stopped when he put pressure on it with a towel. He wouldn't let me call the ship's doctor for him."

"Did he know the guy who did it?" Alan asked.

Phil shook his head. "Well, I don't think so. But here's the skinny. I offered our help to figure out who tried to kill him."

"Who would want to murder the captain? And why? He seems to be a likeable guy," Kelley chimed in. She didn't bother to mask the blaze of anger in her eyes.

Phil sighed and looked around the table. "That's exactly what I thought. That's why I agreed to help him find his attacker."

Steve's eyes flashed as he leaned toward his father-in-law. "Do you have any idea how many passengers and crew there are on this ship, Dad?"

"A lot?"

"I heard there are twenty-five hundred passengers and a crew of nine hundred. It'll be next to impossible to find the guy," Steve added bitterly.

Alan looked over at Steve and thought for a few moments. "Not so fast, Steve. We'll just have to narrow it down as to whom on board knew the captain and could have something against him that is serious enough to attempt murder."

"Yeah. That should narrow it down quite a bit," Ashley smirked.

"We're going to meet with the captain at eight tomorrow morning to see if we can help him before this develops into something even more serious," Phil replied.

The rest of the group nodded, looked at each other and quietly finished their drinks.

As they stood up to leave, Phil said, "See you tomorrow for breakfast. And, I promise you—I won't spoil your cruise. And remember, the captain asked us not to say anything to anyone about this."

Grinning, Ashley grabbed him by the arm and walked him out of the lounge. "My goodness, Daddy, you can't help yourself. Once a sleuth, always a sleuth."

The Willis family met with Captain Lodger the next morning in a secluded part of the nearly empty dining room. Over juice and coffee, they talked about the incident the night before.

"Captain," Phil said, "my family has gathered here to help you search the ship for your assailant."

The captain opened his mouth to protest, then thought things over for a moment and nodded reluctantly. "But no one on the ship must know this search is going on or that we have a problem on board. It could cause panic."

Phil glanced down at the bandage on the captain's hand. "I can assure you no one will learn anything from us."

"But what about your personal safety while we make the search?" Alan asked.

"My security force can keep an eye on me," the captain responded.

"Is there anyone on board you suspect at this time?" Kelley asked brushing the hair out of her eyes.

"Perhaps one of the passengers or a member of the crew?" Steve chimed in.

The captain considered that. Then answered quietly, "Not at the present time."

"We can try to screen all of the passengers if you can

give us access to the personal information you have on them," Alan said.

"I can arrange for you to have entry to all our files on the internet," the captain replied. "But, you'll have to be very discreet in your search so none of the crew suspects anything."

Kelley had been lost in her own thoughts momentarily. Then spoke up. "From my past experience as an investigator, I know that usually a personal attack on an individual is done by someone who has past ties to the victim. Think carefully, sir. Do you know of anyone who might want to seek retribution on you for something?"

The captain look startled. "Let's see. Yes, it's been a number of years ago. One of my most trusted officers was involved in a string of burglaries from the passengers and was caught. His name was Hans Bluhm. In fact, he had an accomplice, his brother, Alfred. After, I testified in court against them, they were found guilty and sentenced to five to seven years in prison."

"Could they have been released by now?" Alan asked.

"Could be. I didn't keep track of them. Believe me, Mr. Willis, I run a tight ship, I've been commanding vessels for over twenty years now. Since that one incident, there have been only the usual minor crimes that take place occasionally on a ship. You know—like drunken brawls—minor thefts. But, I wasn't personally involved in any of those. I'm fairly certain it wasn't one of the crew who attacked me."

"Well, we can start with that," Phil declared. "I'll have my son and son-in-law start to check the manifest of passengers on this ship for those names."

He stood up and said to the captain, "I give you my word we'll be careful. Now, I think my family and I are famished. We'll order some breakfast if it's okay with you?"

Before he left the dining room, the captain arranged for
Alan and Steve to meet with him later that morning in
his private office on the bridge. After getting his personal
code to the files, they planned to search the manifest for
clues as to who might be the captain's assailant.

"While you're doing that, I'll layout what you four can
do to help find the captain's assailant," Phil said.

Later in the afternoon, Kelley and Phil retired to their
cabin to go over the passengers manifests Alan and Steve
had given them earlier. They heard a knock on the door.
There stood Alan and Ashley and their spouses.

"What's up, Dad?" Alan asked.

"I looked through the manifest records you printed out.
But didn't discover anything significant. Now, let's go out
on the balcony and have a chat," Phil said.

He opened the door and waved for the others to follow
him. They sat in chairs looking out at the water. "Here's
your assignment," Phil said, "I want you four to head up to
the gallery where the ship's photos are posted. Look them
over carefully. See if you can spot anyone suspicious. Then
meet your mom and me in the dining room for dinner."

"Yeah," Ashley said. "I thought the fellow who didn't
want his picture taken when we boarded the ship acted
mighty suspicious."

Alan, Laura, Ashley, and Steve reviewed the photos that
had been taken during the cruise. Ashley suddenly spied
something dubious in a couple of the pictures.

"Hey guys, look at this photo that was taken when we
boarded the ship. See those two men behind us in the
picture? They are ducking down and hiding their faces
from the camera."

Steve nodded. "Look at this next picture. The photographer got a shot of the one man from the side. Doesn't he look suspicious to you, Alan?"

"He sure does," Alan replied, grabbing the two pictures. "I'm going to buy these two photos and show them to Mom and Dad."

They met Kelley and Phil in the dining room and showed them the pictures. Alan and Steve explained their suspicious to Phil, who decided to show the photos to the captain. He knew the ship was scheduled to dock in the morning.

After looking over the photos carefully, Captain Lodger said, "These two men do resemble Hans and Alfred Bluhm, but I can't say for certain. It's been several years since the trial, they didn't have beards then."

"If these men want to attack you again Captain, they will probably strike tonight, since it may be their last opportunity," Phil replied, looking concerned. "And somehow, I have a feeling they will be back."

"Please Mr. Willis, give me the photos and leave this matter to my security force. I thank you and your family for your help, but I really must insist you enjoy the rest of the cruise and not trouble yourself with this."

Phil nodded in apparent agreement, while thinking to himself. I'll just let the captain believe we are dropping the matter. But, recalling his undercover days, he was determined to help catch the person or persons who were out to kill the captain.

Chapter 25

After the Willis clan finished dinner, they headed to the
Las Vegas show for the eight o'clock program. It was
scheduled to last about one hour with a comedy show
immediately following.

During the comedy show, Phil found he could not
concentrate on what was being said. He shut his eyes
and dropped his forehead as his mind drifted... lost in
his own thoughts. He was pre-occupied with formulating
plans to protect the captain and capture his assailant.

When the show ended, he turned to Alan and Steve
and took a deep calming breath. "Follow me guys. One
of you is going to hide in the captain's cabin in case his
attacker strikes again."

Phil knocked on the captain's cabin door at about ten-
thirty. There was a long pause before the captain yelled
out, "Who's there?"

"It's Phil Willis with my son and son-in-law. We're here
to protect you."

The captain reluctantly opened the door and shot
back, "Thank you, but I believe I can handle the situation myself."

Phil brushed past him, flung the door open, and
stepped inside followed by the two younger men. "No

arguing Captain, I insist. This is the last night of the cruise and we're taking no chances. Steve, you hide in the captain's bathroom. Alan, you come outside with me and we'll patrol the hallway. Captain, you go to bed as you normally would."

Phil could see the lines of strain on the captain's face, as he nodded.

Each of the men took their assigned posts. All was quiet for some time. Then, just after midnight, Phil spotted a man, clothed in dark clothes, come unhurriedly down the hall. An entry card was inserted in the captain's cabin door, and it slowly opened.

From behind the partially opened bathroom door, Steve could hear the sound of the door opening. A sudden prickle of awareness slid up his spine and settled in his nerves, an instinctive alert. He shifted his gaze slightly and caught sight of a man clothed in a dark hooded jacket creep into the room and move toward the captain's bed.

As the intruder crept forward, Steve burst out of the bathroom and his shout split the air. He jumped on the man from behind, hollering, "Stop. You're under arrest. Stay out of the way, Captain. He's mine."

From their positions down the hall, Phil and Alan heard the loud scuffle in the cabin and came running . As they ran through the doorway of the cabin, they could see the two men brawling on the bed and the captain standing against the wall.

Phil hit the light switch just inside the doorway. He spotted a knife lying on the floor beside the bed and Steve was sitting on top of a hooded man. Within seconds, Steve and Alan had the assailant subdued and his hands tied behind his back.

"We've got him," Phil shouted out.

Alan whipped the hood off the man's face. "Do you know this fellow Captain?"

Taken by surprise, the captain gasped and took a hasty step backwards. Then he paled dramatically and swallowed. "Yes. I recognize him. He used to work on one of my ships." He uttered a crude word beneath his breath. "He's the fellow I testified against in that theft case. His name is Hans Bluhm. But now, he has a beard."

"Well, this is one of the fellows we spied slipping past the photographer to get on the ship," Steve said in a controlled whisper. "Now, all we have to do is find his accomplice."

"What room is your partner in?" Alan asked, as he slanted a sharp look at Hans.

Hans glared and blinked in his direction, his gaze not quite focused. After hesitating only a second, he whipped around, malice twisting his lips, "Go to Hell."

"No need to ask him that," the captain said, making no attempt to hide the outrage in his voice. "Just look in his pocket for his room card. We can look up his cabin number from that."

Steve went through Han's pockets and pulled out his card. The captain picked up the phone and called security and gave them the information.

Within a few minutes, the captain turned to Phil and said tersely, "Hans is registered with his brother, Alfred. My security men are on the way here to get Hans. We have a holding cell downstairs near the engine room where we can confine him until we dock tomorrow. His brother is registered in the same cabin. It's 414 on Promenade Deck."

"Good. Alan, you come with me, we'll use Han's card to enter the cabin. Captain, please call your security men back and have a couple of your men come here and a pair meet us in Cabin 414." There was a note of caution, as he added, "Steve, you stay here with the captain, until his men pick up Hans."

Shortly after one, Phil decided to call it a day and he headed for his cabin. The captain's two assailants were safely locked up in the holding cell, the ship's security force had taken over.

The next morning, upon Kelley's suggestion, the whole family ordered breakfast delivered to their rooms, so they could get an early start.

After a sleepless night and a quick breakfast of coffee and sweet rolls in their room, Phil and Kelley were getting dressed, when they heard a knock on their cabin door. Phil opened it and saw the captain standing outside.

"I've notified the authorities to meet us at the dock," the captain said. "They'll take care of the Bluhm brothers. The authorities will want a statement from you, but I just wanted to tell you I can't thank you enough for all you have done for me, Mr. Willis."

"You're certainly welcome," Phil replied.

"By the way, I want to give you something in return for your kindness," the captain answered. He had a warm smile on his face as he reached into the pocket of his jacket and pulled out several items. "Here is a letter enrolling you in our 'Platinum Club' and a card for each of you three couples. From now on, you will receive VIP treatment whenever you sail with our cruise lines. Also, I'm issuing your entire family a certificate for a free seven-day cruise. It is good indefinitely. Use it whenever you wish to sail with us again. It's the least I can do to show you my appreciation."

Taken off guard, Kelley looked up, her eyes widening. "Thank you. But, that's too much."

"Nonsense. This is just a small appreciation for saving my life. By the way, with the cards, you may be among the first to leave the ship this morning."

"Well, sir," Phil said, extending his hand. "My family really enjoyed this cruise. We'll be delighted to sail with you again."

After the captain left, everyone finished packing their carry-ons. Taking advantage of their platinum cards, were among the first to exit the ship. They picked up their suitcases from the terminal and pulling them behind them, they went through customs in no time.

Phil and Alan took the transport bus to the parking lot where they met the shuttle van. Steve waited with the ladies and the luggage by the curbside. After loading the luggage in the van, they headed home.

As the van headed west toward Tampa, Kelley looked over her shoulder at the four younger people who were sitting in the two rows of seats behind them—sound asleep. Laughing, she said, "Look's like our sleepy heads are napping, Phil. It'll be good to get home. I know Laura and Alan can't wait to see little Michael."

Phil nodded enthusiastically. "By the way Kell, it was a good idea about ordering room service this morning. Gave us a good head start."

After the cruise, life in the three households changed dramatically.

Alan and Laura were delighted with their young son and purchased a three-bedroom house with a sizeable yard for him to play in.

With discourse in its ranks and the people of Tampa discontent with the running of the police department, a major shake up was instigated by the police commissioner. A whole new command was set in place.

Jude Minor, a man who took no prisoners, was named acting police chief and an investigation of the detective department and the police personnel was started.

Captain Minor asked Lt. Willis to try to establish an improved police relationship policy with the people of

Tampa.

Alan was also committed to negotiating better interaction with the news media. As part of his ongoing agenda, he started giving talks at the various schools to cement a warmer association between the city's youth and the police department.

Laura was delighted this new assignment kept her husband off the streets as he tried to improve the image of the police department.

At times, Alan would take two-year old Michael and Laura along with him to the talks. Alan now appeared to be more of a politician than a cop. Laura was a big part of Alan's progress. She typed speeches for his talks, and a solid bond developed between them.

At all of Alan's talks, it was Michael who stole the show. All of the students thought he was just darling with his red hair and baby blue eyes.

Phil and Kelley needed to see Michael at least once a week. It gave Alan and Laura the opportunity to sneak off to New York City or points west for a weekend now and then.

When he thought about his lovely family, Phil would occasionally lean over and kiss Kelley on the cheek and whisper, "You did good, girl."

Ashley and Steve started out married life with a "You Light up My Life" mentality and both meant it. But as time went on, the glow seemed to disappear from the marriage.

Steve started to spend more and more time away from home while Ashley worked ten to twelve hour days. Then, to her surprise, Ashley discovered she was expecting a baby.

After a full nine months of nausea and troubles, Ashley had a little girl by Cesarean section. The baby was beautiful with dark eyes and blonde hair and weighed in at just over six pounds.

The parents had a long discussion over names. Ashley leaned toward "Bonnie" but finally gave in to Steve's suggestion of "Tiffany." She decided that letting Steve name the baby might bring the love that have been dimming back into their lives.

As time passed, nothing seemed to satisfy Steve, not even his daughter. When Tiffany was a couple of years old, Steve met a cocktail waitress in one of downtown Tampa's bars and was spending more and more of his evenings with her. Soon, Ashley and Steve were "Lovers no More."

As the months went by, Ashley continued to work long hours at the law office. Steve was still employed with the Tampa Police force. One afternoon, after Ashley picked Tiffany up from day care, and returned home, she found a note on the end table from Steve.

It read—"Ashley, I'm moving out. Don't know where I'll be staying yet. But, I'll send you money when I can. I've just got to get away."

She talked this devastating situation over with her parents. "Even though I kind of expected it, you just can't get ready for something like this, Dad. But, Tiffany must always come first."

"Steve's a low down..." Phil started to say, before Ashley waved her hand and interrupted him.

"No, Dad. Maybe it's my fault. I was spending too much time at my job. But Tiffany and I will be okay. I promise."

"I feel that someday, Steve will be back," Kelley said, putting her arms around her daughter. "In the meantime Ashley, you've just got to keep on going. Keep your chin up."

Chapter 26

"Ashley, how many kids did you invite to Tiffany's birthday party?" Kelley asked, as she stood in Ashley's kitchen preparing a snack tray for the party. Nearby, Phil was busy pouring lemonade into plastic glasses on a large tray.

"Most of the children are from her class at school, a few from the neighborhood, Cousin Michael, and Laura and Alan, who are in the back yard supervising the games."

Ashley sat down on a chair in front of the granite island. "Say, where is the birthday cake that you picked up, Mom? How did you get it decorated for our Tiffany?"

"It's still in the refrigerator. And because she's now thirteen, I got the cake decorated with red, white, and blue balloons. No little pink ballerinas for our teenager."

Phil turned around and looked solemnly at his daughter. "Well, you've done an excellent job raising her. But, what about her father?" His eyes were troubled. "Have you heard from Steve? It's been about ten years since he left you that note and took off."

"Yes. I realize that, and I want to thank you two for not reminding me of the past all the time," Ashley replied. A shaft of pain darted across her face. "But to answer your question. Only an occasional Christmas card with a small check for Tiffany."

Kelley shook her head. She made no attempt to hide the anguish for her daughter. "I just can't believe he would treat you and Tiffany like that."

She and Phil looked at each other and shook their heads. "Life goes on," Phil commented.

There was a note of caution in Ashley's voice as she said, "Well, after he left us, I heard he moved into an apartment in Tampa. Later, his old partner called me to see how I was doing. He told me Steve just walked into the police chief's office one day, laid down his badge and gun, and said he was taking a leave of absence. He said he was all burnt out. He picked up his last pay check and split. Didn't even tell his partner 'good-bye'."

She forced herself to take a deep breath and continued, "A week later some guy came into the police station, looking for Steve. He said that Steve owed him over a hundred bucks for a bar bill. He said his bar maid had suddenly quit, and he believed she and Steve might have left town together."

Phil walked over to Ashley and put his arms around her. She laid her head on his shoulder. "Did I do something wrong, Dad? What caused Steve to change so much?"

He shook his head and anger contorted his features. "I can't answer that Ashley. Sometimes men just seem to go through a mid-life crisis, but Steve was a little young for that."

Ashley looked sadly up at him, her face darkening, her eyes anguished. "I'm certain that it's partly my fault. Maybe I spent too much time concentrating on my work and the baby. Maybe I didn't listen enough to him or spend enough one-on-one time with him."

"Well, there's not much you can do about it at this point," Phil interjected.

Kelley stopped what she was doing and her eyes grew sad. "Well, I think that it's a crying shame that he gave up his good job with the department."

Ashley looked at her mother, a wave of melancholy washed over her and tears came into her eyes. "He said he was burned out Mom and needed space to find himself."

"Well, today is not the day for tears," Phil said firmly. "It's Tiffany's birthday and a time for celebration."

Ashley sniffed and raised her head. "You're right, Dad. Only, I wish that Tiffany had a father in her life. And deep down, I still love Steve."

Just then Tiffany walked into the kitchen. "Grandma, when are you going to bring out the cake and ice cream? It looks like it's going to rain."

"We'll have you open the gifts and do the cake and ice cream in a few minutes, Tiffany," Ashley replied. "But first, you have to see your special birthday gift from Grandma and Grandpa."

"You're still my little princess. I have something special for you," Phil said.

"It's hard to believe that she'll be starting high school next year." Ashley took a steadying breath as she led the way out of the kitchen and up the stairs.

"Where are we going, Momma?" Tiffany asked.

"To your room, sweetie." As Ashley opened the door to her room, Tiffany let out a scream of joy when she saw new bedroom furniture. Kelley and Phil had bought her an antique white four-poster bed with a matching dresser and night table. Alan and Phil had smuggled it into the house the previous evening and had set it up when Tiffany was at her friend's house for a sleep-over.

"Now I know why you made me get dressed for the party in your room, Mom," Tiffany exclaimed.

After admiring the new furniture, they started down

the stairs to join the group outside. On the way down, they heard the front door bell ring.

"I'll get the door, Momma," Tiffany said, running ahead of the rest. "Maybe, it's my friend, Sonya. She's the only one who's not here yet. She said she was coming."

"Okay," Ashley answered. "I'll go out to the kitchen and help Grandma take the refreshments out to the back yard."

Tiffany opened the inside front door, and looking through the screen door, she could see a tall well-dressed man.

"Hi. You must be Tiffany. And today is your birthday," the man said peering through the screen. "I'm Steve. And that's a pretty party dress."

Tiffany stared at him. "Thank you. But I'm not allowed to invite strangers in. I'll go and get my mother."

At that moment, Ashley walked up behind her . "Tiffany, Grandma wants you to come to the back yard. She has cake and ice cream ready."

Without moving, Tiffany glanced over her shoulder at her mother. "Mom, this man just rang the door bell. And he knows my name."

As Ashley peered through the screen door, a startled look appeared across her face. It turned a gray ashen color. She recognized her husband, Steve.

"Hi Ash," Steve whispered.

Before Ashley could say another word, Steve continued, "Just wanted to drop off a gift for my daughter."

Even though Tiffany was in the eighth grade, she acted more like an adult than other girls her age. Her head jerked up in surprise at his words. She turned calmly to Ashley and asked, "Is my Father back?"

Ashley looked solemnly at Steve with concern. "We'll see."

"Please, may I give my gift to Tiffany?" he asked.

Tiffany looked up questionably at her mother. "Please, Mom?"

Ashley thought for a moment. She unlocked the screen door and opened it. "Yes?"

Without coming in, Steve handed his gift through the open door to Tiffany. "Have a happy birthday, sweetheart."

She reached out and took it. "Thank you. I'll open it when I open my other presents." She turned slowly and with the gift under her arm, headed for the back yard. It was time to continue the celebration with her friends.

"What brings you back after all these years without a word?" Ashley asked. Her voice was thick with emotion—mostly anger. Ashley could not believe that Steve, who had so abruptly left her years ago, was now standing calmly in front of her. Chills ran up and down her spine. She was lost for words.

"I saw Tiffany's picture in the paper, she won the science fair trophy. The article mentioned due to her excellence in science she was going to work personally with a prominent scientist at USF this summer. You must be very proud of her. Anyway, the article reminded me of her birthday. I thought I should stop by personally and say hello."

Ashley raised an eyebrow and snapped coldly, "Well, then hello and good bye. Sorry I can't ask you in."

"That's okay. I can't stay anyway. I've got an appointment, later today, with the Tampa Police Chief. I think he might be willing to take me back and maybe even give me my old job back." He studied her face and smiled, "And by the way, our daughter is just beautiful."

"Yes. Isn't she?"

Steve took a step backwards at the chill in her voice. "Well, I'll be going. But, I would like to see you again. Soon? May I call you?"

Ashley looked down at her feet and considered that question for a few moments. She hadn't seen nor heard from Steve in years. And now, he suddenly showed up at her door step.

After a short pause, she stepped back into the living room, took her purse off the desk, and pulled out a business card. She walked back to the door, opened it, and handed the card to Steve.

"Thanks. I'll call you sometime next week after I get settled in." He put the card in his shirt pocket and took a step closer. He smiled and looked down into her eyes. "You look terrific, Ash."

She smiled briefly at him. "And so do you, Steve." Ashley sighed and stood still, watching him as he turned and walked down the sidewalk. She closed the inside door, turned, and started back through the living room to the kitchen. With her head down and tears misting her eyes, she almost walked right into her father.

Phil stopped in his tracks and stared at his daughter. "You look like you've seen a ghost."

She looked up at him and sighed. "You could say that. Steve is back, Dad."

The next couple of hours were filled with fun. The children sat at covered tables in the back yard, where birthday cake and ice cream were served. Tiffany then opened the pile of gifts her friends had brought her.

After the guests left, a slight rain started to fall. Tiffany was in her room, going through her many gifts. Kelley and Phil were in the kitchen washing the serving dishes and bowls.

"It seems so quiet with all the children gone," Phil said.

"And Tiffany and Ashley's lives are changing so rapidly," Kelley added. "I can't believe that Tiffany is in her last year of grade school."

"Yes. And I think it's terrific that Tiffany has developed such a big interest in chemistry and science. By the way, how did Ashley get that professor at South Florida to offer help with Tiffany's science project?" Phil asked as he dried one of the serving platters.

"Oh, Ashley was doing some legal work for him and told him about Tiffany and her science project. He suggested that she help him in the lab at the university. She is so excited about going there to work with him this summer."

Phil and Kelley were finishing up in the kitchen, while Ashley entered Tiffany's bedroom. "Well, Tiffany, have you decided what your best gift is?"

"Here it is," she reached under the pile of gifts on her bed and pulled out a large white coat box. "It's from Daddy."

She opened the box and held up a white lab coat. "A lab coat. I can't believe he got me this. He must have heard that I'm going to work at the university this summer. And it has my name embroidered on the pocket."

"Yes. He said he saw the article in the newspaper about you," Ashley responded. She was glad that her daughter had adjusted to seeing her father for the first time with such adult calm.

"I'll have to thank him for it, next time I see him," Tiffany added.

"Yes. You'll have to do that. Why don't you try on the coat, let me see how it looks on you."

Tiffany jumped up, put on the coat, and twirled around with excitement.

"My goodness, how grown-up you look," Ashley said. Her happiness for her daughter was apparent in her voice. "And now, I have your birthday gift from me." She handed Tiffany a small wrapped box.

Tiffany ripped off the paper and opened the box. "Oh my God, Mom. Just what I wanted. A new cell phone."

"You'll have to transfer all your friend's numbers from your old phone into it. But, I'm sure that you will figure out how to use it in no time."

"I'll do it now." Tiffany threw her arms around her mother. "Thank you. Thank you."

Ashley gave her a big hug. "I love you so much, Tiffany."

"I know. I love you, too." Both of them had tears in their eyes.

Tiffany started to dial a number on the phone. "I have to call Grandpa on my new phone and tell him that my bedroom set was the best present I received."

Ashley chuckled, "Grandpa's in the kitchen, you know. But that's okay and somehow, I have the feeling that you're going to tell everyone that their gift to you was the best."

Chapter 27

Three weeks passed since Ashley and Steve saw each other at Ashley's birthday party. Since then, they had met privately for coffee a couple of times and discussed the past in detail.

Steve accepted a new job with the Tampa Police Department. Even though he and Alan were working out of the same building, neither had sought the other out during the work week.

Alan was busy working on public relations for the department, and Steve had been assigned to investigating a list of cold cases.

Today, Steve had taken the time to give his wife a quick call. "Hi Ash, how about driving over to Tampa and meeting me for lunch in the headquarters cafeteria?"

There was a long pause before she replied. "I don't have much going on at the office right now. But, I was going to head home, because Tiffany's coming home from school early. She only had a half-day because of a teacher's meeting."

"Great. Bring Tiffany. I would love to talk with her. I go to lunch at one. Maybe, you could come about twelve-fifty and hold a table for us."

"I do want you to get to know Tiffany better. But, you'll

have to give her some space. You're almost a complete stranger to her, you know."

At exactly twelve-fifty, Ashley and Tiffany entered the cafeteria. Both were dressed in blue jeans and casual cotton tops. Everyone who saw them could readily see that they were mother and daughter—their features were so identical.

They looked around the room and spotted a table near the windows. Moving like jack rabbits they dashed for the table and claimed ownership. As they sat down, Ashley asked her daughter to turn off her cell phone and to not text her friends while they ate lunch.

The cafeteria was busy and noisy. Within a few minutes, they looked up and saw Steve entering. Ashley stood up, waved at him, and yelled, "Over here."

When Steve approached the table, Tiffany jumped to her feet, ran to him and clasped her arms around his waist and placed her head on his chest. "Hi Daddy."

He gave Tiffany a brief hug and said, "Great to see you. Say, can you hold the table, while your mom and I get the food."

"Just soup and a salad for me, Mom," Tiffany replied.

"Yes. I know. And blue cheese dressing on the salad," her mother said as she suppressed a smile.

Steve put his arm around Ashley's shoulders and guided her to the cafeteria line. He gave her a slow squeeze as he whispered, "I'm so glad that you both came, Ash."

The noise in the cafeteria grew louder as they ate their lunch. It was difficult for them to talk.

After they finished eating, Steve suggested. "Let's step outside and visit. I still got about fifteen minutes left on my lunch hour."

They walked out of the building,. Steve guided them to

a couple of park benches on the side lawn.

"Thank goodness these benches are in the shade," Ashley said, wiping her brow.

Steve helped her sit down on one of the benches, and Tiffany plopped down on the end next to her mother.

Steve took Ashley's hands in his. "I've got lots to tell you, both. I want to bring you up to date on my future plans."

Ashley looked quietly at Steve and then looked upwards toward the Heavens. "Before you say anything Steve, I want to thank you for inviting us to lunch. It gives Tiffany a chance to get to know you better."

Steve nodded. "Thank you, I appreciate that." He looked fondly at his daughter.

Tiffany stood up, walked over to Steve, and gave him a generous hug. "Thank you for the lab coat for my birthday, Daddy. I love you had my name embroidered on it in gold. I know my friend, Colleen, who's staying at the USF dorm with me this summer, will be green with envy."

He shot her a wide grin. "I'm so glad that you liked it."

"What about you, Daddy? Where do you live now? Can't you come back and live with us? There's so much I need to talk to you about."

Ashley looked up, startled at her daughter's statement. Her heart started to beat like a muffled drum. "Slow down, Tiff," she said. "Give your father a chance to talk."

Steve smiled at his daughter and replied gently, "First things first. But thanks for asking."

Turning to Ashley, he said, "I wanted to tell you that I get my first pay check Friday. It's been two weeks since I started the job. I plan to head to the bank and open a new checking account. Then, I'm going to the police car auction. The guy that runs it is holding a year-old Rav4 for me."

"That's great, Steve. Sounds like you're starting to get

back on your feet," Ashley said, struggling to keep her emotions under control. Her heart fluttered in her chest. Although she had told Tiffany that her father wanted to reunite with them, she could not believe Tiffany had actually asked her father to move in.

"I'm off at noon on Friday and was hoping you could meet me. Maybe you can drive me to the bank and join me at the auction. Tell me what you think of the car."

Ashley looked at him and smiled gently. "Sure. I can do that."

"That sounds great." He looked at his watch and stood up. "I've got to get back to work."

"Where are you staying ,Steve?" Ashley asked, trying to keep her emotions in check.

"With one of the cops from the precinct. He put me up in his guest bedroom."

Not knowing quite how to react to that statement, Ashley decided to change the subject. "Have you noticed how bright our daughter is?"

"Yes. She's very intelligent." He broke out in a big grin. "She thinks we should get back together. And I want you to know if you let me back into your lives you'll never regret it."

Tears came into Ashley's eyes. She cut him off before he could say anymore, swallowed, and took a step back. "You have to realize that you broke my heart when you left. I spent many difficult years raising Tiffany by myself. I don't know what I would have done without the support of my family. Now, I'll have to think long and hard about getting back together."

"Please do. You know that I never stopped loving you," Steve replied humbly. "Now, I have to go."

Resisting the urge to pressure Ashley any further, Steve gave her a quick peck on the cheek. Then hugged Tiffany affectionately.

Ashley looked over at him with a gentle smile. "I'll pick you up at noon on Friday, and we'll talk some more."

Steve seemed reluctant to leave. "You're both really special to me."

Ashley's gaze followed him as he walked away. She liked the way he was trying to ease his way back into her life. If this is the new Steve, I really like him.

The following Friday, Ashley picked Steve up and they went to the bank, where he opened up a checking account, then to the auto auction and purchased the Rav4. The auctioneer told Steve he could pick the vehicle up on Monday, when he would have the paperwork completed.

As they drove away in Ashley's car, she reflected on the recent conversation she had with her parents about Steve's request to get back together. She remembered the one positive thought that they had always installed in their children, was never to dwell on the past, but rather to move forward at all times.

The only thing worthwhile remembering about the past are the good times, they said. Weddings, birthdays, family trips, and of course, the famous Sunday family night movies and snacks—and—oh yeah, Christmas and Easter were special.

Ashley turned toward her husband, "You know, Steve, I've prayed long and hard about the thought of us getting back together. And I've come to the conclusion that for Tiffany's sake, we should try to start over. She deserves to have a father in her life, so we both want you to come home. Let's head over to your room and pick up your things. It's time for this family to re-unite."

So, as time passed, Ashley and Steve tried to focus on the future for themselves and their daughter, who was now ready to enter high school.

The transition to living together was not easy at first,

but with their daughter's happiness always foremost in their minds, Ashley and Steve worked their way through the difficult times. Much thought went into balancing their work and private lives, to give them stability. Ashley made sure she no longer worked twelve-hour days, but rather spent more time with her husband and daughter.

Working on the cold case list at the police department kept Steve in the office and off the streets. He said that he enjoyed working inside and having his own office. So far, with the help of detectives, he had helped to solve two cases.

Steve and Alan spent many Saturday mornings playing golf. "You call this bonding, Alan?" Steve asked.

"No. You're still a better golfer than me." Alan chuckled.

Ashley left the law firm of Bella and Bella and started her own practice. She and her father worked together on family law and tax cases.

After some time, Ashley grew tired of that and began taking on smaller criminal cases. The judges liked the fact that she volunteered for pro bono cases and she was forever being courted to run for different political offices.

However, at the present time, Ashley was content with her legal work. But most important, Ashley and Steve's commitment and love were growing stronger every day.

Chapter 28

Ashley opened a small law office of her own in Tampa where the rent was cheap. She could now schedule her own hours and her father came in occasionally to give her a hand. But, she soon discovered this type of practice was boring to her. She was anxious to get back to court on criminal cases.

Tiffany was in high school and her major was in chemistry. Ashley, Steve, and Tiffany were now not just a family, but a real team.

At this stage in her life, Ashley realized her daughter and husband must be her first priority, but the thought of being center stage in a court case once again, made her juices flow. She had hinted to several of her legal colleagues that she was considering returning to criminal law.

Saturday morning, Ashley went into her office to finish some billing on a nasty divorce case. As she completed her work, she received a call from the District Attorney, Miles Mentor.

"Ashley, I heard that you are considering going back to criminal law, and I would like to hire you to become part of a special prosecution team in Tampa. I'm certain you've heard we have a serial killer on the loose in the area. I need you to get involved in the case. When we catch this guy, I need a strong attorney like you to take this fellow to court and to get a death penalty conviction. So far, he has attacked three females. The first young lady escaped from him alive, but wasn't able to give us any clues as to where he held her hostage. The second two were prostitutes and he raped, mutilated, and murdered them."

The tone of his voice worried her—it was very serious and rough, as though he had thought his request over for a long time before calling her.

"Are the police getting near to catching him?" she asked.

"The police have an all counties alert in the area." His intense concern vibrated though his words. "They are advising females not to walk the streets alone at night, but rather travel in groups. That would be sensible at the present time. I'm just trying to give you a heads up about the case and see if you would consider working for us."

Ashley struggled to control the surge of panic that had gripped her at his request. Was she capable of handling a case as important as this?

"Here's my office number and address. Please plan to meet with me to learn more about the case," Miles added.

After the call, Ashley sat back in her chair, silently thinking the surprising offer over. She decided she should confer with both her husband and father before taking on this case. Before she had a chance to call Steve and tell him about the DA's offer, she heard a brief knock on her door.

"Hello. Anyone here?" Ashley stepped out of her office and poked her head around the corner into the reception area, where she saw a slender young man. Standing just inside the entrance door, he appeared to be in his early twenties and stood about five feet nine. He was wearing a Notre Dame ball cap. "Are you Ashley Clarke or Ashley Willis Clarke?"

"Okay, you know my name, and you've got my attention. It's a bad time. Whatever you're selling, I'm not interested." Her voice reflected her impatience as she asked, "And you are?"

He grinned and pointed to his hat. "N.D. That's me. Nick Dyer at your service."

Ashley was not amused. "Don't look now my friend, but that blue cap with the gold N.D. initials on it stands for Notre Dame."

He broke into a hardy laugh, "Well, if you don't tell I won't. I've got most people believing that it stands for my name."

"Sorry, I don't have time for games. I'm closing up for the day. Come back next week when I have more time."

"I heard that you might be considering a job with the district attorney's office. I used to work there, and I thought you might need a special investigator assigned to you for your case. The city's my beat. I know it inside and out."

"Boy, news sure does travel fast." She slanted an intense glance his way. "I just got the job offer. How did you find out so quickly?"

"I'm Nick Dyer. Judge Dyer's grandson." He pursed his lips. "And he knows everything that goes on in this town."

"Yes. I know the judge. He's tops in the Tampa court system." Ashley eyed Nick carefully. "If I do take the job, I'll probably need my own investigator. Why don't you come back on Monday and we can talk."

"Okay." He turned to leave the office.

She gestured toward him. "Wait, I was just leaving. I'll lock up and walk outside with you."

Ashley locked the door and turned to walk to her car.

Nick put on a bike helmet and got ready to drive away on a motorcycle.

"Nice bike," she called out as he drove away.

She spent the weekend talking over the pros and cons of the job offer with both Steve and Phil, and made her decision. After talking the situation over with the District Attorney, she decided to accept the job and keep her office open for the time being, since the rent was already paid for the next several months.

Shortly after nine, the following Monday, Ashley parked her car outside of her office. Coming from behind her, she heard the sound of a motorcycle, and turned to see Nick driving up. She looked at him and a smile flickered in her eyes. "I like that you're very prompt."

He took his helmet off and grinned. "I try to be. Where can I park my bike?"

She gestured toward a nearby electric pole. "Lock it up next to that pole."

She unlocked the office door and entered with Nick right behind her. She stopped at the computer in the reception area, sat down, and turned it on. "You can use this computer."

"I guess I got the job then?" he teased. "And what about the pay?"

Ashley wrote a figure on a legal pad and pushed it across the desk to him.

Nick looked at it. "Yes. That seems very generous. Believe me, I'm worth every penny."

"Well, we'll see. Do you know how to get into the files on here?" she asked.

"Sure. Piece of cake." He reached out and punched a few keys. "All set, Mrs. Clarke."

She located a program on the computer and printed

out several sheets of paper and looked up at Nick. "Grab those papers and take these two file folders. I have to take them to my husband at police headquarters."

He muttered a polite response as she added, "I've been having trouble with my old Corolla. I think it needs a new battery and maybe a starter. Why don't you follow me to the car dealership so I can drop off my car? Maybe, we can go on to police headquarters on your bike. Can two people ride on it?"

"Sure. I carry an extra helmet in my carrier."

Ashley took the files from Nick and stuffed them in her briefcase. With Nick following behind her, Ashley walked outside and locked the office door. She jumped in her car and turned on the ignition. It wouldn't start.

"Say, I know cars. Let me look under the hood for a moment." Nick said. He tinkered for a while, and then shouted. "Pump the gas a few times and give it a crank."

Ashley did as she was told. The engine turned over. With Nick behind her on his motorcycle, she drove to the dealership. She pulled into the service bay and told them the problems that she had been experiencing. The service manager informed her they could squeeze her car in and would have it finished in a couple of hours.

Exiting the building, Ashley walked up to Nick, who was waiting on the curb. She donned the extra helmet, strapped her briefcase on the back of the bike, and plopped down behind Nick. She grabbed him firmly around his waist and held on as they roared off.

She soon discovered riding a motorcycle wasn't the most pleasant way to get somewhere dressed as she was. The skirt of her business suit was hiked up around her thighs and gave everyone a good view of her shapely legs. But, his cycle was certainly faster than a car. With much expertise, Nick weaved in and out of traffic.

"You okay, Mrs. Clarke?" Nick asked a short time later,

as he pulled up in front of police headquarters.

She glanced at him, shrugged, took off her helmet, and pulled her skirt down. Patting her hair into place, she laughed. "That was fantastic. No wonder my mother said she used to love her cycle. Maybe I'll get a bike for myself some day. It certainly would be cheaper than that car."

Inside the police headquarters, Ashley led Nick to Steve's office. She knocked briefly and entered with Nick behind her.

"Hi, honey. How's it going?" Steve asked looking up.

"Okay. But first, the ladies room is calling to me. Then, you can bring my young friend and me up to date on this killer."

He nodded, and she introduced Nick to him. "My husband is working on catching the serial killer ."

When Ashley returned to Steve's desk, she was carrying three coffees. "Thanks. Just what I needed," Steve said, taking the coffee from her hand.

He motioned for Ashley and Nick to have a seat in front of his desk. "Say, Ash, did you bring the personal information that you looked up on the two murder victims?"

"Got it right here." She pulled the folders out of her briefcase and handed them to him.

Steve looked briefly through her notes. "Good work. Thanks." He pulled out his files on the murders and added Ashley's papers to them.

"This is one vicious killer," he said, as he looked through his official police notes on the murders. "Let's see victim number one. She was mutilated and killed in one place and then moved. We found her placed inside a dumpster in back of a supermarket. Someone carved her up good. A real psycho," he said in a cold voice, placing the photo on the desk in front of him.

He opened the second official police folder and pulled out a picture of a female's body in what appeared to be an empty sandy field.

Looking across the desk at the photos of both women, Ashley stared at them and shuttered. In addition to deep cuts all over the bodies, she could see that the index finger on each woman appeared to have been severed. "Wow! Whoever murdered these two must be insane," she whispered.

Steve nodded. "Yes. This second was found in an old baseball field. She, too was mutilated, but the coroner said that she was still alive when the murderer discarded her in the field. She bled out there and appeared to have died about an hour after she was dumped. A city maintenance crew went to cut the weeds in the abandoned field after receiving complaints from the neighbors and discovered the body."

"I saw a couple of billboards around town offering a reward to anyone who can give clues to the killer's identity," Nick added.

"Right. It's up to a hundred thousand already," Steve added.

"May I look at the files a little closer?" Nick asked.

"Sure." Steve handed him the folders.

After shifting closer in his chair, Nick studied the photos and the papers carefully. He frowned and muttered a curse word under his breath as he stared at the photo of the body in the baseball field. He turned the photo around and looked closely at it. "Say, it looks like there's a drawing in the sand."

He studied the photo thoroughly and then bolted upright in his seat and shouted, "I think this girl was trying to tell you something."

Steve's head snapped around.

"What is it, Nick?" Ashley said, jumping to her feet.

He gave her an arrogant grin. "I'm just about to become brilliant."

Chapter 29

Nick stared intently at the photo for a few minutes. His eyes widened as he fixed his attention on it. "Yes. I know this place. It used to be a softball field, then a kids' play ground."

Ashley and Steve leaned forward in their seats as Nick continued, "Look at the woman on the ground."

Steve's gut clenched.

"Yes. I'm looking at her. What?" Ashley's heart was hammering .

"Look above her left hand," Nick ordered. "She was trying to tell us where she had been held and tortured."

"So?" Ashley stared at the photo carefully.

"I said look above her hand," Nick said. "She drew something in the sand."

Ashley stiffened and peered at the photo. "It's a box."

"No. She drew a picture of a house," Nick replied, his lip twitching.

Steve grabbed the photo and looked intently at it. His eyes clouded. "That's a house?" There wasn't a great deal of conviction in his voice.

Nick nodded his head with certainty. "Yes, and that's the letter 'R' above it."

"And you think you know where she was tortured and

mutilated because of that?" Ashley shook her head in disbelief.

Steve felt distinctly uneasy as he sat upright in his chair. "Slow down, Fella. Start over."

Nick drew a deep breath and continued with fervor, "You said that the coroner stated the victim was still alive when she was dumped in the old baseball field. She drew a picture in the sand to tell us where she was held before she was murdered. The 'R' is for the 'Railroad House.' It's an abandoned railroad car. A bunch of us kids used to hang around there years ago to smoke weed. Then, a couple of homeless guys chased us out and turned it into a ramshackle house for themselves."

"You think that you could find this place again?" Steve muttered abruptly.

Nick glanced at him, then nodded and said with confidence, "With my eyes shut."

Captain Jude Minor had walked into Steve's office in time to overhear the later part of the conversation. "What's this I just heard? You might have a lead on our killer?"

"Yes, sir," Steve answered. "Might be possible."

Steve stood up, walked around the desk to the captain and gestured toward the two sitting in front of his desk. "This is my wife, Ashley, sir. She's going to work for the District Attorney's office, this is her private investigator, Nick."

The captain reached over and shook Ashley's hand. Turning to Nick, he asked, "I didn't get your last name."

Nick held out his hand. "Dyer, sir. Nick Dyer." He pointed to his head. "N.D. —like the hat."

The captain grabbed Nick's outstretched hand. "Glad to meet you. What's the lead, kid?"

Nick replied in a confident tone, "I'm not a kid, sir. I'm a lot older than I look."

The captain warmed, but without much emotion. "I'll

take your word for it. But time's wasting. What's the lead?"

"I think I know where the place in this drawing is located." Nick picked up the photo from the desk and handed it to the captain. "It's been a few years since I was last there."

Taken off guard, the captain's eyes widened and his mouth opened as he asked, "Close by?"

"About five miles outside of the city. Off the Selmon Expressway." Nick closed his eyes for a moment and tried to recall the location. "I can't tell you the exact turnoff. I'll have to see it to remember."

The captain's gaze was steady as he turned to Steve and snapped his fingers, "Clarke, you get a squad car and take your wife and this young man to the site and check it out. If it looks promising, give me a call back. In the meantime, I'll tell Lt. Willis to notify his SWAT team to get ready in case we need them."

"Yes, sir," Steve replied. He picked up the phone and ordered a squad car and a driver to pick them up at the side door of the station. "We'll be on our way in a minute, Captain."

"Good. Let me know how things look when you get there. You're in charge, Clarke," he ordered as he walked out of the office.

Steve opened the file cabinet in back of his desk and pulled out his shoulder holster and weapon. After putting them on, he motioned for Ashley and Nick to follow him.

At the side entrance of the station, they found the patrol car and the driver awaiting them. They jumped in the car and with the siren blaring, the car raced through the side streets of the city and onto the expressway.

Lt. Steve Clarke was determined to apprehend the serial killer and give the city of Tampa and its residents some peace and quiet after the recent bout of panic that had gripped it.

Suddenly, Nick snapped, "Slow down, we're almost there, I think. Get off that next exit."

Steve ordered the driver to turn off the siren. Nick directed him to make a right turn off the highway and onto an old dusty dirt road.

They drove a half mile down a road that appeared to be deserted and flanked on both sides with overgrown vines and wild looking shrubs.

"Stop," Nick called out. "Pull up by that wooded area and that old gate." He pointed toward a large rusty iron gate that appeared to be the entrance to a weed covered driveway.

"We're almost there," Nick warned. "The old railroad car is back in there."

"Before we go up there, I'm going to call the captain and give him directions to this place," Steve said, his eyes narrowing.

After giving the directions, Steve concluded his conversation. "Captain, we're going in to investigate the situation."

"Be careful Clarke. Willis and his SWAT team are ready when you need them. Don't do anything foolish. Remember if the murderer is there, he could be armed and dangerous. And we want to take him alive."

They got out of the squad car. "Follow me," Nick ordered. He walked around the gate and headed down the overgrown path through the woods. "It's back here a few hundred yards."

Ashley brushed the burrs off her skirt. "It's a good thing that you didn't try to drive down here," she said, turning to the officer who had driven them. "You probably would have screwed up your tires."

Nick nodded. "Yeah. And there are a lot of boulders down this road. That's why my buddies and I used to like to drive our dirt bikes down here. Made us feel like we were playing the X Games."

Within a short time, they worked their way through the shrubbery and underbrush until they came to a small clearing. They spotted what appeared to be an old Jeep parked next to a decrepit looking boxcar covered in vines.

"We used to call this the 'Railroad House'," Nick said as they cautiously inched closer.

Steve suddenly stopped. "You and Nick stay here, Ash," he ordered.

Ashley gave him a disapproving glare, but silently, did as she was told.

Steve and the officer advanced cautiously. When he got close enough to the Jeep to read the license plate number, Steve wrote down the number. He stood still and listened carefully to see if there was anyone moving inside of the boxcar.

Motioning for the police officer to follow him, he crept back to where the other two were standing in a thicket of bushes. Putting his finger to his lips, Steve signaled for the three to follow him as he walked away.

He whispered, "Let's head back to the squad car. I want to call in the license number and find out who that Jeep belongs to."

Back at the squad car, Steve called the captain. "Sir, I've got the license number of a Jeep parked outside the old boxcar. Can you run it? Didn't see anyone around the place, but I suspect there might be someone inside because of the vehicle. Can you dispatch Willis and his SWAT team so we can move in?"

The captain answered, "I'll check out the license number. We're on our way, wait until we get there before you make any move. By the way, Clarke—good work."

"And Captain, the house is only a few hundred yards in from the highway, so I wouldn't use any sirens," Steve cautioned.

They waited inside the squad car for about twenty minutes, until Captain Minor arrived with two police cars.

The captain stepped out of his car and walked up. "I brought four police officers with me. That should be enough man power until Lt. Willis and the SWAT team arrive."

He turned to the officers that were exiting their vehicles. "Remember, men, if our killer is in there, we want him alive."

Chapter 30

The captain stepped closer to Steve. "Got a name off that license plate. The Jeep belongs to a Doctor Victor Minoso. He's a physician from Tampa. The vehicle hasn't been reported stolen, so I don't know if the doctor is involved or not, but we'll proceed carefully at this point. He could be inside the place."

Within a couple of minutes, the SWAT team pulled up with an ambulance behind it.

Lt. Willis and the team jumped out and geared up. Looking at the team, Captain Minor commanded, "Okay, men, let's take this guy down. I want to emphasize that we need this man alive, so I don't want anyone getting trigger happy. Clarke, you're in charge of this operation after he's apprehended. Remember to read this bastard his rights. Let's not make any legal mistakes."

"Sir, I checked the location out carefully," Steve said. "The place is back a few hundred yards down this old road. I suggest that we proceed on foot from here. Someone was using the old abandoned railroad car as a house. However, I couldn't determine if anyone was inside at this time."

Looking at Ashley with apprehension, the captain

added quietly, "Mrs. Clarke, I want you and your associate, Nick, to stay here by the vehicles."

Then turning back toward the SWAT team, he lifted his cap and raked his fingers through his hair and asked, "Willis, you got tear gas in case you need it to smoke this guy out?"

"Got it, sir."

"Good." The captain's teeth clenched. "Take your men slowly down the road and be careful. Remember, I said, I want this man alive. The rest of us will cut through the underbrush and proceed in."

Lt. Willis smiled briefly at his men and waved for them to follow him. "Let's move."

As the SWAT team approached the house, Alan assigned two men to the back, two men to each side, and two men next to him facing the front doorway.

Crouched down inside a stand of brush, Alan pulled out a bullhorn and ordered, "Dr. Minoso, this is the Tampa Police. We have the place surrounded. Come out with your hands up."

Captain Minor and the rest of the men watched quietly, waiting for some sign of life. Nothing happened.

After waiting several minutes, Alan looked around quizzically. He made the announcement again over the bullhorn. Still, no response. Then, talking into the phone on his shoulder, he issued an order to his men in a hard voice, "Get ready with the tear gas. Looks like we might have to smoke him out."

Suddenly a dirty disheveled looking man exited the back door of the building with his hands in the air. After he observed that the man was not armed, one of the SWAT team members grasped his arm with lightning speed and unbalanced him with a firm twist of his wrist. A moment later, the man landed flat on his face and was handcuffed.

"We've got a man out here in the back, Lt. Willis," one

of the members shouted over his phone.

Alan and the rest of the team raced around to the back where he saw his men already had the man cuffed. "He came out peacefully, sir," one of Alan's men said with a sigh of relief.

Captain Minor and a couple of police officers dashed around to the back. "Good job, Willis. Now, read Dr. Minoso his rights."

"I'm not Minoso," the man responded humbly. "I just found this place today. I was looking for a place to sleep. A guy in a long white doctor's coat was here. Boy is that place a mess inside. When I said that it looked weird, the doc said he used it for medical experiments. Before we could talk much, he got a call on his cell phone. Said his wife had an emergency, and she was going to pick him up down the road. So he left his Jeep here and went out on foot. He sure left in a hurry."

Captain Minor shook his head, uttered a few curse words under his breath, and said, "Great, we caught a homeless old guy. Costello, you and Abbott go inside and check the place out and don't destroy any evidence."

The two detectives slipped inside the railroad car and looked around briefly. When Costello came out, he had a disgusted look on his face. He went up to the captain and whispered, "It's Hell in there. Looks like the place where the murders could have occurred. There are a couple of chains attached to the wall and what looks like dried blood on the floor. Found a box on the table with a couple of small fingers in it."

Minor shook his head sadly. "Too bad we missed the bastard. Get the place sealed off. Go inside and bag and tag everything. Take lots of pictures, too. Then, you and Detective Abbott meet me back at the precinct."

"Yes, sir."

The captain had his men put the homeless man in one

of the police cars and they headed back to the precinct with Steve, Ashley, and Nick following them.

Inside the building, the captain turned to Ashley, "Well, Mrs. Clarke, you and your young friend here might have found the murder scene. It appears that this doctor guy was kind of sloppy. And, from the sound of things, right now he's on the run."

"And don't forget his wife might be involved. Could be she's be running with him," Ashley added.

"Any reward?" Nick asked, with a grin on his face.

Captain Minor uttered a bark of laughter. "I doubt if you would be eligible for it, since you work for the DA. But, in any case, we have to find this Dr. Minoso and determine if he is the serial killer before we proceed any further. It will be days before we can go over all the evidence. I have a feeling that Dr. Victor Minoso and his wife are planning on skipping town."

"You might be right." Suddenly, Ashley was hit with a staggering notion. "I'll bet that they're heading to Cuba," she said.

After giving her a doubtful look, Steve asked, "What makes you think that?"

Ashley smiled and shrugged her shoulders. "The Jeep had a plate on the front that read, 'I love Cuba'."

"Good observation," the captain responded. "Our info says that the Minoso's are originally from Cuba. And Victor is a doctor so he can easily obtain documentation to fly there. The flights go out from the St. Pete-Clearwater International Airport all the time. Steve, call there and see if there are any departures today. In the meantime, I'll have my men get a picture of our doctor and his wife and issue a BOLO on them."

Steve got up and ran to a desk in the back of the room, where he made a phone call.

Returning, he said, "All morning departures for Cuba

were cancelled. But, there's a plane leaving at three-fifteen."

Detective Costello walked into the room and threw a photo on the desk in front of the captain. "Here's a news-paper picture of Dr. Victor Minoso and his wife, from some society event."

"Nice looking couple," the captain said with some scorn. "From what we learned so far, Dr. Minoso left in a hurry, and without bothering to clean up the crime scene. That means he had an idea we were on to him. I think you should head for the airport right now, Lt. Clarke."

Within a few minutes, Steve, Ashley, and Nick were back in the squad car with their driver. With the siren blasting loudly, they headed toward the St. Pete-Clear-water Airport.

When they arrived, the driver turned off the siren and pulled up in front of the main entrance to the terminal.

"Nick, you stay with the car," Steve directed as the police officer and he jumped out of the car. "Ashley, you can come with us. You can check out the ladies room for Mrs. Minoso."

The terminal security guard approached the vehicle, and Steve flashed his badge. "Tampa police. Here on official business. Okay, if we leave the squad car here while we search the terminal for a suspected criminal?"

"No problem," the guard said.

Inside the terminal, they ran over to the ticket coun-ter. "You have a flight leaving for Cuba at three-fifteen. Where are they boarding?" Steve asked the woman at the window.

"Yes. National Airlines. Direct to Cuba. Leaving at Gate 6. They're boarding right now," the clerk promptly responded.

"Which way to Gate 6?" The clerk pointed to her left.

Looking around, Ashley spied a cart passing by used to transport people who could not walk easily. She pointed to it. "Let's take that," she suggested.

They jumped on the cart. When the driver saw the two men in police uniforms he asked, "Where to fellows?"

"Gate 6 and hurry?" Steve answered.

"Yes, sir. Hang on." The driver started the cart and raced down the terminal toward the gate.

Approaching Gate 6, they could see about fifty people waiting in line to board. They jumped off the cart and with photos in hand, started to look for the infamous Dr. Minoso and his wife.

Ashley spied the doctor coming out of the men's restroom. He walked toward a tall, dark-haired lady, who was in line with several Ralph Lauren alligator bags at her feet.

Ashley gave Steve a nudge. "There they are."

Steve turned to the officer standing next to him. "Let's proceed with caution. We don't want them to run and cause an uncomfortable situation with this big crowd. Try to arrest them as quietly as possible."

Steve slipped up on the pair. The other officer approached from the other side. Steve quietly laid his hand on the doctor's arm. "Tampa Police, Dr. Minoso."

The doctor turned around and looked frantically for a means of escape.

"Don't even think of it, Minoso," Steve said. "You're not going anywhere. You're under arrest."

The doctor drew himself up indignantly. "Let me alone or I'll miss my flight. You have no reason to arrest me."

"That's where you're wrong doc," Steve hissed. "You are suspected of the murder of two women, and I have a warrant for your arrest."

As she listened, Mrs. Minoso stood there stunned. She started to cry as Steve pulled out his handcuffs, jerked the doctor's hands behind him, and cuffed him.

Ashley picked up the Ralph Lauren designer bags from the floor, and took Mrs. Minoso by the arm. "It's better if you just come along quietly," she whispered in the woman's ear. "Don't make us handcuff you, too."

The waiting passengers stood nearby, somewhat stunned as Steve and the officer took Dr. Minoso back to the cart and quietly placed him inside. Ashley threw the bags onto the floor of the of the cart and pushed Mrs. Minoso in ahead of her.

The shocked airport driver took several breaths, and said, "Where to officers?"

"Back to the entrance," Steve snapped.

The driver turned the cart around and headed back to the terminal entrance.

Back at the precinct, the captain asked Steve if he had read Dr. Minoso his rights. "Yes, sir. I followed procedures to the letter. He didn't give us much resistance. By the way, Captain, how did you get that arrest warrant so fast?"

"It's easy; when you know how," the captain chuckled. He turned to the other officer, "He's all yours now. Print and book him. Get his airport parking ticket and have his car towed so we can check it out."

"What about the wife?" the officer asked.

"Book her as an accessory to the murders. Then, question her. I have a feeling she might be charged later. She must know something. After all, she's the one who alerted the doctor we were on to him and helped him to get away."

"I need to call my lawyer," Dr. Minoso squealed.

"In due time," the captain snapped back.

In the next week, Steve Clarke watched as the district attorney lined up all the evidence and filed numerous charges against the doctor and his wife.

"I'm sure after we present all our evidence, and the one surviving witness against this man, we can prove him guilty and put him away for a long time," the district attorney stated with confidence.

However, it took months before Dr. Minoso was put on trial. In the meantime, Ashley Clarke had decided that she did not want to get directly involved in the trial. She turned down the job with the district attorney's office and instead, continued on with her own private practice.

Nick stayed on with the district attorney's office and helped two of the assistants with the trial. They sought the death penalty for Dr. Minoso and charged Consuelo Minoso with assisting him in his escape.

During the trial, Dr. Minoso took the stand in his own defense. He said he killed the women in a fit of rage when they would not help him with his experiments. When he was sentenced, he showed no facial expression and seemed completely unremorseful.

After the trial, most of the jurors said they were surprised he didn't plead insanity, because they really felt that he was insane.

Eventually, it was all his lawyer could do to save Dr. Minoso from execution. He was sentenced to two life sentences without the chance of parole.

Consuelo Minoso was found guilty of being an accessory to the crime and was sentenced to five years in prison.

Later, the families of the murder victims sued Dr. Minoso and his wife in civil court. Each family was awarded a million dollars. Dr. Minoso's socialite wife was forced to sell their mansion on Coffee Pot Bayou in order to pay the obligations and the lawyer's fees for both the criminal and civil cases.

Ashley's slate of personal injury and family law cases kept

her office up and running. Steve continued to work cold cases for the police department.

Both of them found that working five days a week, from eight to five, offered them plenty of time to spend with their daughter, Tiffany.

Chapter 31

The lives of Kelley and Phil and their children and grand-children stabilized in the next few years, and they were all spending more time together.

The budget cuts at the police station offered Alan the opportunity to reduce his hours to three work days of ten hours each and still retain his benefits.

Laura had her real estate license and now that the economy had turned around, house sales were finally picking up. Sports were a large part of young Michael's life as he attended high school. He played third base his freshman year and was considered one of the area's leading players. A good education was still his top priority, and he became very interested in law enforcement.

Steve had cut down on his working hours at the department. Ashley was working fewer hours at her private law practice. Tiffany, who was not only beautiful but very intelligent, attended an all girls' high school and continued to be very gifted at science. On weekends, twice a month, she would go to USF to work with her professor in his chemistry lab.

Kelley and Phil had made a decided effort to enjoy their golden years. Phil devoted part of his time helping seniors with their taxes and doing some pro bono legal work. The two of them together volunteered twice a week at Hospice and kept in shape with their regular Senior Silver Sneakers exercise classes.

And to Phil's surprise, he completed writing his novel. He discovered that when he sat down to write, he couldn't write fast enough. His book, published with a terrific looking cover, was about an undercover agent.

Kelley's old friend, Veronica Miley, stopped by their home for a three-day visit. They spent the time reminiscing about Kelley's late mother, Ann. Veronica left Kelley a photo album with many pictures of Ann. After she left, Kelley decided to copy the photos to a DVD and mail a copy of it back to Veronica.

It was eight in the morning, when the phone at the Willis household rang. "Hi, Mom. Just wanted to tell you that Tiffany, Steve, and I are off to Orlando for a four-day science fair, where Tiffany's presenting her project. What's going on with you and Dad?"

"Well, neither of us could sleep last night. One of our dear neighbors, Mrs. Carmen, has a son named Hector. He's one of three young boys charged with murder. She asked your dad to defend him. It looks like the case is going to get quite complicated, we think that your father might need your help. The other two boys involved in the case will have public defenders, but your dad decided to defend Hector Carmen. You might have been following the story in the newspaper."

"I think I read something about it. All three boys are out on bond, I believe."

"Yes," Kelley replied, smothering a sigh. "It's a big relief to Hector's mother that he can at least sleep at home until the trial begins."

"Well, tell Dad that he can count on me no matter what

it involves. I'm always here for you."

"Okay. Love you, Ashley."

Later that morning, Alan entered his parents' home. Smelling the scent of freshly made coffee, he ran to the kitchen where he found his father, standing at the counter pouring a cup. Phil whirled around when he heard Alan enter the room.

"Morning, Dad. I just heard from Ashley that you're taking on a new case. The Misti Woods' murder trial. Want to talk about it?"

"Sure. Have a seat." Phil shot back, his eyes lighting up. The excitement in Phil's voice reminded Alan of his father's old zeal for the law.

Phil poured a cup of coffee for his son, went to the refrigerator, and got out the cream. He put the coffee and cream down on the table as Alan sat down. He took out a package of Alan's favorite sweet rolls and placed them in front of him. "Help yourself, although it doesn't seem like you need the sugar rush this morning."

Alan laughed as he sat down beside his father and moved his chair closer to him.

"Now, bring me up to date on what you know about the murder of Misti Woods, and the boys accused of the crime," Phil asked.

Alan reached into the package, grabbed a Bear Claw, chewed on it for a while, then started to talk.

"Well, three teenage Hispanic boys were arrested and charged with the rape and murder of the girl, a high school senior. And without even knowing the evidence, the kids seemed to have been already convicted by the media."

Phil glanced at him and shrugged. "They always are. Anything for a good headline."

Alan leaned back in his chair and looked thoughtfully at his father. "Why did you decide to get involved in this mess, Dad? Do you know one of the boys involved?"

"Yes. A neighbor, Mrs. Carmen, called me and asked me to defend her son, Hector. Kelley said she's really a nice lady and very religious. Mrs. Carmen said her son has been hanging around with the wrong gang lately. She pleaded endlessly with me on the phone to take the case, I agreed."

"I see," Alan said. Then his cell phone rang. "Excuse me for a minute."

He looked down. "It's Officer Abbott calling." He switched on his phone. "Good morning, Felix."

"You better sit down. Guess you haven't heard the news yet this morning."

"No. What's going on? Tell me."

"The Misti Woods' case we're working on is getting more complicated by the minute. The news media hasn't gotten wind of it yet, but you know they found Jorge Mendosa, one of the accused murderers, dead a couple of days ago."

"Yeah. I know." Alan blinked a couple of times.

"Well hang onto your hat, as they say. Early this morning, they found his brother, Carlos Mendosa, dead in an alley in Tampa. He was found lying next to a dumpster. He was beaten badly and choked to death. All hell is going to break lose today in the papers and on TV."

"Oh, my God," Alan exclaimed as he leaned back in his chair and closed his eyes.

"Right now, it looks like some kind of revenge for the girl's murder. I think the Hector kid should be concerned for his life. At this point, things don't look too good for him," Abbott added.

After Alan hung up the phone, he told his father what he had just heard.

Two of the accused murderers were dead and his client

could possibly be next.

After a few moments of silence on his father's part, Alan added, "You might want to give defending Hector Carmen a second thought. He's the cousin of those two dead boys and the last of the accused."

Phil felt sick to his stomach. "I'm going to talk things over with your mom, Alan. Then, I'll come into the station and get all the facts from you and Detective Abbott. Are you going to be there later?"

"Going there right now," Alan answered as he stood up. He gave his father a pat on the back and left the house.

Later, Phil filled Kelley in on what he had just learned from Alan. They both realized that the case was becoming even more complicated than they at first anticipated. Kelley looked at Phil with great concern, "Are you sure that you're ready to get involved with this?"

He sighed and looked at her with compassion in his eyes. "I did agree to help poor Mrs. Carmen and her son."

As they were finishing their conversation, the phone rang. It was Hector's mother, who was screaming with fear. "My nephew, Carlos, has been found dead. I'm afraid that they will try to kill my son, next. Can you get him some protection? Can you help us?"

Phil spoke reassuringly to Mrs. Carmen and finally calmed her down somewhat. He told her that he was on his way to the police station. "Don't worry; I'll get protection for your son. Now, I want you to lock the doors and keep Hector inside. Don't let him go anywhere."

He hung up the phone and looked at Kelley, "Who would want to kill those two?"

Kelley shook her head. "I would start with the girl's relatives. And, I hope that you'll be very careful, Phil."

Phil's head was spinning. Should he take this case? But the thought of being back in the courtroom had his heart racing.

Chapter 32

A short time later, the phone rang again and Phil answered it. It was Ashley. "I know you had plans to work on your new case today, Dad, but Tiffany was hoping that you could join us for the weekend. She said you helped her develop her science project, and she wants you on stand-by in case she runs into a problem. Her science teacher can't go and she's frantic. Do you think that you could come with us?"

Phil thought for only a few minutes. He realized his granddaughter's situation was more important than anything he might have planned. He turned to Kelley and placed a hand on her shoulder. "Tiffany needs me to go with her to Orlando; do you think you could fill in for me here? You could go to the police station and get all the information on the murder case from Alan and his buddy, Officer Abbott."

Kelley flashed him a broad smile and nodded. She was delighted to be given the opportunity to get involved in the case.

After telling his daughter he would be at her house in a few minutes, Phil ran upstairs, packed an overnight bag, and was off to Orlando to help Tiffany.

Soon after Phil left, Kelley jumped into her car and

drove to police headquarters. This new development of the death of the second young man involved in the murders had taken everyone by surprise and put the police department on edge. Of the three young men accused of the rape and murder, only Hector Carmen remained alive. And now, their intuition led Kelley and Phil to believe that Hector also was in imminent danger.

After parking in the lot, Kelley strolled into police headquarters and headed to the detectives' department where Alan and a large group of detectives and officers were gathered.

When he saw his mother enter, Alan looked up from his work and waved her over. "I thought Dad was coming."

"I know. But Ashley called and said that Tiffany wanted him to come to the science program with her. So he agreed to go, and sent me in his place."

Suddenly a loud voice called out, "Everyone into the conference room." Kelley immediately turned toward the door on the opposite side of the room and recognized Captain Minor standing in the doorway.

She followed the detectives as they quietly shuffled into the adjacent room. As she stood just inside the room, the captain instructed, "Take a seat, men." Glancing back at Kelley, he added, "Mrs. Willis, please close the door and have a seat."

Kelley narrowed her eyes, gave him a brief nod, and sat down.

He strode to the front of the room. "I want to bring everyone up-to-date on the murder of Misti Woods and the deaths of two of her suspected assailants. First of all, for those of you who have not seen it yet, the sergeant is putting a photo of the dead girl up on the screen."

Everyone's eyes went to the screen in the front of the room. The captain grimaced and continued, "Misti was just shy of twelve years old when she was viciously raped and murdered."

Kelley's heart clenched, her eyes filled with tears, as she stared up at the picture of the lovely young school girl, dressed in shorts and a tank top, and smiling happily. She silently thanked the Lord that something like this had not happened to her precious granddaughter, Tiffany.

The captain sighed as he waved at the officer who was working the video, and grimly added, "Misti's mother passed away five years ago."

Kelley's tears suddenly stopped, and she felt a deep anger replace her sorrow, as the captain continued. "Her only survivors are her father and grandfather. So, I don't have to draw you a picture to tell you how devoted both of those men probably were to her. Next is a picture of her father, Gavin Woods."

A photo of Misti's father became visible on the screen. He was tall and brawny and was dressed casually in an open-collared shirt and blue jeans.

"The only shot we have of the grandfather is rather obscured. It is a picture of him in a wheelchair at the girl's funeral."

The photo of an elderly man, with a thin ungainly body, flashed on the screen next. He was bent over in a wheelchair and appeared to be sobbing with grief into his hands. His face could not be readily seen as it was obscured by a shock of long white hair.

"Next, here are the photos of three young men suspected of murdering Misti," the captain said angrily. "Of the three, two are already dead, the first a couple of days ago and the second boy last night. The first young man was found next to a strip club. Whoever killed him beat him up horribly. The second boy's body was discovered last night in an alley in the same area. He was badly beaten also and choked to death."

He looked over at the sergeant who had been running the projector. "The sergeant will now pass out a report on what information we have on the case at this point."

The men looked over the report. The captain walked up and said quietly, "Mrs. Willis, it is my understanding that your husband has agreed to be Hector Carmen's attorney."

Kelley's chin went up with a deliberate confident movement. "Yes, sir, that's correct. He had to go out of town for the weekend for an unexpected situation. That's why I'm here in his place. He talked to Hector's mother this morning, and she is in mortal fear for her son's life. She wants immediate police protection for him. I plan to meet with her this afternoon and tell her what steps the police department is prepared to take to protect her son."

The captain avoided her gaze. "We anticipate that Hector will eventually stand trial for his participation in the death of Misti Woods. But, you are correct; we need to provide him with protection in the meantime. My present problem is trying to determine who killed those two boys. I have a feeling that it was someone seeking revenge for the girl's murder."

Kelley stiffened and her heart caught in her throat as the captain continued, "The father of the dead girl was in Los Angeles when the first kid was killed. And he was in Jacksonville last night on business. So, he has a solid alibi for both murders. Our detectives checked him out thoroughly, and I don't believe he's our man."

"Of course, he could have hired it done," Detective Abbott said as he and Alan walked up.

The captain snapped his head around and glared at him. "That's a thought."

Alan suggested, "Maybe, it's related to a gang war. Those boys were part of a well known gang and had a couple of rival gangs after them."

"So far, we don't have any links to that." The captain shrugged.

A sudden thought clouded Kelley's eyes. "What about the grandfather? Both he and his son had to be considering revenge."

The captain's eyes were thoughtful as he looked at her. "I doubt it Mrs. Willis, since he is in a retirement home and wheelchair bound. It would be almost impossible for him."

A sudden shiver ran through Kelley. "What retirement home, Captain?"

"I believe it's called 'The Homestead'."

"Would you mind if I checked on him? And would you mind if Alan helped me?"

The captain shrugged his shoulders. "No. I welcome the assistance. We need all the help we can get on this case."

After everyone else left the room, Kelley turned to Alan. "The Homestead is where our friend, Harvey Younger, lives. I haven't seen him since he moved there. Why don't we head over there when your shift is over and visit him? We can check up on the little girl's grandfather at the same time."

"Good idea. Her father and grandfather have a good reason for wanting those kids dead. The captain said the girl's funeral was extremely sad; you could see those two men were really hurting."

Later in the afternoon, Alan and Kelley drove to The Homestead Retirement Home. "There it is on the left," Kelley said, pointing to a large two-story stucco building.

"Looks like they fixed this place up really nice," Alan said. He pulled in next to a painter's truck and viewed the newly painted brown and beige building.

"Remember, we're here to visit Harvey," Kelley said as she exited the car.

Alan shook his head in amusement. "Got it."

As they entered the building, a young man came strolling out of a side office and called out, "Hi there. I'm Larry Jones, administrator. Can I help you?"

Alan walked over to him and shook his hand. "Alan Willis, and this is my mother, Kelley. We're here to visit our friend, Mr. Younger."

"Oh, sure. No problem. He's most likely in the dining room waiting for supper. That way." He pointed to the corridor on his left. "If you want to join him, you're welcome. Its five dollars each," he added.

"No. We're just visiting," Kelley said as she started to walk away. She stopped abruptly. "Do we need to sign in or something?"

"No," Larry replied. "This is a retirement home—not a nursing home. The people who live here come and go all the time."

He reached into his pocket. "Here's my card. If you know of anyone who would like to join us here, we have room for a few more residents. We have twenty four-hour hour security."

Alan took the card, put it in his pocket, gently grabbed his mother by the arm, and strolled down the hall toward the dining room.

Entering the dining room, they spotted Harvey sitting at a small table in the back corner. He looked up just as Kelley waved at him, and his face lit up with joy.

He jumped to his feet and gave Kelley a big hug. "Harvey, this is my son, Alan," she said.

Harvey gave him a firm hand shake. "What a nice surprise. And you look great, Kelley." He motioned for them to have a seat at his table. "And where is Phil?"

"Went to Orlando with our granddaughter. A big science

fair up there. We were just passing by and thought we would look you up," Kelley said.

Alan tilted his head to the side and chuckled at her little white lie.

Kelley continued, "And there's a gentleman here named Vern Woods that we wanted to ask you about. But first, tell us what you have been up to, Harvey. How do you like it here?"

"It's okay." When he spoke, Harvey's voice was low. "But, it's not like home. I made friends with a few card players, but now they're gone. In fact, I'm going to be moving to Knoxville, Tennessee, at the end of the month. My daughter and her husband bought a five-bedroom home. My son-in-law makes good money, and they've invited me to live with them."

"That sounds wonderful," Kelley responded.

He nodded. "I'm going to take them up on their offer since I want to get to know my three grandchildren better. So good-bye Homestead. And remember, if you're in the neighborhood, call and stop by."

Kelley reached into her purse. "Here's my husband's card with our email address. Have your daughter or son-in-law email me with your new address. Perhaps, if we take a trip north sometime, we'll visit you"

They looked up as they saw a tall, thin man with a shock of white hair, walking slowly into the dining room.

Harvey pointed toward him. "There's your man. That's Vern Woods. He's leaving here soon, I heard."

"Oh, do you know him well?" Kelley leaned forward forcing Harvey to tilt his head to meet her gaze.

Harvey frowned and swallowed his hurt, hoping his pain didn't show on his face. "Yeah. We used to be really good friends," he answered sadly. "But after his grand-daughter got murdered, he became very bitter. Went into seclusion. Won't talk to anyone. Not even me."

"He doesn't look like the guy that we saw in the photo at the funeral," Alan said, staring at Vern. "He was hunched down in a wheelchair then."

"Had knee surgery not long ago. Just started walking again, and he's getting around pretty good now," Harvey said. "In fact, for a couple of months, before his surgery, we used to go to Walmart after supper in his black Toyota Corolla. He won't go anywhere now."

Harvey's chest felt tight and heavy, but what was the use of thinking about his friend's situation. Looking forlorn, he continued, "Just stays in his room. Anyway, we're both moving out of here. I heard the administrator say that Vern was going to live with his son."

Kelley and Alan sat and chatted with Harvey until the staff started to fill the water glasses and bring out the supper trays. As the young server headed for Harvey's table, Alan leaned over, "Listen Harvey, we'll let you enjoy your supper in peace. We've got to go."

"Sure you don't want to stay? We're having meat loaf. I'll treat."

"Got to get home to my wife and son," Alan said.

"We'll try to see you before you move," Kelley said. "That's a promise. And be sure to email me your new address in case we miss you before you leave."

"Thanks," Harvey said.

"Oh Harvey, you have my husband's card and phone number. If you notice Woods going out in the next few days give us a call," Kelley stated.

"Why is that?" Harvey scrunched lower in his seat and looked at her with confusion racing across his face.

Kelley's chin lifted and she smiled briefly. "Oh somehow, I've just got a hunch about him."

Chapter 33

After leaving the retirement home, Alan called Captain Minor at the precinct. "Captain, this is Lt. Willis. I've got a hunch about the person who killed those two young kids. My mother and I just visited the retirement home where Misti's grandfather lives. Remember, he was in a wheelchair and all hunched over when he attended the funeral?"

"Yeah. I remember," the captain responded. "What about him?"

"Well, his friend at the retirement home said he's a changed man after his granddaughter's death. The guy's a real loner and very bitter. I think he might be responsible for the murder of those boys. I want to do a stake out on him in case he decides to go after Hector Carmen. I know that it's too late for you to assign some officers for this evening, but I'm willing to do it on my own. "

"Why do you think it's important that we start the stake out on the grandfather right away?" the captain asked.

Alan answered without hesitation, "Because Woods is leaving the retirement home soon to move in with his son. My dad told Hector Carmen's mother to keep her son off the streets tonight, make him stay at home, and lock the house up. But, you never know what kids will do, and my parents are worried about him. After tomorrow, you'll have him in protective custody so he should be safe."

"Well, what do you propose, Willis?"

"The other two boys were found near the Sunrise Laundromat. That's where their gang usually hangs out. I want to watch the grandfather and see if he cuts out from the retirement home tonight and looks for Hector. Somehow, I think the kid might sneak out of the house."

There was a slight pause before the captain answered, "That sounds like a bit of speculation. But, if you want to, okay. Do you need backup?"

"I've got it covered for now."

" I'll have a black and white in the vicinity tonight just in case. Be careful, Willis, whoever killed those boys carries a lot of hatred. And, most likely he'll have a gun. People filled with extreme grief aren't always rational. And if the old man did kill those boys, we want him alive."

"Right. I'll keep in contact," Alan replied and hung up his phone.

At seven that night, Alan and Kelley returned to the retirement home and sat in the rear parking lot, where they kept an eye on Vern Woods' black Toyota Corolla. About an hour later, Woods came out the back door of the building, got in his car, and drove off.

Keeping a safe distance behind, Alan followed the Corolla as it headed north on Mabry Road. He waited patiently nearby as Woods stopped at a 7-11, went in, and came out carrying a six-pack of beer and drove off.

Alan and Kelley followed Woods for the next ten minutes until he parked his car near the Sunrise Laundromat at Dale Road. Alan turned down Euclid Avenue, a side street, and parked where he could keep an eye on Wood's car and still have the building in his sight.

"That's where the kids always hung out," Alan whispered.

He pulled his field glasses out from under the seat and handed them to Kelley. "Here, keep an eye on things for me while I call in to the captain and tell him where we're at. And that Woods is here, too."

As Alan was talking on the phone, Kelley tapped him on his arm. "Alan, look. There are four boys down there in the alley next to the Sunrise Laundromat. One of them is wearing an orange Miami Dolphins cap."

Suddenly her eyes widened and she shook her head with a look of disbelief. She looked as though lightning had just struck her. "That's what Hector Carmen was wearing a couple of days ago when I saw him and his mother. Oh, my God, what's he doing out? We advised his mother to keep him home."

Alan hung up the phone and grabbed the glasses from his mother. "Sure, it's Hector all right. Why in the hell, didn't he stay home, like you told him to?"

"Okay, let the play begin." Kelley's face was deadly white and her eyes were filled with concern.

The four boys were sitting on the ground in the alley with their backs to the Laundromat. Looking through his glasses, Alan saw Vern Woods sitting in his car at a spot where the boys couldn't see him. He appeared to be just watching .

Suddenly Kelley's head snapped up and she called out, "The boys are getting up. Looks like they're on the move."

Woods' car started up and headed slowly toward the boys. When the car was parallel to them, Woods stopped, leaving the motor running. He jumped out, ran over to Hector, put a gun to his head, and grabbed him by the collar. Dragging Hector behind, he staggered back to the car, opened the passenger side door, and threw him in.

He ran around to the driver's side and jumped in, still waving the gun.

"Woods has a gun," Alan yelled out. Then, an ugly curse flew from his lips after he watched Woods push Hector into the car. "Damn, he grabbed the kid."

Kelley's mouth dropped. She felt the breath leave her body.

Before Kelley and Alan had a chance to react any further, Woods put the car into gear and sped off.

"Where the hell is he headed with the kid?" Alan shouted out. Reacting quickly, he turned on the ignition, whipped the car around, and followed Wood's car down the street.

Woods drove slowly for several miles, heading south on Mabry Road. As he drove along, Alan called Captain Minor and reported Hector's abduction and that he was following Woods. When Woods got to Gandy Boulevard, he made a right turn.

"Now, where's he headed?" Alan asked, lowering his voice to a near whisper.

"I think that he's headed to the cemetery on Gandy, where his granddaughter was buried." Kelley's soft reply drifted into Alan's troubled thoughts.

"Yeah. Palm Cemetery. I know the place." Being careful to stay far behind Wood's car, Alan followed him into the cemetery as he called into the department, gave them his location, and asked for backup.

Kelley pointed to a side road. "Over there. He just parked the car."

Alan parked his vehicle and turned toward Kelley. His chest tightened. "You stay here and wait for backup."

In a controlled whisper, she quietly said, "Okay. But I don't like this. Maybe you should just wait."

Ignoring his mother's suggestion, Alan turned off the ignition, got out of the car, and preceded slowly toward Woods' car. As he crept to the car, both Woods and Hector exited.

He heard Woods scream out, "Get down on your knees, you bastard. My revenge is almost complete. You're the last of the three who raped and killed my granddaughter. And, you'll be the last to die. But first, I'll give you some real pain."

Alan could hear the sound of blows, as Woods punched the kid in the face with his clenched fist.

Alan raced toward them. As he came around the car, he saw Hector kneeling on the ground. Woods was standing above him, holding his gun to the kid's head. "And now, you die!"

Alan tackled Woods from behind and threw him to the ground. Within moments, he had Woods' hands drawn behind his back and snapped the handcuffs on him. "Your killing days are over, Mr. Woods."

Woods shot an angry glance at him. "Let me up. I want this kid dead and in his cold grave like my granddaughter. He deserves to die like those other two."

The backup police car pulled up beside Alan's car

Jumping out of the car, Kelley yelled out to the officers, "They're over there." The officers sprinted toward them with Kelley on their heels.

Alan looked up as the officers approached and a deep frown crossed his face as he said calmly, "I just read him his rights. You can take him in."

After the officers threw Woods into the squad car, a relieved Kelley put her arms around Hector, who was now shaking and crying. "I thought we told you to stay home with your mother. And look at your face—your eye is bruised and your nose is bleeding."

Hector wiped his nose with his sleeve. "I know. He just tried to kill me. I should've listened. But I was going nuts at home, and I wanted to hang out with the gang."

"Well, it's all over now," Alan said compassionately.

"Will your husband still help me with my trial?" Hector asked Kelley, as he swallowed hard.

"Yes. He promised your mother."

Before Vern Woods could go to trial for the murder of the two boys, he entered a plea of guilty. Rather than giving him the death penalty, the judge sentenced him to spend the remainder of his life in prison.

Hector Carmen was tried as an accomplice to the rape and murder of Misti Woods; after it was proven that he had only driven the car, and did not realize the other two had killed Misti until after the deed was committed. With Phil's competent defense, Hector was sentenced to twelve months in a juvenile facility followed by five years probation.

After the trial, Kelley looked at her husband and said, "You may want to wait a while before you decide to take on another case like this. It was just too hard emotionally for us."

The next few years passed by quickly with Tiffany and Michael now in high school. Both Alan and Steve decided to take early retirement since the budget at the police station was slashed drastically. Eventually, Alan joined his wife, Laura, in the real estate business. Both were very successful in the following years.

Ashley took only small uneventful cases in the next few years—divorces, accidents, and small claims.

Steve started a small business out of his garage; fixing and selling used bicycles.

Phil spent a good deal of his time on his computer, writing crime stories.

One Sunday, at their customary once a month dinner

with their children and grandchildren, Phil announced that he had rented a villa in Key West for five days for the entire family.

"Great, Dad," Alan said.

"Yes. And count us in, too," Steve chimed in.

"Yes. And I hope that now it's "Final Justice" for all of us," Kelley said, smiling. Her family saw love and happiness in her eyes and felt their own love and happiness expand astronomically.

"Tomorrow, I plan on going to my office for a short time to get some billing out of the way," Ashley commented. "And no more crazy adventures for any of us, especially murder trials."

"But then again, you never know, who or what might pop up," Phil added.

Kelley smiled at him, "Yes, I know. Never say never."

Chapter 34

Ashley sat at her desk and mumbled mockingly to herself. "What am I doing in the office on a Saturday morning?" After she finished her paperwork, she planned to head to the Blood Mobile. She and Steve made a habit of giving blood once a month in return for two tickets to the AMC theatres. Not only was it a good and charitable thing to do, but it would be tonight's entertainment.

Just as she was getting ready to sign off her computer, she heard a tapping on the front door. She pushed her chair back, stood up, and walked into the front reception area. Ignoring the sign on the front door that read 'closed,' the person outside rapped repeatedly. As she stood there trying to decide what action to take, the tapping grew increasingly louder and more persistent.

It's can't be Steve, she thought. He volunteered this morning to help finish painting the local church hall. Afterwards, he's supposed to meet me at the mall where the Blood Mobile is parked.

"Hello in there," a voice called out with more than just a touch of impatience. "I saw through the window that you have a light on inside. So I know someone is there. Please answer your door."

Peeking through the glass in the door, Ashley saw a tall, attractive, blonde young lady standing outside. Reluctantly, she opened the door, with a smile that was obviously forced and asked, "Yes? Can I help you?"

The young woman appeared to be extremely nervous. Her words ran together as she spoke. "Are you Attorney Clarke? May I come in? I have something I must discuss with you."

Ashley shrugged, stepped back, and waved for her to enter. "Sure, but slow down. Please catch your breath. Then you can tell me how I can help."

The woman sighed and with a determined look on her face, eagerly followed Ashley as she walked into her office.

Ashley motioned for the woman to have a seat in front of her desk. She studied the young woman's ashen colored face and walked to the small refrigerator that sat in back of her desk. She reached inside and pulled out a bottle of cold water. After unscrewing the cap, she placed it on the desk in front of the young woman. "Take a small sip of water. Calm down. Give me your name."

The woman took a long sip. She forced a half-smile. After taking a deep breath, she said, "My name is Kathleen Sullivan. I'm here because my brother, Sean, was arrested. We need your help."

Ashley sat down and with characteristic bluntness asked, "And why was he arrested?"

"The police believe that he murdered our parents," Kathleen said as she hung her head and a mist filled her eyes.

Ashley's head snapped up. "Murdered them?"

"That's what they say." Kathleen's voice was now filled with searing despair. "But I'm sure that he's innocent, and I want you to defend him. Sean wouldn't hurt a fly, much less our own parents."

Ashley pulled a legal pad out of the drawer, and started

to take notes as she studied Kathleen's care-creased face. "And your parents' names?"

"Ryan and Maggie Sullivan," Kathleen replied. "They adopted us when we were very young."

"Where is your brother now?" Ashley sat forward in her chair, her voice deep with interest.

Kathleen straightened, frowning. "He's in jail, he called me a little while ago. He sounded so frantic. I hope you can get him out, because I know he's innocent. When you meet him, you'll see that he could never do anything like that."

All of a sudden, something clicked in Ashley's brain. Her shoulders rose and fell in a thoughtful sigh. "Sure, it was on this morning's news. Your parents owned a brewery."

She pondered the situation for a few moments. "I know someone at police headquarters who I can call and who might be able to help." She picked up the phone, dialed the number to police headquarters and asked for Detective Costello.

"Detective Costello, and his partner, Detective Abbott, were transferred to another precinct. Detective Orsini and his partner are taking over their cases."

"May I speak to him then?"

After a short time, Ashley heard, "Detective Orsini, here. What can I do for you?"

"I'm Attorney Ashley Clarke, my husband is Detective Steve Clarke. I understand that you are working with him now. You have a Sean Sullivan locked up in your jail I believe."

"Wait a second," he said as her words cut into his thoughts. "It's noisy as hell in here. I'm going into the next room. I'll pick up the phone in there."

"Okay, Mrs. Clarke, I'm back. It's quieter here. You say you're calling about a guy named Sullivan?"

"Sean Sullivan. You have him there. Right?"

"Just a minute." Ashley heard him call out, "Hey, Mitchell, do we have a Sean Sullivan booked in here?"

"Yeah. Supposed to have killed his folks," Mitchell yelled back.

"We've got him," Orsini said into the phone. "What can I do for you?"

"Just wanted to be sure he's there." Ashley replied. "I'll call you back in a few minutes, Detective."

She hung up the phone and turned to Kathleen. "Yes. He's there. Now tell me the facts of the case as you know them."

"You may have heard on the news this morning," Kathleen said softly, hesitantly, her voice trembling. "My parents were found dead inside their home. Stabbed to death. And for some reason, the police seem to think my twin brother is responsible."

She sank into her chair, deep in despair. "The TV news showed pictures of the house roped off with yellow tape. But, they didn't give any details on the deaths. Only said that my brother was arrested. I just don't know what to do to help him."

Ashley's brows lifted as Kathleen continued, "I hope that you'll agree to defend him because I know he's innocent." She took a handkerchief out of her pocket and wiped her eyes. "We'll pay you whatever you want. Money is no object."

Ashley pondered the situation for a few moments, then whipped around and snapped her fingers. "Well, to tell you the truth. My practice has not only been slow lately, but quite dull. I think I might be ready for the challenge of taking on your brother as a client."

"Oh, thank you. Thank you," Kathleen said, with a sigh of relief. "I heard you are one of the very best lawyers in town. That's why I'm here."

Ashley shrugged her shoulders. "Thank you, that's very flattering. I would like to talk to your brother before the detectives have a chance to interview him. He definitely shouldn't talk to anyone without his attorney present. However, it's Saturday, and there's not much I can do for your brother today, except to interview him and get his side of the story."

A frustrated breath escaped from Kathleen as Ashley continued, "He won't be arraigned until Monday morning. Right now, I just want to talk to him."

"That at least is something encouraging."

Ashley picked up the phone and called Detective Orsini back. "I'm on my way into headquarters to talk to my new client, Sean Sullivan. Can you do me a favor and make sure that no one talks to him until I get there?"

"Sure. No problem," he answered. "But from what I just heard, I think you'll have quite a challenge on your hands defending this guy."

Ashley accepted that with a wry nod. "I think I'm up to it. See you in twenty minutes." She hung up the phone.

Kathleen sank back in her chair somewhat relieved. "So you'll take my brother's case then?"

"We'll see. First let's get to the jail," Ashley leaned toward her, warming gently. "And I'll need to know everything about your brother's relationship with your parents."

"Let's take my car," Kathleen said. "I'll fill you in about my brother and my folks on the way."

Ashley nodded, grabbed a legal pad and a pen, and shoved them in her briefcase. "Let's go."

As they headed for police headquarters, Ashley dug her notebook and pen out of her briefcase. She turned toward Kathleen. "You said you'd give me some background information."

"I'm prepared to tell you everything I know."

Ashley gave her a reassuring smile. "Okay. Let's start with the basic stuff. Names first."

"My parents are—were—Ryan and Margaret Sullivan, everyone called her Maggie. My brother is Sean. We're the only children. Our real parents were killed by a drunk driver when we were very young, and the Sullivan's adopted us. Sean and I are twins. But, I guess I mentioned that before."

Ashley jotted the information down. "And when did the police arrest your brother?"

Kathleen looked over at her and heaved a sigh. "Right after the murders. One of the neighbors saw someone wearing dark clothes run away from my parent's house. He called the police. When the police pulled up to the estate, they caught Sean running down the driveway. He told them he had been downstairs in the library, and when he heard a scuffle upstairs, he ran up and found our parents, lying in pools of blood in their bedroom. He could see they were already dead. So, he ran out of the house because he thought the murderer might still be in the house. That's why he was running away."

Ashley nodded and took notes. "Tell me something about your parents. When you say 'estate' I assume that they had a great deal of money?"

Kathleen paused, listening to directions from her car's GPS system, then forced herself to continue. "My adopted dad, Ryan, owns a beer distillery in Tampa. You may have heard of it—Sullivan's Brewery. His father came from Ireland and opened up the brewery years ago. Over the years, the beer has become very popular, and the brewery was expanded several times. In fact, there was talk of another large expansion again soon."

Kathleen stopped talking as she whipped the car into

the parking lot next to police headquarters. "Here we are." She parked the car in an empty space and they exited.

Inside the building, Ashley told the desk sergeant that Detective Orsini was expecting her. "He's back in the detectives' office. Do you want me to show you the way?"

"No. I've been here a few times. I know the way."

Ashley led Kathleen down the hall and to the detective's room, where she knocked briefly before throwing the door open and entering. When Detective Orsini saw Ashley, he jumped to his feet. "You must be Attorney Clarke." She smiled and shook his outstretched hand. "Glad to meet you."

Ashley turned toward Kathleen. "Kathleen this is Detective Orsini. This is Kathleen Sullivan, Sean Sullivan's twin sister."

Orsini reached out and shook Kathleen's hand. "Sorry to meet you under these circumstances."

He directed them to his desk and pulled out a chair for each before he walked around to the back of the desk, pulled out his swivel chair, and sat down.

He looked at Kathleen and said quietly, "We've got your brother back in a holding cell, miss. I heard that he's calmer now than when he was first brought in. He kept on yelling 'I'm innocent.' His speech is a little difficult to understand at times."

Then he directed his attention to Ashley. "Because it's Labor Day weekend, the captain tried to give a lot of the men a three-day weekend. We're running with a skeleton crew. Also, the courts are working on a reduced schedule and won't be open until Tuesday. So we don't expect Sean to appear before the judge until then."

Ashley shook her head and said to Kathleen in a soothing voice, "Sorry. I forgot that it's a holiday weekend. Guess we'll have to wait until Tuesday to get Sean out."

Kathleen looked at the detective and tried to hold back the tears. "Can't you make an exception for him? He's innocent. And he's so scared—he's never been in jail before."

"Everyone who comes in here says that. Sorry—no exceptions." He looked at Kathleen with compassion.

He leaned forward in his chair and placed his arms on his desk and looked intently at Ashley. "You're going to represent Mr. Sullivan, counselor?"

"Looks like it. Right now, I just want to talk to him."

Orsini gave her a steady look. "By the way, the news media is all over the murders. Two of our detectives are out at the house right now, working the scene with the medical examiner. They'll probably want to take a statement from Sean later. No rush, he's here for the weekend."

"I understand. I'll want to be present when they do."

"Okay, then. I'll have one of the officers bring Sean into a private room and let you two visit with him."

He stood up and led the women into a room nearby. They sat down at the long metal table and waited silently for Sean to arrive. A short while later, the door opened and a tall, slender, disheveled young man with long sandy brown hair, was led in by a uniformed officer.

When he saw his sister, Sean ran to her and flung his arms around her. A shudder seemed to flow through him. "Oh my God, Kathleen. I can't believe—this is happening. Mom and Dad are dead and the police think—think—that I did it."

"I know. I can't believe it either. But I brought a highly recommended attorney." She struggled to sound confident. "This is Ashley Clarke, and she has agreed to help us."

Sean looked at Ashley and his voice quivered, "I didn't do it. I'm innocent!" With a slow stutter, he repeated, "I'm—innocent." His head dropped to his chest, and he nibbled on his lower lip.

Ashley helped Sean into a chair and spent several moments trying to calm him down before she started to interview him. She made a point of trying to ask him questions slowly and calmly. However, still very upset and shaking violently, Sean couldn't seem to rap his mind around what had occurred nor could he understand her questions.

Suddenly, he jumped to his feet and started to pace the room, repeating, "I didn't do it. I didn't—do it."

Ashley got him to sit back down and continued to try to interrogate him. After he told them what he knew of the incident, Kathleen looked desperately at Ashley and pleaded, "You will defend my brother, won't you?"

"Please—help—help—me," Sean pleaded.

"Yes. I'll take the case. I'll be back for the arraignment on Tuesday. In the meantime, when you're a little calmer, Sean, I want you to try to remember exactly what happened and write all the details down. Remember, everything is important. So don't leave out anything."

The door opened and Detective Orsini entered with another man walking behind him. Ashley didn't recognize the tall, broad-shouldered man with a strong-boned face and thick slightly curly hair.

"Mrs. Clarke, meet Detective Falco. We've just learned we've both been assigned to this case, counselor."

Ashley stood up and shook hands. "I have just agreed to represent Sean Sullivan. So I will be the attorney of record."

"Please have a seat counselor," Detective Falco said.

"Thank you. My client is planning to plead innocent to the crime."

"Of course," he responded. He turned to Sean and said coldly, "Now that your attorney is present, Sean Sullivan, we have a few questions for you."

Chapter 35

On Tuesday, the day after Labor Day, Attorney Ashley Clarke sat behind a long wooden table in Room 304 of the Tampa downtown courthouse. Seated to her right was her co-counsel, her father, Phil Willis. Seated to her left was their new client, Sean Sullivan.

The back of the courtroom was filled with local news media. Two of the major networks had sent people over for the hearings.

"All rise," the bailiff ordered as Judge Judy Ott entered the courtroom. The judge took her seat behind the bench and wrapped her gavel loudly to quiet the crowd. The bailiff announced, "Court is in session. All be seated."

After everyone settled down, the judge looked at the bailiff and asked, "Who's up first this morning?"

"Sean Sullivan. He is charged with the murder of Maggie and Ryan Sullivan, his parents," the bailiff called out.

The judge looked down at both the prosecuting and defense teams. "Is everyone ready to proceed?"

"Michele Bain, Assistant District Attorney." A tall dark-haired woman stood up. "My assistant, Dawn Cardamane and I are ready."

She was wearing a Donna Karan suit; a smart cream short-sleeved tailored jacket, nipped at the waist, which fit like a glove and teamed with a short, straight black skirt that ended two inches above her knees. On her feet were black Italian leather shoes. Placed on the table in front of her were a matching purse and briefcase. Michele Bain gave the appearance of a very professional and prosperous lawyer and looked right at home in the courtroom.

Ashley stood up. "Ashley Willis Clarke and Phillip Willis, here for the defense."

The judge looked briefly at her papers. Then quickly put them aside said to Ashley. "Okay, now let's get started, Mrs. Clarke. Your client, Sean Sullivan, has been accused of the murder of his adopted parents, Ryan and Maggie Sullivan. And the evidence as reported by the police seems to substantiate this. How does your client plead?"

Ashley leaned over and conferred with Sean. He jumped to his feet, then in a loud and confident voice, cried out, "Not—not—not guilty, your Honor."

"And Mr. Sullivan not only has a clean record, but he is not a flight risk. Therefore, we ask that he be released on bail." Ashley said and motioned for Sean to sit back down as she took the seat beside him.

After hearing arguments from both sides concerning bail, Judge Ott said, "Bail is set at two hundred fifty thousand. Mr. Sullivan will wear an ankle bracelet, and reside with his sister, until the trial begins. The trial will commence five weeks from today."

She pounded her gavel and announced, "Next case."

Ashley gathered up her papers and left the courtroom with her father and Kathleen. They planned to wait for Sean to trade his orange jail suit for his everyday clothes and to join them shortly.

While waiting for Sean in the corridor, Michele walked up to Phil. "Good morning, Attorney Willis. We meet again."

"Morning. You're looking terrific as always. And I believe you have met my daughter, Ashley Clarke," he replied, shaking Michele's hand.

Michele nodded her head. "Yes. It was some time ago that we were in court together. But, good to see you again, counselor."

Turning toward the young woman standing beside her, she said, "This is my assistant, Dawn Cardamane." Dawn was an attractive woman of average height, in her early twenties, and immaculately dressed in a gray business suit.

"Glad to meet you," Ashley said, shaking Dawn's hand.

"Same here. I've watched you from afar the last couple of years. You seem to be doing very well in your law practice," Dawn commented.

"Yes. Maybe someday, you'll even come over to my side," Michele added smiling at Ashley.

"Maybe. Here's' my card with my fax number if you want to send me any additional information of the case," Ashley replied. "Both sides have five weeks to investigate all the evidence, and I'm certain that my investigator will come up with a strong defense for Sean."

Michele smiled sweetly. "By the way, after you review all the evidence we have against your client, and you decide to make a deal, just let me know. I'm always willing to accept a plea. If we can't come to agreement before, I'll see you in court."

Ashley glared at her and nodded. After Michele and her assistant walked away, Ashley looked at her father, "As soon as Sean comes out, let's go Dad."

Phil, Ashley, and Kathleen sat on a bench in the hall waiting for Sean to arrive. Kathleen reached into her purse, pulled out a slip of paper, and handed it to Ashley.

"Here's a check for your retainer fee. I already made arrangements with a bail bondsman to take care of the bond. Thank you for taking my brother's case."

Ashley took the check, glanced at it briefly, and put it into her briefcase. As Sean, now dressed in casual slacks and a white-collared shirt approached them, they jumped to their feet.

Kathleen threw her arms around her brother and patted him on his shoulders consolingly. He leaned toward her, warming slowly. He hung his head and tears came into his eyes as he looked at Ashley and Phil. "Thank you. Thank you..." he stuttered.

Phil looked at him and frowned. He had just discovered that the young man was not only extremely shy for his age, and never looked anyone in the eye, but, he stuttered tremendously when he was nervous. Phil found himself wondering if the young man was slightly retarded. He realized that it may not be a good idea to put Sean on the stand. He hoped that his concerns about the young man did not show on his face.

Ashley smiled at Kathleen. "I want you to take Sean home now, and try to keep him calm. Then, I would like both of you to come into my office later to talk over our strategy. Or better yet, I can come to your house, so Sean won't be so upset and confused."

Ashley looked at Sean. "In the meantime, I want you to write down everything that you did on the day that your parents died—put it down hour by hour. I was disappointed that you didn't do that while you were in jail, as I asked."

Pain seemed to jerk through him. "I'll—try—," he stuttered, looking down at his feet.

Ashley laid a gentle soothing hand on Sean's arm. "Try not to worry. Our job is to have you found innocent and to eventually find out who really killed your parents."

He swallowed hard. "My—adopted—parents—Mrs. Clarke," Sean stuttered back, his mouth dropping.

After they left the building, Ashley and Phil jumped into her car and headed to her office. On the way, Ashley glanced over at her dad and said fondly, "I'm so glad that you agree to be my co-counsel."

Phil regarded her affectionately. "Yes. And your mother is anxious to start doing some investigating for you."

"God, I love you two. When we get back to the office, I'll get on the computer and make a list of possible suspects. We can give that to Mom to get her started on the case."

"Good idea." Phil pulled out his cell phone. "Hey Kelley, this is your better half. Ashley and I just finished up in court. We would like you to meet us at her office. Wear comfortable clothes and good walking shoes. We need you to spring into action. This is one tough case."

"I'm ready," she answered.

"And by the way, my dear wife, the assistant district attorney prosecuting the case is none other than my old friend, Michele Bain. You remember her. When I was up against her before, her nickname was 'top gun'."

"Sounds like you and Ashley have your work cut out for you," Kelley responded.

Back at the office, Ashley took control. She reviewed all the information that she had to date on the Sullivan family. "Dad, I need you to visit Mr. and Mrs. Sullivan's private attorney. See if you can learn what the Sullivan's estate is worth and when the will is scheduled to be read. Try to learn who gets what. If all the money goes to Sean and Kathleen, the prosecutor will probably try to use that against Sean as a motive for the murders."

"Mom, you go to the Sullivan brewery, talk to the General Manager, Larry Keller. Maybe he can give you some insight into what, if anything, unusual might have been happening with Mr. Sullivan's business lately. While you two are doing your part, I'm going to do some paperwork."

"Aren't you scheduled to meet with your client, Sean?" Kelley asked.

"Yes. Kathleen called a little while ago and asked if we could meet at her apartment. I said no problem. So, I'm going there to see both of them. Sean is supposed to provide me with the time frame of his where-a-bouts the day of the murders."

"Talk to you later," Phil and Kelley said, before they went on their respective ways.

The rest of the day proved to be most interesting for them.

Phil met with Ryan and Maggie Sullivan's attorney, Harold Gross. To Phil's great surprise, he told him that Larry Keller, the man who had been general manager of the brewery for years, would inherit fifty-one percent of the business. The Sullivan children, Kathleen and Sean, would jointly inherit the house and the remaining forty-nine per cent of the brewery together with one million dollars in bonds each. The contents of the house were to be sold and the monies donated to Hospice. Also, he learned from Attorney Gross that there had been a lot of anger and bitterness between Ryan Sullivan and his son, Sean, when earlier Sean had refused to enter into the business.

Kelley headed to the Sullivan Brewery to interview Larry Keller, the General Manager, hoping to get more information about Sean's relationship with his father and to see if he knew of anyone who might have had it in for the Sullivans.

Later that afternoon, Ashley arrived at Kathleen's apartment on Bay Shore and rang the bell. Within a few moments, Kathleen opened the door and stepped outside into the hallway. She drew Ashley to the side and said quietly, "Before you come in, I must tell you something about Sean."

Ashley looked puzzled. "Yes?"

Kathleen put her hand on Ashley's arm. "Well, first of all, as you might have noticed, my brother is extremely shy."

Ashley nodded. "Yes. And I noticed that he tends to stutter when he gets nervous."

"That's exactly why I hoped you would try to hold your questions to him to a minimum," Kathleen said imploringly.

"I'll do my best," Ashley sighed. "But, you realize that in order to defend him properly I will have to ask him several questions."

"I know that. But, please try not to upset him too much. He is very fragile emotionally," Kathleen answered as she opened the door and led Ashley into the living room.

At Kathleen's directions, Ashley took a seat on the sofa. She placed her briefcase beside her, opened it, and drew out a pad and a pen. She looked at Kathleen and simply said, "I'm ready."

Kathleen nodded, left the room, and walked down the hall to a bedroom door. She knocked and told Sean that his attorney was here to see him.

Sean slowly opened his door and peeked down the hall into the living room where he could see Ashley sitting. He took a deep breath, and quietly followed Kathleen to the living room.

Ashley smiled reassuringly at him and gestured to the sofa beside her. "Hi Sean. Please sit. I have a few questions for you."

He stopped in front of her, hesitated for a few moments, then reached into his back pocket and pulled out several sheets of yellow legal paper. "Mrs. Clarke—I have your—list," he stuttered as he handed it to her.

"Good. Let me look it over." She motioned for him to sit down.

Sean slowly took a seat at the far end of the sofa from her, while Kathleen sat down on a nearby chair. Sean scooted far back into the corner, sank into the cushions, and whispered, "You know—you know—I'm innocent." He hung his head and wouldn't look Ashley in the eye.

"Yes. I know. And, that's how you pleaded," Ashley replied firmly. She slid a little closer to him and placed her hand gently on his arm.

He finally lifted his head just a little and whimpered, "Do you have any idea of who might have killed—my—step-parents?"

"No. But, I won't exempt anyone who knew your folks from being a suspect. My investigators are on the case as we speak. Now, let me look over the log that you gave me."

Both Kathleen and Sean sat silently as Ashley looked over the information that Sean had given her. Finally, she placed the papers on the coffee table and staring at them, asked, "Do either of you have any idea who might have wanted your parents dead?"

Sean's head suddenly lifted, and he jumped to his feet. "Kathleen, tell Mrs. Clarke— about that guy who—works at the brewery. You know—the one who is so nasty to me when I visit there."

Kathleen looked puzzled, and then thought for a few moments. "Oh, you mean Conrad Volt."

Sean clapped his hands." Yeah. Yeah. That's the one. Tell her—about him."

Ashley could see the lines of strain in her face as Kathleen leaned forward in her chair. "Well, Mrs. Clarke, when my grandparents opened the brewery years ago they had a partner, Julius Volt. Everything went well at first, and then, he and my father started to disagree a lot. In fact, you could say that they became bitter enemies, so my father decided to buy Mr. Volt out after he took over the brewery. Mr. Volt took the proceeds from the sale and returned to Germany to live. But his son, Conrad, stayed behind. There was a binding agreement in the sale that my father would continue to employ Conrad at the brewery with a good salary, for as long as he chose to work there. So you see, Julius Volt didn't completely let go of control of the brewery."

"And?" Ashley asked, now quite interested in this bit of information.

"And—well, my father and Conrad were always arguing. Conrad acted as though his father still owned half of the place, and he liked to boss everyone around. So in return, my father gave Conrad a crummy, insignificant job. And Conrad seemed to hate all of us. Because of all the constant tension at the brewery, Sean and I wanted no part of the place. We both had other interests; but this also brought tension between our father and us."

Sean's head bobbed up and down as he listened to his sister. Then, he said, Yes—He was one strange guy—and—he hated my father and me. Mrs.—Mrs.—Clarke, you might want to check—him out."

"I heard from Mr. Keller that Conrad Volt called his father almost daily to report what was going on at the brewery," Kathleen added.

Ashley considered what the two had just told her. After scribbling down a few notes, she said, "Yes. I'll do that. In the meantime, I want you both to stay close to home. I'll call you when and if my investigators or I uncover any information about him."

Sean jumped to his feet. "Be careful when you're around that Volt guy. He's—a mean one." Suddenly Sean spun around on his heels and said to his sister, "I'd like to lie down—and take a nap now. I'm kind of—tired."

Kathleen stood up, walked over to him, and placed her arm around his shoulders. "Do you think that you have everything you need from us for now, Mrs. Clarke?"

"Yes. Of course. I'll call you tomorrow and keep you updated."

"If you decide to come over, please call first," Kathleen said. "We might be out. We need some groceries, and I want to buy Sean a new suit."

Ashley placed her note pad and pen in her briefcase, zipped it up, and bid the two good-bye.

In the car, Ashley dialed her mother's cell. "Mom, are you at the brewery yet?"

"Yes, dear, "Kelley responded.

"I would like you to check out a fellow by the name of Conrad Volt, who works there. I would prefer that you don't talk directly to him, but rather ask the general manager and some of the other workers about him. Try to be discreet."

"Will do, honey."

Chapter 36

After visiting with Sean and Kathleen, Ashley decided to call Detectives Orsini and Falco at police headquarters. The desk sergeant answered the call and forwarded it to the detective's department. "Good morning. Detective Falco speaking."

"Hi. This is Ashley Clarke. I was wondering, if I stop by about eleven or shortly thereafter, will either you or your partner have a few minutes to talk with me about the Sullivan case?"

A brief pause, then, "Sure, I'll even buy you lunch in the basement cafeteria, after we talk."

"I'd like that."

At about eleven thirty, Ashley strolled into police headquarters. Detective Falco was standing in the lobby waiting for her. "Good to see you again, Mrs. Clarke."

She shook hands with him, then posed the question that was foremost in her mind. "I stopped by to see if you know if they've assigned anyone permanently to the Sullivan case?"

"As a matter of fact, my partner and I got it. You said that you wanted to talk to one of us about the case?"

Ashley nodded, sighing with relief. She knew that she could readily work with these two friendly detectives.

He shot her a piercing glance. "Let's head back to our office. Detective Orsini is there working right now."

Ashley followed him to the detectives' office where his partner was seated at his desk. He looked up from his work and saw Ashley following Falco. "Hi, Mrs. Clarke," he said warmly.

"Don't get up detective," Ashley said as she took a seat in front of his desk. She placed her purse and briefcase on the floor beside her. "I was wondering if I could ask you two a couple of questions about the Sullivan case and give you an update on what I've learned."

Detective Falco took a seat next to Ashley and looked at the other detective. Orsini brushed his hair forward over his receding hairline and replied, "Sure. Why not? You know something we don't know?"

Ashley sat on the edge of her seat, now somewhat nervous. "I was present when you questioned Sean Sullivan, and I know that you didn't get too much out of him. But, have you discovered anything new on the case since then?"

Orsini leaned back in his chair. He didn't smile. He looked like a man who didn't have much use for polite talk. "Not much. We talked to a witness who saw the Sullivan kid leaving the house, but as you know, he claims he's innocent. The Sullivan's were stabbed numerous times, and the murder scene was extremely bloody. Usually people are just shot in a robbery so we don't believe that was the motive. You have to be able to get pretty close to a person to stab them to death. Whoever killed the Sullivan's did it in a passionate rage. But, so far, we haven't found the murder weapon."

Ashley thought for a few moments, then a frustrated breath slipped from her. "Now, let me tell you a few facts that my investigators and I have discovered."

Orsini looked at Falco with a slight bit of amusement.

"Not only is this lady mighty pretty, but she is one hell of an investigator."

"Thanks." Ashley decided to let that compliment pass by her. "Well, not only do I think that my client is innocent, but I've been checking out another possible suspect."

Detective Falco leaned forward in his chair, put his elbows on the desk, and tilted his head to meet her gaze. "You have someone else that you believe killed the Sullivans?"

"Yes." Ashley leaned over, pulled some papers from her briefcase, and put them on the desk. "A Conrad Volt. He works at the Sullivan Brewery. His father, Julius Volt, and Ryan Sullivan were partners in the brewery for years. A lot of bitterness developed between them, and Ryan Sullivan bought the older Volt out."

Both of the detectives listened intently as she continued, "The sale itself was very difficult, and Julius Volt forced Mr. Sullivan to put a clause in the sales contract that his son, Conrad, would have a job at the brewery for the rest of his life. The senior Volt and his wife went back to Germany to take care of his ailing mother, but the younger Volt stayed here. He never got along with the Sullivans or anyone at the brewery. And he wasn't afraid of showing his dislike for Mr. Sullivan."

"Sounds interesting," Detective Orsini commented as he shot a piercing glance at her. "Is there more?"

"Young Mr. Volt and the now sole owner, Ryan Sullivan, had been feuding for the past several years. My mother, Kelley, who does my investigative work, has been out to the brewery. She talked to the general manager and some of the other employees and learned that the day before the Sullivans were murdered Ryan Sullivan and Conrad Volt had a heated argument at the brewery. Loud yelling and cursing was heard coming from Conrad Volt's small office. One employee said that she heard Conrad Volt shout out, 'I wish you were dead, you bastard. You screwed my father and forced him to leave."

That information seemed to have gotten Detective Falco's attention. He frowned and lifted his head. "That could give him a motive to kill Ryan Sullivan. But, it's hard to believe that he would have attacked both of the Sullivans so violently."

Ashley studied his reaction intently and continued, "But, that's not all. We learned from one of the ladies at the brewery that on the day of the murders, Conrad Volt was gone from the brewery for over two hours and he was very upset when he returned."

"Slow down, Mrs. Clarke," Orsini said bluntly, leaning forward and looking at her sternly.

"Well, anyway, may I make a suggestion?" Ashley asked.

"Go ahead," Falco responded, as he exchanged a grin with his partner. "You're on a roll, lady."

Ashley sat forward in her chair and suggested in a controlled tone of voice, "Maybe you could get a warrant and check out Mr. Volt's residence. You haven't found the murder weapon yet you said, and who knows? He certainly sounds like he had a motive to murder Mr. Sullivan. And maybe Maggie Sullivan just happened to walk in after he killed her husband. So, he had to kill her too!"

Her simple words ate at him, and Detective Orsini replied, "While this is all speculation, Mrs. Clarke, you've certainly given my partner and me something to work on. We'll talk it over and then plan our next move. We'll keep you up to date."

"Sure," she answered softly and then stood up. "Guess I'll be going then."

"What about that lunch I offered you?" Detective

Orsini asked, his gaze looking up. "I'm still good for it."

"Thanks. That's very kind of you, but I have a lot of work to do. So I think I'll just grab a sandwich on the way back to my office."

She picked up her purse and briefcase and started to leave. "My client has suffered a lot of trauma due to this, but I'm sure he's innocent. Put yourself in his shoes, you would be frightened and nervous too."

Falco looked at his partner, shrugged, and the two exchanged knowing glances.

Detective Orsini stood up, walked over to Ashley, and shook her hand. "Thanks for coming in and offering us some new insight on this case. We'll keep you informed if anything new breaks on the case."

"I appreciate that."

Heading back to the office, she called her mother and father and asked them to meet her at four that afternoon. "Lots to go over with you two."

Before Phil could hang up the phone with Ashley, Kelley grabbed it. "Oh, Ashley, something I forgot to tell you earlier. The general manager at the brewery said that old man Sullivan ran the brewery like a military camp. It was 'His way—or—the highway' as they say. That was one of the reasons that his son, Sean, hated the business. The kid loved the arts, especially writing poetry. I don't want to worry you, dear, but I learned that Mr. Sullivan and his children were never very close according to the workers at the brewery."

"Thanks for the info, Mom. Talk more about it to you later."

Chapter 37

Ashley hoped she had planted a seed in the minds of the two detectives and they would check out Conrad Volt and his activities on the day of the murders. She realized the investigation was now in their hands.

When Phil and Kelley arrived at her office that afternoon, they found her at the computer busy reviewing the recently discovered information about her client.

She beamed when she saw them enter her office. "Boy, Mom, you sure helped me with this case. You just may have found the real killer. And when I told the two detectives on the case what you had learned about Conrad Volt, they appeared to be ready to follow up on your lead."

"Glad that I could help you," Kelley said as she sat down on a chair in front of her daughter's desk.

"Well, it's been so difficult trying to get anything out of Sean Sullivan. But, I hope that further investigation will lead to the real murderer," Ashley replied in exasperation.

After they discussed the case for some time, Ashley suggested, "Why don't you two head home now. I'll call you when and if there are any new developments."

Ashley spent the rest of the afternoon looking over photos of the deceased victims and reviewing the information. About five that afternoon, just as she was getting ready to leave the office, Detective Orsini called her.

The tone of his voice was high with excitement, "Boy, have I got news for you, Mrs. Clarke."

She scooted forward in her chair, and her head lifted in anticipation. "Okay. I could use some good news."

"Detective Falco and I took your advice. We went out to the brewery and interviewed the general manager and a couple of the ladies there. Then, we went to a judge with the information we had gathered about Volt and got the judge to issue a search warrant for his residence. Guess what we found?"

"Please, tell me. I'm ready to explode," she shouted into the phone.

"We found incriminating evidence in the Sullivan murders. Hidden in a shoebox on the top shelf of the closet was a blood stained towel with the letter 'S' on it. And inside the towel was a silver bloody letter opener with initials 'R.S.'"

"Yes. Yes," Ashley replied. Now torn with anticipation, she tried to force her voice to sound calm.

"Wait, that's not all. We brought it back to headquarters, and the medical examiner confirmed that the blood found on the weapon matches that of Mr. Sullivan. And the blood on the towel matches Mrs. Sullivan's, A positive. Of course, we have to do more conclusive DNA tests to definitely tie the blood to the Sullivan's. But right now, we think that we've found the murder weapon and our murderer."

"Any fingerprints?" Ashley asked.

"I doubt it. The killer probably wore gloves."

Ashley could not contain her excitement. "Still, I love the news. I can't wait to tell Kathleen and Sean."

"Slow down. We've got more to do on this case."

"Is that it for now?" she asked.

"We got a warrant for the arrest of Conrad Volt. We're charging him with the murder of Maggie and Ryan Sullivan. Tell your mother the information she got about the heated argument between Ryan Sullivan and Conrad Volt was just what we needed to get the search warrant for his residence."

"Thank you. I'll tell her."

"We arrested Conrad Volt and brought him in... charged him with the double murders. At first, he just kept screaming, 'I'm innocent. Just because I hated old man Sullivan, you can't pin the murders on me.' Then, after he calmed down, he asked for a lawyer. My partner is waiting for Volt's lawyer to arrive before we question him."

"I hope that you're going to bring Michele Bain, the prosecuting attorney, up to date on all this," Ashley replied, as she brushed some strands of hair out of her eyes and sat back in her chair, relieved that her client may now be freed of the charges.

"As soon as I hang up with you, I'm giving her a call," Detective Orsini replied.

Later that afternoon, Ashley received a call from Michele Bain. "I talked to the detectives on the Sullivan case. Can you and your client meet me tomorrow morning at nine in courtroom six, second floor?" she asked warmly.

"We'll be there with bells on," Ashley answered, not knowing what Michele Bain was up to.

Shortly before nine the next day, Ashley, together with Kelley and Phil arrived at the courthouse where Kathleen and Sean Sullivan met them on the bottom floor. Together, they took the escalator up to the second floor and walked into the court room.

They saw Michele Bain and her assistant, Dawn Caramane, seated at a long table on the left side of the room. Ashley waved at them and directed her client to a seat next to her and Phil. Kathleen and Kelley took seats in back of them.

They waited patiently as a few media people and spectators came into the room and sat down. Finally, the bailiff entered from a side door and called out, "Please, will this courtroom come to order? This court is now in session. Her Honorable Judge Ott presiding."

The judge took her seat behind the bench and looked down at some papers in front of her. She smiled and looked at the assistant district attorney. "Ms. Bain, you wish to make a statement, I understand."

Michele jumped to her feet. "Yes, your Honor, the state now has new information regarding the murders of Maggie and Ryan Sullivan. A Mr. Conrad Volt has been arrested and charged with the killings. With this new information, the state wishes to drop all charges against Sean Sullivan."

A loud intake of air was heard from the audience, and Kathleen Sullivan gasped and yelled out, "Yes."

The judge rapped her gavel on the bench. "Quiet in the courtroom. I do not tolerate any outbursts in my courtroom."

Looking at Sean, Judge Ott added, "The case against Sean Sullivan is dismissed. You are free to leave, sir." She looked at the two police officers standing nearby. "Please remove Mr. Sullivan's ankle bracelet." Then, standing halfway up, she tapped her gavel. "Court is adjourned."

After the judge left the courtroom, the small audience started to clap. Ashley turned to her client and clasped him gently on his arm. "We did it, Sean. You're free."

Sean shot her an annoyed look. Clearly and distinctly, he said under his breath, "You mean I did it, bitch."

Ashley whipped her head around in shock, every bit of color draining from her face. She could not believe what she had just heard. Sean Sullivan had spoken clearly without any trace of a stutter. She swallowed hard and sat there almost frozen in her chair.

Sean gave Ashley a mocking grin, stood up, and walked over to two policemen who took him out of the courtroom to remove his ankle bracelet. His expression was now smug and secretive.

Phil leaned over, tapped his daughter on the shoulder and eyed her doubtfully. "What did Sean just say to you, Ashley?"

Ashley shook her head, trying to ward off her chilly premonitions. She hugged her elbows, feeling cold and almost painfully brittle.

Then, she swiveled around backwards, twisting her head to look at her father. He avoided her eyes, said nothing and glanced away. Finally, she muttered, "Let's get out of here, Dad."

As they started to leave the courtroom, Michele walked up to them. She grasped Ashley's hands in hers. "Nice going, counselor. I heard that your investigator gave the police the information that they needed to nail the real murderer. I don't know who your investigator is, but you should definitely give him or her big raise."

"Thanks. It was in the family," Ashley replied.

Michele turned to Phil. "Let's not lose track of each other in the future, Phil. Why don't you give me a call next week? We can have lunch and get caught up."

Phil smiled at her. "You got it."

When Ashley, Phil, and Kelley got downstairs they saw Kathleen and Sean Sullivan standing near the exit door. Ashley walked up to them and gave Kathleen a hug. When she turned to Sean to hug him, he stared coldly at her and kept his arms to his side, indicating that he wanted no part of the warm fuzzy greeting. He frowned and snapped, "Prepare your bill, and send it to me. You'll be paid in full. No thanks to you, I'm free. It's me who got me free." He gave her a lazy slow grin that was a taunting slap in the face after what he had just said.

Ashley winced at his angry tone and his words tore through her. She was affronted and hurt. She pursed her lips, refusing to reply.

He grabbed his sister by the arm. "Let's get the hell out of here," he snarled, talking plainly, and no longer stuttering at all. With that statement, he and his sister headed out of the building, trying to avoid the media, while the others stared in amazement after them.

"I can't believe that he was so abrupt and rude." Kelley's voice was shaken as she frowned and looked at her daughter, who was standing there dazed and pale to her lips.

Ashley gave a skeptical snort. "Well, he's certainly not the quiet, slow talking and shy Sean Sullivan that I had for a client, Mom."

"Not very grateful for our help either," Phil added.

As they walked out of the building, a short middle-aged man with thinning gray hair walked up beside them. Ashley whispered to her mother, "I recognize that guy. He was seated in the back of the court room and he talked to Kathleen Sullivan several times." She stopped abruptly and tapped the man on the arm. "Excuse me, sir, do I know you?"

He looked smugly down at her. "Everyone knows me. I'm Jason Fountain, the locally famous theater director. I'm presently directing a new show, 'The Innocent.' It will be showing at the Capital Theatre in four weeks."

"Oh, yes. I've seen an article in the paper advertising it," Ashley said.

He smiled briefly at her. "And, thanks to you, my

leading man Sean Sullivan, will be the star. I was afraid that I might have to use the understudy in his place if his legal situation didn't end quickly."

Ashley looked puzzled. "He and his sister never mentioned that he was an actor."

"Yes. And I must say, one hell of a good one. He can play any role. Here's my card. Call or come to the box office. I'll leave four tickets for you there. If you love theatre, you'll love the play."

Ashley and her parents stood silently, staring after him as Jason Fountain walked quickly away.

"Well, doesn't that beat all? Sean Sullivan is an actor," Phil said. Then he looked at his wife, "How did the police and you manage to miss that fact, my dear?"

"And why didn't he or his sister mention it?" Ashley added in disbelief.

Chapter 38

They stood silent and just stared at each other for a few minutes, unable to believe that Sean Sullivan was an actor, and they knew nothing about it. Phil shook his head. "Doesn't that just beat all?"

"Well Dad, let's get out of here and head back to my office," Ashley said, some of the tension fading from her face. "I want to close out the file on this case and send the Sullivan's my final bill. Then, I want to put them out of my life."

As they drove back to Ashley's office, she suddenly called out, "Wait, Dad. Turn around. Pull up to the corner near that red building."

Somewhat alarmed, Kelley asked, "What's up Ashley?"

"That's Conrad Volt's apartment building. "

"And how do you know that?"

"I got a picture and the address from the computer. And I've got a hunch."

"You've got a hunch, and you want to stop at Volt's apartment?" Phil said. He did as his daughter directed and turned around.

"Yes. But, it's just a gut feeling," Ashley answered breathlessly. He parked the car and they got out. As they walked up to the building, they saw a sign outside that read 'Apartment for Rent'.

"That can't be Volt's apartment yet. It's too soon after his arrest," Kelley said as she doubtfully viewed the sign.

"Must be another apartment. But, at least we can look around," Ashley replied as she eagerly took her mother's hand and dragged her forward.

Inside the building they saw a door on the left with a notice 'Apartment Manager'.

"Let's talk to the manager about Volt," Ashley suggested, now with the single mindedness of a steam roller. She knocked on the door and after a short time it was opened by a short heavy-set middle-aged man, wearing thick glasses. "Good day. I'm Ken Daly, apartment manager. Can I help you?'

Ashley executed a dazzling smile. "We see that you have an apartment for rent."

"Are you interested in seeing it?" he asked.

Ashley gave a choked laugh. "I don't think so. I'm Attorney Ashley Clarke and these are my associates. I wonder if I could have a few moments of your time?"

Daly couldn't conceal his confusion at first, then stepped back, "Sure. But, what about the apartment? You don't want to wait if you're interested in renting it. It's priced reasonably for this area, and it will go fast."

Ashley nodded, trying to reassure him. "I'm sure it will, but I just wanted a few moments of your time. I would like to show you a couple of photographs and see if you recognize the people in them. May we come in?"

He mopped his brow. "I'm kind 'a busy."

"Please, sir. I'll make it quick," Ashley assured the man.

He shrugged his shoulders and waved them into his apartment. He gestured for them to have a seat on the sofa. He sat down on a nearby chair.

"This will only take a few moments," Ashley promised

as they gingerly sat down on the well-worn and somewhat dirty sofa. She reached into her briefcase, pulled out a large manila folder, opened it, and placed a photograph of Sean Sullivan on the coffee table.

"Do you recognize this man?" she asked.

Daly tilted his head and studied the picture intently. "Sure. This guy's picture was in the newspaper. He killed his folks. They owned the brewery where my tenant, Conrad Volt, worked."

"Have you ever seen this man visit your apartment building?"

"Nope. Can't say that I have," Daly replied simply.

Ashley reached into the folder and pulled out a photo of Kathleen Sullivan. "Ever seen this woman?"

Mr. Daly scowled and started to laugh. "Where's her red wig? I know wigs, and she was wearing one when she was here."

"She was here?" Ashley sat forward in her seat. "When?"

"A week or so ago. Yeah, she was here with some fellow. They wanted to take a look at the apartment that was for rent. The guy with her was wearing a mask."

At that, Kelley perked up. Her heart caught in her throat. "A mask? What kind of a mask?"

Daly looked shocked at the sudden reaction to his words. "You know the kind that people wear over their mouth and nose so that other people can't breathe on them and give them germs. A hospital mask, a guess you call it."

"And what did the fellow look like?" Phil asked as he stiffened.

Daly's reply was nonchalant. "Couldn't see much of his face. He had a ball cap pulled down low over it."

Ashley put the photo down on the table and looked quietly at her parents, knowing that something had changed. Then, turning to Daly she asked, "What did this couple do while they were here?"

"Well. I have two apartments on the second floor and two on the third. I took them to the apartment on the second floor that was for rent. It's next to Volt's place."

"Would they have known that?" Kelley asked.

"I guess so. His name and apartment number are listed downstairs on the directory. And he has a name plate next to his apartment door to help delivery people find the right place. Anyway, when we got to the apartment for rent, I opened the door, and started to take them in. Suddenly, the fellow said he had to get something out of the car and he left. So just the girl and I went in and looked the apartment over. Funny thing is that she closed the apartment door behind us and spent a lot of time looking around the place. I thought it was strange because there isn't that much to see. It was just an empty one-bedroom."

"I guess she was pretty interested in renting it then?" Ashley asked with an innocent smile.

Daly shook his head. "I don't know about that. She began to ask all kinds of questions about it though. Finally, I got tired of all of it and said, 'Hey, lady, I'm missing my favorite TV program, 'The Price is Right.' She just glared at me. Suddenly her cell phone rang. She listened to it for a few minutes, then said 'okay' and hung up."

"Do you have any idea who she was talking to?" Ashley's innocent smile that she had pinned on, suddenly faded from her lips.

"No. But after that, she said, 'I don't think that I'm interested in the place after all.' Then, she just bolted out the door. By the time I locked up the apartment and headed downstairs both she and the guy were gone. He never did come into the apartment. I don't know where he went."

"Could he have gone into Conrad Volt's apartment while you two were in the empty apartment next door?" Kelley inquired.

Daly shrugged his shoulders. "He could have, I guess. I know that Volt sometimes forgets to lock up his place. He's always rushing around. Said he thought it was pretty secure here since we only have six units in this building—three on each floor. Anyway, I've got two apartments to rent now that Volt's in jail."

Ashley lifted her brows in destain and stood up. "Well, thanks for all the information, Mr. Daly."

"Are you friends of Mr. Volt?" Daly asked.

Ashley shook her head. "No." Her parents got to their feet.

"I hope Volt gets his stuff moved out soon," Daly commented. "I have to be able to show the place." He stood up, walked toward the hallway leading to the back of the apartment, and yelled, "Hey, Ma, almost time for the 'Price is Right'."

"Okay," a voice called back.

Daly reached into a desk drawer, pulled a small card out, and walked over to Ashley. "Give me a call if you change your mind about the apartment."

Ashley put the card in her pocket. "Thanks. Will do." She shook his hand and they walked out of the apartment.

Outside the building, Kelley, Phil and Ashley stood by the car and looked at each other—doubt apparent on each face.

"Are you two thinking what I'm thinking?" Kelley asked abruptly

"Yes," Ashley replied. "Getting into Volt's apartment would be a piece of cake."

"You know, maybe the wrong guy is in jail now," Ashley added, her voice filled with uncertainty.

"Don't know what we can do about it now. The case is closed, and the police seem convinced that Conrad Volt murdered the Sullivans," Phil added.

Ashley sighed and shrugged her shoulders. "Let's go guys. "I don't know if we have any concrete evidence that would lead them to reopen the case at this point."

A few blocks later, Phil slowed down his car and pointed ahead, "Look Ashley—the Capital Theater. And look at the marquee. It says 'Coming soon—The Innocent—Starring Sean Sullivan'."

"I guess that puts the period on the page, looks like Sean is definitely an actor," Ashley replied with sarcasm. "He sure fooled us."

Kelley nodded and added, "And, I'm starting to believe that a disguised Kathleen and Sean Sullivan made an appointment to see that vacant apartment next to Conrad Volt's. Perhaps they used that opportunity to plant the bloody letter opener in Conrad's closet."

"But at this point, I doubt if the police will act upon our mere suspicions. And I have to think that the Kathleen and Sean really pulled the wool over my eyes," Ashley said, her voice filled with self-loathing.

"So, you're just going to consider the case closed?" Phil asked.

Ashley nodded. "For me, the case is closed."

Just as Ashley said that, her cell phone rang. "Ash, this is Steve. Do you and your folks have Tiffany with you?"

"No, dear. We're just on our way home from the courthouse. Why?"

"Well, I just got a call from the school. The office called to say that she never came to school this morning. They were calling to see if she was sick."

"I don't understand, I put her on the bus at eight this morning. What could have happened to her? Where can she be?"

Chapter 39

Kelley's cell phone rang. She talked on it for a few moments; hung up, and turned to Phil. "They've got a crisis at the hospital. All of a sudden, people are bringing sick kids into the emergency room. They want me to come in and give them a hand."

Phil swung the car around and headed to the hospital. After he let her out at the emergency room door, he looked at Ashley. "Now what's up with Steve? You sounded concerned when you talked to him."

She nodded. "Yes, I am concerned. Very concerned. He said that the school called and that Tiffany was absent today. They wanted to know if she was sick or what. I put her on the bus as usual, but she never checked into her first class." Ashley's heart was beating a mile a minute. "Steve said I should go with you to your house and stay there, Dad. He's going to try to call her friends and see if they know where she could be."

"Did he try to get Tiffany on her cell phone?"

"Of course. That's the first thing that he did. No answer."

As they drove to Phil and Kelley's home, Ashley's cell phone rang. She looked at her father with tears in her eyes. "I hope this is Tiffany." She answered the phone, turned to her father, and whispered. "It's Steve."

"I've got some disturbing news for you, Ashley. I went to the school and a couple of Tiffany's friends said that after she got off the bus, she was called over to a blue car parked at the curb. She talked to a man for a while, then waved at her friends and yelled out, 'My mom's been in an accident, and I have to go to the hospital. See you guys later.' She got into the car and went off with the man. One of the girls thought that sounded suspicious and wrote down the license plate number of the car. After she gave it to me, I checked it out. The car was stolen near Stark prison."

"Oh, my God, that's where Jerry Albright was sent. His divorce case was one of the first that I helped with at Bella and Bella after I moved to Florida. Jerry was convicted of beating and raping his ex-wife after she got everything he owned in their divorce case. Dino and I found her all beaten up on the floor of her apartment in Dolphin Springs, and we both had to testify at Jerry's trial. After he was found guilty of the crime and sentenced to fifteen years in prison, Jerry vowed that when he got out he would take care of Dino, me, and his ex. But, he's still in prison isn't he?" she asked as panic surged through her body.

"No. I remember you're telling me about him. So, I called the prison warden to find out if he was still there. He escaped from prison early this morning in a laundry truck. The state police are out in force looking for him."

"Oh, my God. Do you think that he's looking for me?" Ashley asked.

"I just don't know, Ash," Steve answered. "I talked briefly to the prison warden, he said Albright told his cell mate that he planned to take care of the lawyers that sent him to prison if and when he got out. I suspect that it was Jerry who took Tiffany. But, for the life of me, I can't believe that Tiffany would get into a car with a stranger."

"How would he know where we lived and where she went to school?" Ashley asked.

"He probably had someone on the outside keeping track of you for the past several years. Where are you headed now?"

"We just dropped Mom off at the hospital and are on our way to my dad's place."

"Be careful. Have your dad check out the house when you get there. Lock the place down and stay there. I'll send a couple of officers over to the hospital to stay with your mom. The State Police already sent a squad up to Dolphin Springs to keep an eye on Dino and Gina Bella. I'll be over to stay with you as soon as possible."

Phil pulled up to the entrance to the gated community, and recognizing him the security man opened the iron gates. Phil rolled down the car window. "Hi, Winston."

"Morning, Mr. Willis. I mean, afternoon."

"Any strange cars or people coming through here today?"

"Just the usual. And, oh yes, a furniture truck. Dropped off a refrigerator to the Miller's place. You know, Kerry Miller."

"Ya. Sure."

"Something wrong, Mr. Willis?"

"Tell you later."

"Oh, Mr. Willis. Remember you told me the other day about that the back gate lock was broken? Well, maintenance is going to fix it. He said he has to buy a better lock. Should get at it soon."

"Thanks, my friend. Gotta go," Phil responded as he put up the car window and pulled away.

Phil followed the driveway to the side of the house where the garage was located and parked.

"Dad, aren't you going to put the car in the garage?"

"No room. Your mother has several long tables set up in there. She's doing some leaded glass work. Getting it ready for the church bazaar."

Both exited the car and walked to the front door. Phil unlocked it and they entered. The condo was all on one floor with the kitchen located to the side of the building and a door leading from the kitchen to the garage.

Walking toward the kitchen, Phil said, "I'll make us some coffee, honey."

"Good. And make it strong," Ashley replied. "I'll use the guest bathroom while you're doing that."

For a moment, Ashley felt secure in her father's home, but her mind quickly shifted to her daughter. Where is my Tiffany? Please, God, don't let any harm come to her.

She began reflecting about when she had last seen Jerry Albright. She recalled how angry he was that Dino Bella and she had testified against him. And she shuttered as she recalled his words as he left the court room. He yelled out to his wife, "I'll get you for this." Then he looked at Ashley with intense anger in his eyes and muttered loudly, "And you too, bitch!"

Steve had told her that Jerry had escaped and was last sighted in the small town of Lutz, outside of Tampa.

As she walked down the hall to the bedroom, Ashley prayed, "Please don't come here, Jerry. Please leave us alone."

Phil was in the kitchen, preparing the coffee, when he suddenly looked over at the door to the garage. I've got to remind Kelley to be sure to lock that door at all times.

As the coffee started to brew, Phil walked into his bedroom and opened the top drawer of the night stand. He reached in and pulled out his Beretta from beneath a pile of paper. Opening the bottom drawer, he removed a box of bullets, loaded the weapon and placed it in the waist band of his trousers. Finally, he bent over and retrieved a knife and wrist holster from the bottom drawer. He rolled up his shirt sleeve and secured the knife and holster to his arm; then rolled down his sleeve, covering them. "I'm ready for you, Albright."

He strolled back into the kitchen, pulled a couple of cups from the cabinet, and turned to get some cream out of the refrigerator. Just then, he heard Ashley yell out from the back bedroom, "Dad. Dad."

Phil raced to the guest bedroom and saw Ashley standing in the middle of the room, next to the bed. She was pointing toward the closet. Phil stopped dead in his tracks, unable to believe what he was seeing.

Standing in the open doorway of the closet was Jerry Albright, and he was holding Tiffany with his arm around her neck and a knife at her throat.

Ashley whispered, "Jerry. Oh, Jerry. Please don't hurt my daughter."

Jerry snarled. "I'm not only going to hurt her, honey, but I'm going to kill her, you, and that old man standing there. I've waited years for my revenge, and I'm going to take it nice and slow. But first, you're going to watch me carve up your pretty daughter's face. She was so concerned when I told her that you were hurt and in the hospital."

"Please Jerry; Tiffany hasn't done anything to you. Please don't hurt her," Ashley begged.

He glared at her. "She's going to feel pain, like I felt in prison. The other inmates beat and cut me up when I wouldn't become their special playmate. Now it's my turn to inflict some pain and pay you back. When I get done here, I'm going to look for that tramp of an ex-wife and make her pay, too!" Jerry had the look of a crazed man. His face was red as he screamed, "I'll see that she dies a very slow and painful death."

Then he looked at Phil. "Mr. Willis, I presume? Ashley's

famous lawyer father. I see that you have a gun tucked into the waist band of your trousers. You better take it out and hand it to me. And no tricks or your pretty little granddaughter will get her throat slashed."

Phil glared at him and nodded. Then slowly stepped forward, removed the gun from his waist band, and handed it to Jerry with the barrel pointed toward him. "You'll never get away with this. Let my daughter and granddaughter go."

Jerry switched the knife from his right hand to the left one that he had around Tiffany's throat, reached out with the right for the gun and grinned. "Not in this lifetime. I'm about to do justice and even the score."

Phil looked at him calmly. "You know that Ashley's husband is a police officer. He'll be here shortly."

"You'll all be dead by then. And I'll be long gone," Jerry replied calmly.

As Jerry was placing the gun in the waist band of his pants, the sound of sirens could be heard. His head jerked up in alarm.

At that very instant, Phil flicked his right arm toward Jerry and his knife came whistling out. He hit Jerry in the shoulder causing him to drop the knife and release his hold on Tiffany.

Phil leaped across the room and grabbed Tiffany by the arm. "Go to your mother," he commanded. He reached into Jerry's trousers, pulled out his gun and with all the force that he could muster whipped it across the side of Jerry's head.

Jerry dropped to the floor, unconscious.

Phil leaned over him and waved his arm at Ashley. "Quick, get a couple of my old ties off that rack on the closet door. I've got to tie this guy up and make sure that he doesn't go anywhere before Steve gets here."

Phil turned Jerry over on to his stomach and tied his

hands and feet securely with the neck ties.

Noticing the blood that was gushing from Jerry's shoulder, Phil snapped, "Tiffany get me a couple of towels from the bathroom."

Tiffany raced into the bathroom, grabbed two large towels off the towel bar, and ran back into the bedroom. Phil reached down, pulled out his knife, wiped it on one of the towels and placed the other one under Jerry's shirt to stop the flow of blood coming from his wound.

By this time, Jerry was starting to come around. He looked up at Phil and said weakly, "Damn, you Willis. I'm hurt."

"Too bad. You're lucky that I didn't aim for your heart," Phil said angrily. "But, I don't want you to die, asshole. I want to see you back in prison for the rest of your life."

"That won't happen. I'm never going back there, you bastard Willis."

Ashley walked up to them and tapped Phil on the shoulder. "Dad, I can hear more sirens. I think that Steve and the police are here."

"Let them in and hurry. We don't want this scum to bleed to death. It's too good for him," Phil answered as he kept his gun trained on Jerry.

Ashley, with Tiffany on her heels, ran to the front door and threw it open. She saw Steve racing up the walkway with several uniformed cops behind him. "Hurry, Dad's got Albright in the guest bedroom."

Within a few moments, the police had Jerry on his feet and were hauling him out the front door of the condo.

"Back to jail for you, Albright, where you'll probably rot for the rest of your miserable life," Steve snapped. "You'll never hurt my family again."

Pushing Jerry ahead of them toward the squad car, the police hurried down the walk. Steve whirled around and embraced both his wife and daughter.

"Grandpa saved us," Tiffany said as she snuggled in her father's arms. "He had a knife up his sleeve and threw it at that horrible man."

Suddenly, they heard the sound of a gunshot. They flew out the front door and saw that Jerry Albright was lying on the ground with blood covering the front of his shirt.

One of the officers walked up to Steve. He was shaking as he said, "There was nothing else that I could do except shoot him. He grabbed my partner's gun and was going to shoot us."

Within a few moments, another police car pulled up and the captain exited the car. As the shooting officer tried to explain to the captain what had occurred, the other officer leaned down and checked Jerry. "He's dead, Captain."

Phil tapped the captain on the arm. "Suicide by cop. He said that he would never go back to prison, and I guess that he meant it."

The captain looked at the officer. "You make out a full report when we get back to headquarters. Right now, let's get the medical examiner out here."

As he spoke, the neighbors came out of their condos and gathered in bunches along the driveway. Suddenly, the captain noticed several media trucks that were parked nearby. "Did you guys catch the shooting out here?"

"Yes," the Channel 8 news lady answered.

"Well, I need the tape," the captain ordered. Then turning to Steve, he added, "We'll need a statement from your family as to what occurred inside the place earlier."

"Yes, sir. I'll take care of it," Steve replied. Turning to his wife, he added, "Well, Ashley, Jerry will never harm anyone again. Why don't we all head back to our place?"

"Good idea," Phil replied. "I'll have to call Kelley and tell her that I'll pick her up at the hospital and that we're going to your house for a couple of days. I'll call the maintenance man and have him get someone to clean up the place. And by the way, Ashley, don't plan on cooking supper for us tonight. I'll pick up some Chinese for all of us after I get your mother."

As Ashley, Steve, and Tiffany started toward Steve's car; Tiffany turned around, rushed back to her grandfather and threw her arms around him. "Oh, Grandpa. I love you so much. You saved me and my mom's life. But, I couldn't believe it when you threw your knife at that horrible man. Where did that come from?"

"Yes, Dad," Ashley added. "How did you do that?"

"When Grandma and I worked years ago for a private investigator, he sent us to Sarasota to train with circus people. An English fellow, named Sterling James, gave me the holster and taught me knife tricks. Showed me how to hide the holster up my sleeve, and in one swift motion how to whip the knife out and fling it at a target. Over the years, I would get the holster and knife out and practice."

His family stood there and stared at Phil, with their mouths open, as he concluded his story. "Now, I'll just put them back in my night stand and pray that I'll never need them again."

Chapter 40

When Phil picked Kelley up at the hospital, he told her what had happened with Jerry Albright at their condo. He said that the guest bedroom floor and the drive way had blood on them and that the maintenance man had contacted a hazardous waste crew to come and clean it up.

He said he told Ashley they would stay at her place for a few days, and he was going to take Kelley back to their house to pick up enough of her clothes for the next few days.

When they arrived back at their home, Jerry Albright's body had been removed, and the police had left the scene. Kelley walked into the guest bedroom and looked at the blood that smeared the floor.

"You know Phil, I don't know if I want to live here anymore. I would always be reminded of the fact that Ashley and Tiffany could have been killed here and that Albright fellow died on our front driveway. I think we should sell the place immediately and move."

As they started to pack a couple of suitcases, the maintenance man, Tom, rang the doorbell. He had the hazardous waste crew with him. Phil took them to the guest room and showed them the mess.

After they left the crew in the bedroom to start work, Phil turned toward Tom and said, "Now, my wife doesn't want to live here anymore, and she wants to sell the place."

"Funny you should say that. My son is moving in with me and the place where I rent is too small for the both of us. We're thinking of pooling our money and buying a condo. I might be interested in purchasing your place if the price is right," Tom said.

"I'll give you one hell of a deal, my friend," Phil replied.

Grabbing several suitcases, Kelley and Phil loaded them up with enough clothes to last for an extended stay at their daughter's. "We can come back later and pack up the rest of our stuff," Kelley said.

"Yes. I'll get some boxes for the dishes and we can clean out the garage, too. We can always put everything in storage," Phil added.

"I'll take my glass works to the hobby shop and work on it there," Kelley replied.

A couple of days after the incident, Ashley and Steve returned to work and Tiffany resumed her normal school days. Kelley and Phil returned to their condo only to pack up the rest of their belongings. Within a few weeks, the sale of their home was complete, and they moved to another community.

Following the autopsy, Jerry Albright's ex-wife claimed his body from the morgue. After the body was cremated, she took the ashes out on a boat ride from Dolphin Springs and sprinkled them across the waters of the Gulf of Mexico.

The case of the State of Florida against Conrad Volt did not end well for the prosecution. The defense team had proven that the only evidence against Conrad were the letter opener and the bloody towel, which could have easily been planted in his apartment. At the end of the short trial, Conrad was judged innocent by the jury.

After the trial, Conrad Volt left the brewery and joined his father in Germany.

No one would ever be convicted of the murders of the Sullivans.

Sean Sullivan did only two performances of the play before he and the director came to physical blows over their differences. As the months went by, Sean became more and more irrational and even his sister, Kathleen, could not control him. After he physically attacked her, she had him committed to a mental hospital under the Baker Act where he resided for the next year.

When he was released, he got into a confrontation with a police officer and assaulted him. For this crime, he spent two years in jail. After his release, his sister convinced him to sell the house and their share of the brewery and to move permanently to Ireland with her.

Eventually, Ashley closed her office and retired.

After he retired from the police department, Steve got a call from the Schwinn Bike Company, and they put him in charge of designing and improving their line of bicycles.

Alan and Laura continued working part-time selling real estate.

And both couples started to travel extensively.

"Final Justice" was seen by all.

The Justice Series Summary

Kelley Ryan's adventures started in *Tightrope to Justice* where she worked as a private investigator to locate her uncle's murderer in Dolphin Springs, Florida. There, she teamed up with an extraordinary young fellow, Phil Willis. He joined her in her private eye work.

In the second novel, *Miami Justice*, Kelley and Phil had several adventures in Miami, Florida, involving the high fashion world of expensive clothes and jewelry.

In the third novel, *European Justice*, Kelley and Phil married and headed to Europe on their honeymoon. There they visited Kelley's grandmother and helped Scotland Yard solve several crimes. The book concludes with their adventures in Sicily.

It was Phil's turn to shine in the fourth novel, *Justice 4 Willis* where, as a young attorney, he handled cases with the help of his able investigator and assistant, his wife, Kelley.

Finally, in this, the fifth and final novel in the "Justice" series, their two children, Ashley and Alan, take center stage. Ashley follows in her father's footsteps as a capable attorney, and Alan works with a police SWAT team. All of the Willis family's adventures come to a peaceful end in *"Final Justice."*

Articles and Short Stories by Ray Weaver

"It's a Poem" published in *Chicken Soup for the Soul-Inspirations for Writers*, May 2013, a story about an elderly woman in a nursing home who inspired me to continue writing.

"A Star is Born" published in *Chicken Soup for the Soul-Inspirations for the Young at Heart*; August 2011-a story about Ray's appearance in a play at the local theater.

"The Cell Phone" published in *Chicken Soup for the Soul-Inspirations for the Young at Heart*; August 2011-a story about Ray's first experience with carrying a cell phone.

"The Past Sixty Years" published in *Chicken Soup for the Soul: Twins and More,* March 2009, a story about Ray and his twin brother, Ed.

"A Grandfather's Dream," "the Wieliczka Salt Mines", "Ground Zero in New York," "So this is Canada, Eh," "Ray and Ellie visit Lourdes" among articles published in the Safety Harbor Florida, newspaper, *The Tropical Breeze.*

"So this is Sterling" published in the Dunedin Florida's newspaper, *The Highlander.*

"Make your Memories" published in the "Seniority Section" of the *Tampa Bay Times.*

Second place in "June Times Remember Section" of the *Tampa Bay Times* with a story about his granddaughter.

Story about Grandpa Weaver's 1902 Grocery Store, published in *Bend of the River* magazine.

Numerous articles published in the *Suncoast Hospice Newsletter.*

Author's Bio

Raymond P. Weaver is a resident of Clearwater, Florida. He and his wife, Ellie, have been married for over fifty-four years. They have two children and six grandchildren. Ray has been writing for eleven years and has had numerous short stories and articles published in major magazines and local newspapers.

He is very proud of the stories he has had published in the *Chicken Soup for the Soul* books. "It's a Poem," "The past Sixty Years," "A Star is Born" and "The Cell Phone."

A prolific and dedicated writer, his first full-length novel, *Tightrope to Justice* was published in 2010. *Miami Justice* in 2011, *European Justice* in 2012 and the fourth, *Justice 4 Willis* in 2013. *Final Justice* is the fifth and final book in the Willis family series.

Coming Next

Three Courageous Women

The story of three different and courageous ladies
and their individual struggle to overcome
personal difficulties in their lives.

Due out in Spring 2015

www.ingramcontent.com/pod-product-compliance
Lightning Source LLC
Chambersburg PA
CBHW070218260626
47160CB00002B/595